KU-799-115

The Irish Widow

The Irish Widow

Harriet Herbst

CUMBRIA COUNTY LIBRARY HJ

PIATKUS

Copyright © 1988 by Harriet Herbst

First published in this edition in
Great Britain in 1991 by
Judy Piatkus (Publishers) Ltd of
5 Windmill Street, London W1

British Library Cataloguing in Publication Data
Herbst, Harriet
  The Irish widow.
  I. Title
  823.914 [F]

  ISBN 0-7499-0011-3

Printed and bound in Great Britain by
Billing & Sons Ltd, Worcester

For
    Joan, Eve, Jon, Karla, and Noah
         and
With thanks to
    Adele Bowers and Frances Goldin
    for their loving friendship

*Well you know it or don't you kennet or
haven't I told you, every telling has a taling
and that's the he and the she of it.*

JAMES JOYCE
Finnegan's Wake

1

Little Timothy O'Connell was a diabetic, a terrible hard thing on his mother particularly since she herself had such a sharp sweet tooth, and how was a person expected to be always locking up all the lovely little cakes and pastries, not to mention the preserves and the caramels and bonbons that she kept in the house for her company and herself, hiding them from the poor child, trying to keep him safe from temptation?

Agnes O'Connell was a widow — lusty, busty, and fortyish — a sociable sort of a woman, still with a fine figure, if a bit plump, and the same high color she'd brought with her as a young girl from Ireland. Timmy's father, rest his soul, hailed from County Cork and she herself grew up in Kilkenny, until just turned twenty-nine and despairing of ever getting married, she'd crossed the ocean by plane from Shannon to New York — what a trip that was, and herself so green and scared — to take a job at Schrafft's. Oh, those were the days, with the young men all chasing after her and buying her all the sweets she could eat! But they were long since gone, together with Schrafft's and the fine strapping man she'd finally married—James Ward O'Connell, the best of the lot—a skyjack who'd fallen, God help him, from the twentieth floor of the skyscraper he was working on. He'd left her with his trade union pension, a good bit of insurance (double indemnity for the accident), and a pair of diamond drop earrings he'd just given her as a gift to celebrate their tenth wedding anniversary. And, of course, there was Timmy—a gorgeous golden-haired bouncing rosy-cheeked boy of five, who seemed to have inherited his father's grand physique and her own high color and taste for sweets.

Well, James Ward O'Connell had been a provident doting man, if a bit careless when in his cups. The lawyer had a fine time convincing the jury O'Connell hadn't been drinking before he fell. "Contributory negligence" the other lawyer called it, but she'd won the case. And not a day passed now that she didn't miss him. Still and all it was a blessing he had gone to his peace before he could learn of the terrible lifelong curse that was to be laid on his son.

After a year of mourning she moved back to the old country, to the outskirts of Dublin, where her widow's pension kept her in much finer style than ever it would have done in Queens, New York. She bought a nice piece of land with a sweet little house from part of the insurance money and settled down to properly enjoy her new life. As an attractive widow with a comfortable income, her social position was assured, and as an expatriate now repatriated, she was much sought after. She made a number of friends, mostly men. Timmy was growing fast and already started in school when she began to feel something was not quite right about him. She just couldn't put her finger on it.

Actually, it was Detective Thomas Francis O'Hare, one of her newer male friends, who made her take notice. The boy seemed listless. He'd lost his color and was thin as a rail. He seemed always thirsty and would drink huge quantities of fruit juice and pop. It was strange how his appetite fluctuated; sometimes he wouldn't eat at all, sometimes he wolfed his food as if his hunger would never be satisfied. She thought at first it was due to his sudden spurt of growth — he'd sprung up so in the few years since his father died till she hardly recognized him. Or it might be the change from living in New York, though she would have thought the fresh Clontarf sea air would hearten him. Maybe it was that he missed his father, though he never seemed interested when she talked to him about O'Connell. Still, children sometimes had a way of keeping their grief secret. Whatever the reason, she put it down to growing pains of one sort or another. But O'Hare wouldn't let it rest and kept after her to have the boy checked over by a doctor. She'd really been meaning to follow his advice and make the appointment, but what with one thing or another she kept putting it off; which was a shame really, because there was very little she wouldn't have done to please O'Hare.

Thomas Francis O'Hare, detective first class in the Dublin police force, was a catch any woman in Dublin, including lucky Aggie O'Connell, would have gladly given her eyeteeth for. A widower whose wife had died early, he'd brought up his own two children, grown now thank God and living in the West country with families of their own.

O'Hare was a man in his prime, that is to say in his late forties, and though he'd never remarried, it was clear he must have had plenty of chances. There were more than a few women still chasing after him. It was not that he was exactly a handsome man, certainly no movie star, but he was brawny and cheerful, with a good plain Irish mug on him and a fine sweet disposition. He commanded a lot of respect on his job, and he was handy around the house, always ready to fix things. He was fond of Timmy and he and the boy got on well. All in all, he was as fine a prospective husband as Aggie had ever dreamed of.

O'Hare had gotten into the habit of taking Timmy off on trips around the city, the boy riding on the back of O'Hare's bike. They might go out to Phoenix Park on a Saturday afternoon to play ball or hurley, or on a visit to the botanic gardens or the zoo. Sometimes she'd join them, pedaling along behind on her own two-wheeler, and the three of them would wind up having tea and cream cakes at Bewley's.

It was a lovely time until that day at Bewley's, when Timmy, flushed and excited and seeming happier and more animated than she'd seen him in a good while—he'd just eaten half-a-dozen of the cakes filled with rich whipped cream fresh from the Bewley dairy and drunk three cups at least of sweetened tea—suddenly fell back in his chair with a strange glazed look and wouldn't answer when O'Hare spoke to him. She'd given a terrible cry and knocked over her teacup while O'Hare was trying to calm her and at the same time rouse the boy. He'd been successful at neither. But carrying Timmy, he'd shepherded her out of the place and into a cab and told the driver to take them straight off to the hospital. That was a day—and a night—she'd long remember!

After what seemed like hours of waiting around while Timmy was being examined, the nurse had come out and advised them the boy had regained consciousness and they could see him for a minute, but it would be best not to stay too long. Dr. Vogel wanted to keep the child overnight. They could go home and come back in the morning when the doctor would have the results of all the tests and be able to give them a full report.

Tim didn't want her to leave, holding on to her hand tight and looking so wan and frail it broke her heart. But O'Hare teased the boy into laughing and letting her go by pretending he was getting right into bed with Timmy and staying the night, while the Sister made a big fuss trying to argue O'Hare out of it, and finally the boy agreed and kissed her good-night and made her promise to come get him first thing in the morning. He'd been given a sedative and was almost asleep anyway by the time they left.

Thomas Francis O'Hare comforted her that night as she'd never been comforted before. It was their first time together and she'd tried to resist, thinking they'd only been seeing each other a couple of months and she didn't want him to think her too easy. But he'd had such a gentle sweet way with her, such a lovely wild yet pleading way about him that she couldn't in truth have put him off another minute, even if she'd wanted to.

O'Hare had to report for duty at eight o'clock and crept from her bed at six in the morning—just as well, for her nearest neighbors, the old maid Jenny O'Flaherty and her widowed mother, rose early—saying he hated waking her out of her sleep but would she be sure and call him at least by noon, to let him know how Tim was and what the doctor had to say. She promised and shut her eyes again, but he kept kissing her arms and neck and her face till she could hardly bear to let him go, sleepy as she was. And feeling twice the woman she'd been since O'Connell died (or it seemed now, ever!), she'd gotten herself up at seven, bright and cheerful—usually she hated bustling about in the morning—straightened the house, had a good breakfast, gotten dressed, and been ready by nine to take the bus to the hospital and bring Timmy home.

Delehanty's Sweet Shop near the bus stop was just opening as she passed and she couldn't resist stopping in to buy the chocolate mouse in the window that Timmy'd been hankering for. She had it wrapped in a box with a shiny green paper and bright ribbon to cheer him, and picked up a few peppermints and some toffee for herself.

The bus ride was all too short for the daydream she was having of herself with O'Hare, him asking her that very evening to marry him, and the two of them going off on a month's honeymoon down to the lake country where their days were filled with joy and their nights with splendor.

The conductor called out Donegal Road, Rountree Hospital, and a swift pang of guilt for forgetting all about Timmy and the burden of her present journey cut through the lovely dream like a knife.

She never did get to give him the chocolate mouse, though he saw the shiny package and she had to tell him what was in it. But by then she knew the worst and was already hardening herself for the strict routine she and Timmy would have to endure from now on.

That night after putting the child to bed, sitting with O'Hare and telling him the terrible news, she ate the chocolate mouse herself, sorrowfully nibbling the tiny ears and paws and the delicately molded little body, the tears running down her face as she finished the last sweet morsel of the spun-sugar-candy tail and whiskers.

2

When the doctor first told Agnes O'Connell her son had diabetes, she'd flatly refused to believe it. First of all, Timmy was only just eight, and she'd never heard of a child his age having it. Besides, wasn't it a Jewish disease? And what would a good Irish Catholic boy like her Tim be doing with that kind of a sickness?

Dr. Vogel, a Jew himself, managed to persuade her that diabetes was not purely restricted to the Hebrews — and that in fact Timmy did have it. She took it hard. What with the injections and testing his urine morning and night, and the special diet, it was almost more than a loving mother could be expected to suffer without complaint. But she tried. And Timmy was a good boy. In no time at all he was testing his own urine. She'd made it into a kind of game. "See the color, Timmy? It's blue — blue as the color of your very own eyes. But that's *not* the color we want, now is it, Tim? We can't have that color. It's got to be pink, same as the roses climbing the trellis on the side of the house. I guess we'll just have to keep trying, luv."

Of course, she still had to give him his injections, Lord help her, but he took them like the little man he was, not whimpering at all now as he did the first few times when he watched her preparing the needle.

She tried to keep him off the streets. Temptation was everywhere. She hated the way he'd beg her for a bit of chocolate or a lolly or an ice cream when she took him marketing with her. And the way he was always watching the kids dashing in and out of Delehanty's, licking the icing off their after-school cupcakes or gorging on treats, fair made her sick.

But the hardest part of it was the feeling she had about her ruined chances with O'Hare — her saddled now with a poor sick kid. Not that the man wasn't kind and helpful and considerate still, but all the fun seemed to be drained out of him. He hadn't proposed after their night together, or given her the least hint of his intentions in all the weeks since. And what with Timmy around such a lot and always needing attention, and perhaps out of concern for her own troubled state, O'Hare's lovemaking had become much less tempestuous and a lot more sporadic. Sometimes she wondered if there wasn't another woman. Well, "Swift to bed, slow to wed!" her mother had always told her, and though the times had changed a lot since those days, maybe there was some truth in the old adage. Maybe if she'd held off, he'd be down on his knees to her now; though she was inclined to think if she'd waited, he'd have been long since gone. Or maybe he'd been put out because she'd come home so late from the hospital that day with Tim and hadn't called him as she'd promised. But in all truth, she felt it was Timmy's sickness that was turning O'Hare away from her.

It wasn't until some time later that she learned she was dead wrong about that.

3

Thomas Francis O'Hare wasn't the sort of man to be turned away by trouble. Learning about Timmy's illness only made him all the more anxious to take care of the two of them. In the several months since he'd first met Agnes and Timmy O'Connell, he'd found himself happier than he'd been in a long time. With his own kids grown and off on their own, he hadn't realized how much he missed having a family around.

Agnes O'Connell's son was a quiet well-behaved child with a lovely sweet nature and a great talent for charming people. With his delicate coloring, those wide violet-blue eyes and that golden hair like a shining halo, the boy had something of the look of an angel about him. O'Hare thought Tim was sharp as a whip for his age. He was always asking questions about how things worked and spelling out the street signs and store advertisements and with little more than a year of schooling had already taught himself to read.

O'Hare loved taking the boy about, showing him the town, enjoying Tim's starry-eyed wonder at the strange new sights and delights the city of Dublin had to offer. The lad himself was a sight to see, and wherever they went, people would turn round to stare at him.

Tim had never ridden in a horse-drawn carriage before, or seen a hurling match, and watching the cubs at the lion zoo or tossing crusts to the greedy swans in the lake at St. Stephen's Green could send him into a trance of pleasure. Tim not having a father of his own made O'Hare feel particularly soft toward the lad, and it was plain the boy was attached to him too, always greeting him at the door with a shy grin when O'Hare came to visit, and trying hard not to jiggle with excitement while begging his mother to "Say yes!" whenever an outing was suggested. But it wasn't Tim only that moved O'Hare and brought him so often to the O'Connell house.

The first time O'Hare had met Aggie O'Connell—they'd been introduced by Jenny O'Flaherty on the street—he'd been dazzled by her, by her quick flashing smile, her fine color, and her great hungry zest for life, which seemed to pour over him like the waves of the sea. She was a handful of woman. The way her breasts bounced as she walked, and that beautiful cleavage peeping out of the neckline of her blouse opened to the third button, filled him with a joy he seemed to have long forgotten.

The first time he'd bedded her, he'd felt bewitched. He'd had a few women in the years since his wife had died, but no one who'd moved him to such transports of passion as Agnes O'Connell. He was transfigured. Some of her exuberance must have rubbed off on him, for she'd made him feel like he'd been asleep for years and suddenly waked—a roaring buck again. The day after their first night together, he could hardly keep his mind on his work, he was that distraught with love for Aggie and worry for Timmy. The men at the station noticed how jumpy he was and kept joshing him about what he'd been up to, who was the lady he'd been up with all night, and was he hung over with too much lovemaking or was it just the drink?

He'd been concerned about Tim for some weeks now, the boy seemed so changed, and he'd kept telling Agnes she ought to have him checked by the doctor. The child tired too easily and seemed more delicate, more dreamy than ever. The earlier bright-eyed eagerness and the quick shy smile now had a flickering disembodied quality, while the boy himself—like the Cheshire cat in *Alice in Wonderland*—seemed to fade off into thin air. There was something elusive, shadowy, unsubstantial about Tim lately.

That day, when Agnes hadn't called by noon to let him know how Timmy was doing, he phoned her at home—she had one of the few private lines in Clontarf—but there was no answer, and when he called the hospital to inquire, he was told the boy had just left with his mother. By three o'clock, when he still got no answer, he decided not to wait and took off in one of the patrol cars to see if he could find her, telling Paddy Morphy to look after things and he'd be calling in soon.

He waited awhile on her doorstep when no one answered the bell, then scouted the neighborhood on foot, with no luck. When he came back and there was still no sign of the two of them, he sat in the car waiting, trying to think where they could be and what could be keeping them. Jenny O'Flaherty passed by and gave him a quirky smile and a wink, and he wondered if he was doing Agnes or himself any good hanging around her house in the middle of the day during working hours. To hell with it! Let them gossip all they liked. He wasn't about to give up seeing Agnes and Timmy because of what the neighbors might think.

It was growing dark and he was beside himself, having called the station for messages every half-hour that long afternoon and toured the neighborhood looking in every likely place she might be, stopping off at Delehanty's and making the round of the shops on the High Street. No one had seen them.

When he got back to the house again, it was well past seven o'clock and he was desperate, wracking his brains about what to do, trying to figure out whether to report them missing or what, when he saw her coming along the street. She was carrying Tim, and holding a shiny green parcel dangling by a ribbon. She looked wan and exhausted, and her tam was askew, and she seemed to be staggering under the weight of the child. For a minute he wasn't sure if he wanted to jump out of the car and hit her, or sweep them up in his arms and carry them into the house.

The whiskey on her breath when he took Tim from her almost knocked him over.

4

They thought he was asleep, but he wasn't. He was tired, glad to be in his own bed and home again. He heard them out in the kitchen. They were shouting, but he couldn't make out the words. He was so thirsty he was tempted to call out to his mother, but decided better not.

He got up and went to the bathroom, filled the plastic glass and drank thirstily. The bathroom was something like the one they'd had in Queens, America, when he was little, with a blue basin and toilet, only this one was smaller and had no tub in it. The wall separating it from the kitchen was paper thin, and when the john was flushed you could hear it all through the house. She'd had it put in so he wouldn't have to use the big old one upstairs next to her bedroom, except when he needed a bath.

He could hear her and O'Hare arguing and her saying, "Yes I did! Two Irish coffees is all and a little ginger beer for Timmy. It was just that I was upset and the child was thirsty and I'd never seen the Long Hall before, though I'd heard talk of it and I thought it would cheer him . . ."

He filled the glass again and drank it down. She was still going on, but talking fast and a little breathless, the way she did when she was trying to coax him into doing something he didn't want to do.

"Anyway, the minute he heard we'd come from New York, he came right out to the snug—P. F. O'Brien himself—and invited us into the bar and showed us the old clock—more than two hundred and fifty years old, he said—and the crystal chandelier and all the fine pictures in their gilt frames. It was so beautiful and everyone so friendly, I almost forgot my troubles. And then Mr. O'Brien insisted we all had to have another round on the house to celebrate our coming home to Ireland, and before I knew it I looked at the clock and it was after six and I thought dear God, it's that late and I never called him! Oh Thomas, please don't be mad! I'm that sorry I worried you. I meant to call but what with . . ."

He deliberately flushed the toilet though he hadn't peed and she was always warning him about saving water. "This ain't the United States you know!" she would say. He heard her exclaim "He's up!" and come running into his room.

He knew she would. But it was O'Hare he wanted.

5

O'Hare didn't stay the night. He was torn between pity and anger and hadn't the heart to take advantage of her, the state she was in, not to mention his own. He'd seen plenty of trouble in his time and had handled enough of his own to know the rotten tricks life could play on people. He'd completely forgiven her the worry she'd caused him—how could he not?—she was that shattered with grief. But the thought of the boy and what he'd have to be going through now and for the rest of his life, most likely, filled him with a boiling rage.

When Tim woke, O'Hare went after her to help tuck the boy in and to tell him good-night, asking him to think about what they might be doing together over the next weekend. It might be they'd go fishing on the Liffey if Tim would like that. O'Hare had a rod just the right size for him and could probably dig up another for his mother, if she wanted to come along. But she'd have to promise not to squirm over putting the worms on the hook and not to get seasick if they went out in a boat on the bay. He got a grin from the boy on that, and a drowsy good-night kiss.

O'Hare stayed with her for a while out in the kitchen after the boy fell asleep again, trying to tell her, trying himself to believe, that it wasn't as bad as she thought. New cures were coming along all the time, like the polio vaccine, and who knows — any day now they'd be finding something that would make the diabetes as simple to treat as any of the other diseases that were so dreaded. He'd heard recently about a pill they'd discovered for it. It might be Tim wouldn't even be needing to have the injections for long. They'd talk to the doctor about it. She was to try not to worry so. The thing was to carry on as much as possible as though things were normal — not to give Timmy the feeling he was an invalid — and to see to it that he ate properly, without making a big fuss over it.

She listened dumbly, nibbling away at the chocolate mouse she'd bought for Tim but couldn't let him have now, trying hard to stop the tears from falling, and when he kissed them away, crying, "Oh, Thomas, Thomas! Whatever would I be doing now without you!"

He didn't want to leave her, but it seemed wrong somehow to stay, letting the patrol car sit out there on the street in front of her house all night. Anyway, he had to return it. The late shift would be needing it.

It was raining and gusting up as he drove down the High Street at close to midnight, and he was surprised to see Delehanty's awning still down and the door to the shop open and clattering in the wind.

6

P. A. Delehanty stood one and a half meters tall, if you could call it that, and weighed close to fourteen stone, which made him look almost exactly like an ellipse. Everything about him was round — his mouth, his eyes, the shape of his head under his round baker's hat, and of course his stomach, which bellied out like a soccer ball under his starched white apron. He even thought in circles, his ideas whorling out and around and falling back on themselves to create a perfect philosophical nought, premise and conclusion canceling each other out. People saw him as a cantankerous little gnome of a man or an exuberant cherub, depending on his moods, which were volatile, as befits an artist; but they never for a moment doubted his artistry. Pierre Aloysius Delehanty was a genius, and the fame of his shop had spread far beyond the confines of Clontarf and Dublin, beyond even the shores of Ireland, for many of his creations were ordered by wealthy patrons and visitors to be sent abroad.

He was extremely fond of children, and never having married or produced any of his own, he cultivated the friendship of the youngsters in the neighborhood by providing them with an assortment of confections fit for a king. The ice cream he sold was made of the purest fresh dairy cream, marvelously flavored; his toffee, bonbons, nougat, and chocolates, his tarts and cookies were concocted of the finest ingredients, and so fragrant and temptingly displayed as to prove irresistible. He was always designing some new and unusual delight to capture the children's fancy and inflame their excitement—like the delicately molded chocolate elephant that had a glazed cherry eye and a pink peppermint rose at the tip of its trunk.

Of course, the adult customers had to pay quite a few shillings for these, and for the pastries and cakes they bought, which more than compensated for his impulsive generosity with the youngsters. His cautious, penny-pinching, hard-working French mother and his reckless, improvident, hard-drinking Irish father—both dead, but still very much alive in his spirit—had combined to form another perfect circle of Gallic practicality and Gaelic profligacy.

It was Delehanty's mother who had been the originator and mainstay of MADAME DELEHANTY'S BAKESHOP, EST. 1935, and it was she who had arranged for Pierre when he was in his early thirties to go abroad as an apprentice to the late great Escoffier. Delehanty Sr., having considerably more interest in becoming the star customer at the local pubs than in tending custom in his wife's shop, seemed determined to make his wife an early widow. Ironically, he failed in this as he did in all of his endeavors except the one: he could drink any ten men, jackeen or culchie, under the table without blinking an eye. Apparently, the Grim Reaper placed a higher premium on hard work than on hard drinking, and it was Madame Delehanty whom he chose to take first. She died quite suddenly in 1970 of apoplexy, predeceasing her husband by several months.

Pierre returned from Paris a master baker, in time for his mother's funeral. A week later he altered the sign above the shop to read THE FRENCH BAKERY AND SWEET SHOP, P. A. DELEHANTY, PROP. and promptly added a whole new line of special confections to attract the children in the neighborhood.

Madame Delehanty, had she known, would have risen from her grave at her son's wanton imprudence with *les petites,* but Delehanty Sr. was too inebriate, and too indifferent to matters of business, to pay any notice to his son's innovations. He did, however, remark happily to his pals at the pub on more than one occasion that the shop's till seemed fuller than ever since Pierre had come home.

One midnight, on returning from the Rose and the Thorn, the senior Delehanty found himself with a raging thirst still, and decided to pry open the lock to the cellar and help himself to some of the excellent Haitian rum stored there among the other baking supplies. He managed the lock, but never got to the rum. His son found him the following morning at the foot of the stairs. The poor man had taken a terrible fall and broken his neck.

Pierre buried his father beside his mother, and as the sole surviving Delehanty proceeded serenely and without guilt to cultivate his art, his business, and the very special relationship with the small boys and girls who flocked into his shop. He knew a great deal about each of the children, their names, ages, and birthdates, and their individual tastes and preferences. He teased, petted, and cajoled them all from the littlest bairn in her pram to the ruddiest eight- or ten-year-old tyke (children seemed to lose some of their charm for him when they began to grow bigger than he was), and they in turn were captivated by his jolly elfin appearance, his tender attentions, and of course by his marvelously tempting wares.

P.A. loved them all. They filled his days with delight, his nights with the most delicious dreams. He played no favorites as to sex, but he noticed that at times the little girls seemed to excite him more than the little boys — with one notable exception. But that, like his prized recipes, was the baker's well-guarded secret, and one he was not likely to share with anyone.

It was nine o'clock that Monday evening, and he was just about to lock up, the help having left after clearing the trays and sweeping the floor, making things neat and ready for the morning, when he noticed they'd forgotten to roll up the awning. Neglectful, that's what they were, always needing to be reminded about something or other, and he'd have to speak to them in the morning.

It had started to rain. The wind was blowing hard and the awning outside was rattling away. When he went out to crank it up, he noticed two young jocks hanging about. One of them was carrying a mac over his arm, which seemed to him odd since it had begun to rain heavily and why should he be carrying it instead of wearing it in the downpour? The knife the boy pointed at Delehanty's throat, while he twisted the baker's arm behind his back and marched him into the shop, made the reason clear enough.

The two of them shoved him into the back and made him open the safe, while they stood there stuffing themselves with the cream cakes from the refrigerated shelves, telling him to hurry it up, they didn't have all night. He still had the week's receipts there, not having gotten to the bank that morning as he'd intended, and they took it all, plus the cash in the till that he kept on hand to make change with, which came altogether to something over two hundred quid. Losing the money was bad enough, but the cheap rotten way they treated him filled him with an impotent rage and a ravening lust for revenge. They poked him in the belly, ripping his apron open with a knife, kicked him while he was down on his knees getting the money out of the safe, making nasty jokes about his size and calling him names he didn't want to remember. They took the cash and some more of the pastries, stuffing them into the bag they carried. Tying him up with the strings cut from his apron and pulling his cap down over his eyes so he couldn't see, they left him to sit there all night like a dunce.

Tears of pain and humiliation sopped the band of his cap, which was so tight over his nose he could hardly breathe, and when he tried to call out for help after they'd gone, all that came out was a muffled squeak of anguish. The wind was howling at the open door, and there was no one around to hear him.

7

Aggie hated having O'Hare leave her that night, but as it turned out, it was a lucky thing in some ways that he did. First off, there was her reputation to think of, and Jenny O'Flaherty, the jealous cat, hadn't hesitated to mention the next morning—acting all friendly sweet innocence—how she and some of the other neighbors too had happened to notice the police car sitting in front of the house from early afternoon till close on midnight and they'd all been wondering if maybe something was wrong. Aggie cut her short, telling her about Timmy and the diabetes, and got a lot of cluck-clucking and sympathy. But it made her feel that until she and O'Hare were ready to make a public announcement, they'd do well to be a bit more careful. Not that she gave a hoot what people might be thinking! Still and all, if you wanted to live in peace in a small place like Clontarf, you'd do better to keep your private affairs to yourself, and not be flaunting them in front of a bunch of small-minded gossipy busybodies.

It was a lucky chance that led O'Hare, driving down the High Street that night on his way back to the station, to notice the door to Delehanty's open and swinging in the wind, for if he hadn't, the poor little dwarf of a man might have died of suffocation or fright, which would have meant an end to the French Bakery and Sweet Shop as well. As it was, the shop was closed while P.A. recovered from the concussion he'd got when he fell, crashing down together with the high stool the hoodlums had tied him to. But he was back at work in less than a week, in spite of his injuries and the shock, praising O'Hare to the skies for saving his life, and for catching the hooligans, and boasting to one and all that the next time anyone tried to rob him, he'd make them pay dear for their trouble. He had an old carbine stashed away under some rags on a shelf right next to the safe (it must have been used in the Second World War, or even earlier) and he had it all oiled and polished and the bullets in, ready to use.

He showed it to Aggie one day when she came in to buy a few things and to tell him how sorry she was he'd been hurt and how pleased to see him back and well again. He flushed with gratification at her expressions of concern and took her out back to let her have a look at the gun. He'd every right, of course, to try to protect himself from the thieving ruffians, but the picture of him barely five feet tall holding a rifle bigger than himself and threatening anyone with it seemed pitiful, if not outright comical.

Still, truth to tell, she couldn't help liking the droll little man for all his queer looks and bombastic ways. He was such a pawky baker, and that gentle and loving with Timmy, always offering him a cookie or sweet as a treat, his plump round face wreathed in smiles and his eyes moist with pleasure at the sight of the child. He paid her a lot of attention as well, always leaving whatever he was doing, coming to wait on her himself, whenever she came into the shop. Well, she'd have to put an end to the free treats now and tell him about Timmy, though she hated talking about it, spreading the word about that the boy wasn't well, making him and herself a subject for pity. Still, there wasn't a chance in the world that everyone in and around Clontarf wouldn't be hearing about it before long. She could depend on Jenny O'Flaherty to be advertising it soon enough.

Somehow she never did get around to mentioning it herself to Delehanty, she was that convinced he must have heard the sad news by now. Lately she'd made it a point to do most of her marketing during the hours Timmy was in school, and though P.A. was always asking after him, all she could bring herself to say was that he was fine and doing well at school and busy with his homework and such. And once, when he'd offered her a bag of sweets as a present for Tim, she tried to refuse it, saying thanks very much but really she couldn't think of accepting it. But he wouldn't take no for an answer and kept pressing it on her, saying it was for her as well — he knew how mothers felt about too many sweets for the little ones — till she'd finally given in and taken it, wondering if it was possible the man hadn't heard the word yet about Timmy's condition.

When she and O'Hare talked about it later, they had a terrible row. He'd found a packet of P.A.'s caramels in Timmy's pants pocket and blamed her, and she'd rushed straight off to Delehanty's and given the little man a blistering to scorch the hide off an elephant, though she knew in her heart what had happened was probably more her fault than his.

8

When P.A. learned about Timothy O'Connell's not being allowed to have sweets any longer, he thought it a crying shame. But the manner of his learning of it turned out to be a screaming disgrace.

He had always thought Mrs. Agnes O'Connell a fine lady and a great looker, in addition to her being one of his best customers. The first time she came into the shop, he knew right off she'd come from America by her stylish clothes and her free and easy ways, though it was just as clear she was Irish to the marrow, for she had the true Gaelic beauty. Little Timmy, though fair and delicate, was even more beautiful than his mother. P.A. was terribly taken with him and couldn't resist plying the child with some special treat whenever Mrs. O'Connell brought him into the shop, which in the old days was often.

The day before the excitement with Mrs. O'Connell had been a Wednesday. It was close on to one o'clock in the afternoon and he was just about to put up the half-day-closing sign and lock the front door, having finished waiting on Mrs. Finnegan, always a last-minute shopper, who couldn't decide between the chocolate mousse, which was the special of the day, and the Boston cream pie, her husband's favorite, when he'd noticed little Timothy O'Connell standing about outside peering into the shop window. He hadn't seen the boy in several months, not since before the robbery as he recalled, and he wondered if maybe the child was avoiding him for some reason, though he couldn't imagine why—they'd always gotten on so well. He'd come out of the shop, wiping his hands on his apron—they were still a bit floury from wrapping the Irish soda bread, the "compromise" Mrs. Finnegan invariably settled for.

"Well, if it isn't Timothy O'Connell!" he'd said. "Just the one I've been waiting for. And where have you been hiding yourself all these weeks that I've been looking all over for you, wanting to show you my newest surprise?" The boy looking at him had smiled and held out his hand, showing him the few coppers he was holding. "Well, well!" P.A. said. "So you've come to shop for your mum, is it?"

"No," the boy said, "it's all for me. I'm to buy whatever I want with it."

"Aren't you the lucky one?" P.A. said. "But it's half-day closing. Now, what shall we do about that?"

"It's not too late, is it?" the boy asked anxiously. "I only wanted the chocolate mouse." He looked up appealingly, the wide violet-blue eyes pleading, the enchanting half-smile piercing P.A. to the heart.

"Never too late for a good customer," P.A. had said, and he'd drawn the child into the shop, put up the sign, and locked the door.

That night Delehanty dreamed one of the strangest dreams he'd ever had. He was riding on the back of a tiny pony, and the animal, though small, was fierce and wild and was running away with him. He couldn't stop it no matter how he tried. They were racing madly through a jungle of woods until suddenly, deliberately, the beautiful little animal reared and tried to throw him. A low-hanging branch gave him a terrible blow on the head and he'd fallen, bruised and shaken, the wind knocked out of him — to wake up sweating and breathless, his heart pounding like a jackhammer. He wasn't able to get back to sleep all the rest of the night. If he'd had any sense, he would have known the dream was a warning for the trouble he'd be having that very morning.

Thursday was always a busy time after Wednesday's half-day closing and the shop was filled with customers when Agnes O'Connell came raging in, pushing her way to the back where P.A., who had caught a glimpse of her coming in, was putting aside the brown bread dough he was kneading, thinking to wait on her himself.

"Mr. Delehanty!" she shouted, halfway across the shop. He came out troubled, wondering what it could be was upsetting her, but before he had a chance to inquire, she let fly a barrage that threatened to shatter the windows in all the shops along the High Street, let alone his own. Everyone including the help stopped dead in their tracks and was watching open-mouthed. Was he daft or what? she was yelling at him, her eyes blazing with fury, her hair flying wild, the usual fine high color draining out of her face as she bawled away at him. What in the world did he think he was doing, sneaking behind her back, filling her son with enough sweets to kill a horse, let alone a sick child? He might just as well have murdered the boy, it was pure luck he hadn't! And didn't he know, for God's sakes, the boy had the diabetes, and that candy and cake were pure poison for him? And here she was making herself sick trying to keep the child well and away from temptation, and Delehanty, God knows how often, tempting the poor kid, forcing him to disobey his mother's instructions. And why on earth hadn't P.A. — whom she'd always regarded as an understanding friend and neighbor, not just any ordinary tradesman — at least telephoned her to let her know

Tim was wandering the streets in the middle of the day when he should have been in school?

He was trembling, caught between shame and anger, but he drew himself up to his full height and said in a quiet dignified way that it had only happened the once, and would certainly never happen again, and that he was truly sorry, but so help him, he'd never heard a word about Timmy's having the diabetes and if she'd only told him! He even went on to suggest it was possible he could work out some kind of candy and cake with special ingredients and an artificial sweetener. He'd never done it before but he was sure he could find a way to make it tasty for the boy, and maybe for others who might be avoiding the sugar.

She broke down then, crying bitterly, the women surrounding her and drying her eyes and petting her, trying to soothe her down, and she finally stopped crying, saying how sorry she was and apologizing for her terrible display, but she was that crazed with worry. He said that he could understand that, and all he hoped was that Timmy was all right now, and she said praise heaven he was.

She came over then and put her hand on his arm, looking down at him and asking could he ever forgive her the awful things she'd been saying, and he said, "There, there — not to worry!" But his heart was heavy with the thought that things could never be the same again between him and Timmy, or Agnes O'Connell either.

9

He never got to school at all that day. He knew his mother wouldn't be expecting him home till after four, and he figured by that time he'd be back and she wouldn't even have to know. Only it didn't turn out exactly the way he planned. Anyway, he'd gotten the cookie jar down from the top shelf in the kitchen — she didn't keep cookies in it now, but he knew where she kept them and all the other sweet things she was always hiding around the house, thinking she was fooling him, pretending she didn't really care that much for sweets anymore — and he filched a few shillings from the change she kept there for the gas meter.

She was still asleep. She hated getting up in the mornings, and he liked getting breakfast himself and being on his own without her fussing over him the way she did all the time now. He tested his urine and the key stick turned a bright pink, which meant it was okay. She'd made him promise to call her if it was blue, the color of his eyes. She didn't give him his shot in the morning anymore, only once a day now, mostly when he came home from school.

He was desperate to have one whole day to himself to do exactly as he pleased. He was sick and tired of her bossing him around all the time, watching him like a hawk, keeping on at him about what he was eating and wouldn't he like to have a little rest now, and making a nuisance of herself in and out of his room every minute, when all he wanted was to be let alone.

It wasn't even fun going out with O'Hare anymore. She was always tagging along, and when the three of them would stop off at Bewley's or O'Meara's, she wouldn't let him order what he wanted, until all of a sudden feeling sorry for him, she'd give him a piece of her tart or order him some cream cakes, clattering away to O'Hare about how really it was too bad and the boy ought to be allowed to have a bit of a treat once in a while. And how could the child be always watching them eating things he wasn't allowed, and not be wanting them himself? Then when she'd stop, there'd be a thunderous silence, with black looks passing between the two of them and sometimes an argument, O'Hare flushed and angry but trying to stay calm, asking her couldn't she manage to leave off the sweets herself for a while? Or at least be consistent and let the boy have an occasional treat without always changing her mind every minute. He really thought they ought to have a talk with Dr. Vogel about it. The whole thing wasn't reasonable! By that time Timmy would just look at the cake, his stomach churning with worry, wanting to eat it but scared of what might happen if he did, and he'd end up pushing it away, saying he didn't really feel like having it now. And then she would sulk, or even start to cry, and the whole day would be spoiled.

School was a pain in the neck too. The kids were always poking fun at him because Sister Mary Theresa wouldn't let him run and play during recess. Falling and cutting himself was a danger, she said, and he mustn't let himself get exhausted. So he would just sit there with her and play board games, and a lot of the kids — except for Mike Finnegan who was his friend and okay — got to calling him teacher's pet and sissy. And at lunchtime, there they'd be, chomping away at their great brown bread sandwiches, gorging on chips and cookies and drinking soda pop, while all he had was lettuce and tomatoes, and an egg or a cheese slice, with only milk to drink, and maybe a piece of dry rusk, or sometimes an apple for dessert. Well, at least he wouldn't have to put up with that today.

What he really wanted was a day on his own, a day on the town. There was an American flick O'Hare had told him about playing at the Bijou, and he was dying to see it — *Serpico,* about an honest cop who was framed by the crooked gardai on the force. But it wouldn't start till around two o'clock and he had the whole morning to figure out what else he would do.

There was a variety shop, Madigan's on Market Street, where he'd seen a couple of nifty things he really wanted, and he'd go in and have a look around and maybe buy something if it didn't cost too much. When he got there he walked up and down the aisles and found a Houdini magic set that showed you how to get out of a pair of locked handcuffs and how to breathe under water (through a straw) and a lot of other tricks, and the neat cops-and-robbers game that O'Hare had told him about, and some chemistry and science sets too, but the prices were all too high. Anyway, Christmas wasn't far off and he was making a list for O'Hare and his mother of the things he wanted.

The saleslady kept coming over and asking him could she help. He wondered if she thought he might be going to snitch something (some of the kids he knew did) so he finally left, though he had some time still before the movie.

He wandered around a bit and was beginning to get hungry and was feeling thirsty — he hadn't had his mid-morning snack — when he suddenly remembered he'd left his lunchbox home on the front hall table. That was a mistake! If his mother saw it, she'd be off and running to the school with it and find out he wasn't there! He couldn't think what to do at first, then decided t'hell with it, he'd have his day anyway, and what could she do except scold? She wasn't likely to punish him, "a poor sick kid" like him, and he could always play on her sympathy and tell her he hadn't really felt well enough in the morning to go to school and hadn't wanted to wake her — but then, when he'd got to feeling better, he'd just gone out for some air and a walk around, and never noticed the time passing.

He stopped off at the food shop and had a stand-up lunch, ordering a hamburger and chips and a bottle of orange pop, and felt a lot better, especially after using a penny for the men's. He hadn't realized how late it was — half past one by the post office clock — and he was off to catch the number 13 for town, when he passed Delehanty's. He couldn't resist stopping to look in at the window. It was always such a gorgeous sight, and the smells that came out through the vents were so fragrant they made his mouth fill with spit. Just then, Mrs. Finnegan, Mike's mother, came out of the shop and he quickly put one arm over his head and pressed his face up against the glass like he was shielding his eyes, and she didn't seem to notice him, because she passed right by without a word.

There was a sign in the window that read "Special today — Chocolate Mousse," and he thought Delehanty had spelled it wrong and maybe he ought to go in and tell him. There wasn't a single chocolate mouse in the window, only mounds of cookies and a few cakes and fancy pastries, and the big glass jars filled with the homemade candies. He was thinking maybe he'd rather have the chocolate mouse than go to the movies, if it came down to it, when Mr. Delehanty came out of the shop.

He'd forgotten it was half-day closing, but Mr. Delehanty said it wasn't too late and he had a surprise that he wanted to show him, and before Timmy knew it they were inside and he was sitting on the high stool in the kitchen. It seemed all the chocolate mice were gone and wouldn't be made again until next week, but the surprise was a beauty — a macaroon kangaroo with a brown licorice tail and a sugar-plum baby peeping out of its little pouch. And he said straight off he'd have it. Only Mr. Delehanty wouldn't take the money for it but said it was a present. He'd never tasted anything so delicious and he sat there eating it, and P.A. seemed pleased he liked it and kept touching him, running his hand through his hair and down his back, which made him shiver a little. But he thought it must be the excitement of having such a sweet treat, after going without for so long.

He suddenly thought of O'Hare and how much he missed the fun they used to have when they went out alone together, just the two of them. He remembered the first time they played hide-and-seek in the park, one misty Sunday, and O'Hare's face looking comical and baffled when he managed to give him the miss by a hair's breadth, touching base, yelling "Home free!" Truth was, he didn't mind, almost liked it better, when O'Hare would catch him, shouting "Got you this time!" and toss him high in the air. It stirred some strange memory of something a long time ago. It must have been in America, when he was very little. He was being thrown high up in the air by this big man, it must have been his father. He'd feel light as a feather, then start to fall, the ground coming up at him fast, and be caught at the very last minute. It was scary but exciting, and when O'Hare caught him, it gave him the same breathless shivery feeling.

Mr. Delehanty was asking him if there wasn't anything else he'd like. He said no thanks, he really had to be going, his mother would be missing him, but the little man insisted he have a bag of caramels to take as well. He was startled when P.A., lifting him down off the stool, gave him a hug and a kiss, holding him tight — the baker's eyes all shining and his mouth very wet — but all he said was he really had to leave now. P.A. put him down then, and walked him back to unlock the door, and he said thanks again and ran out of the shop.

The bus was at the corner and he made it on time. He found a seat toward the back, next to an old lady with a lot of packages who kept smiling at him and shifting her bundles around so he'd have enough room. He was feeling kind of dizzy, and even thought he might have to throw up. He shoved the bag of caramels into his pants pocket but some of them spilled out onto the floor. He thought he should pick them up but he was afraid to bend down. The woman leaned over and said something, but he couldn't make out what it was.

They were going over the O'Connell Bridge when the bus veered sharply. The old lady let out a scream that seemed far away. Something exploded in his ear, and that was the last thing he remembered.

10

O'Hare's day started off with a bang. At ten-thirty there was an explosion at the entrance to the Bank of Ireland, housed in the old Parliament Building, and a second bomb went off that afternoon just a few blocks away at the O'Connell Bridge. Seven people were killed and twenty or more passers-by injured, not counting the passengers on a bus that had just missed the second explosion and had run amuck, sheering through a lamp post and careening to a stop after shattering the shop windows of Quinlan Brothers Haberdashers at the northwest corner of Burghers' Quay. The clothing models with arms and legs scattered, lying about amid the broken glass, confused everyone into thinking even more people were hurt and killed, and the anger of the excited crowd that gathered was near-hysterical. A dozen gardai had been assigned to cordon off the bridge area and disperse the crowd and see to it that the injured were taken care of, and O'Hare, who had been working all morning at the scene of the bank explosion, was sent over to supervise. Rumor had it that the Orange Freedom Fighters — the northern extremist Protestant faction — were claiming responsibility. Tempers flared, and the mood of the Dubliners was beginning to turn ugly.

Between getting people to move on to clear enough space for the ambulances to get through and trying to calm the injured and quiet the hot-heads — who were screaming their fool mouths off with cries of "Hang the murderin' Ulstermen!" and "Kill the bloody bastards!" — O'Hare and his men had their hands full. Some of the police were beginning to turn nasty themselves, threatening bystanders who didn't shut up and shove off with the lockup, and O'Hare had to warn them to cool down and just do the job. Not that he blamed them. It was rotten work and he was feeling sour and short-tempered himself, sick with shock at the sudden senseless violent death and the sight of the bloody and mangled wounded being carried away. No matter how often you'd seen that kind of thing, you could never really stomach the horror — though, with time and experience, you learned not to show it while you were working. Well, he'd learned, but he'd been on the force for over twenty years, and a lot of the men were still rookies.

The air was turning cold and it was beginning to drizzle. The men were worn out and could do with a rest and a round or two of Guinness. By four o'clock, the area around the bridge was more or less quiet and O'Hare called in to arrange for some relief help to redirect traffic and keep people away till the debris was all cleared and the crater in the street filled in. The damage to the O'Connell Bridge itself appeared minor. Only part of the marble railing on one side had been shattered, and the bronze plaque that gave its history was hanging askew. He was glad for that at least. He would have hated to see the old landmark totally destroyed. He was reminded of the first time he and Tim, on one of their early outings together, had walked across the bridge, and the boy had been so pleased and excited to learn the bridge had the same name as his.

He was sitting in one of the patrol cars waiting for the relief men to arrive when a message came through that Mrs. Agnes O'Connell had been trying to reach Officer O'Hare all afternoon and would he please get in touch with her as soon as possible. It was urgent.

11

It was eleven-thirty that Wednesday morning when Aggie O'Connell, hat and coat on and ready to be off to do her marketing, discovered Timmy's lunchbox sitting on the front hall table. He'd never forgotten it before and she was annoyed and troubled that he'd done it today — today of all days. It was half-day closing and she had a dozen things to take care of in the scant two hours left her. She was short of cash too. She'd meant to get to the bank to have her monthly pension check changed, and now she'd probably be late for that and for most of the shops as well.

She arrived at the school breathless and irritable, to be greeted in the hall with a fluster of effusion by Sister Mary Theresa, who was getting the children in line for wash-up and lunch, and before she had a chance to say a word or hand her the lunchbox, Sister was telling her how good it was of her to come by to inform them about Timothy's being absent today.

Sick again, was he, poor child! Well, she hoped he wouldn't be missing school for too long this time, he'd been doing so well lately. And had Mrs. O'Connell heard the terrible news about the bomb that had gone off at the Bank of Ireland that morning?

Aggie's heart, still beating fast from the rush, gave a sudden lurch of panic and she had to sit down on the hall bench. If he wasn't in school, where in God's name was he! Sister Mary Theresa was bending over her, blithering away, and she could see the children eyeing them with curiosity. She had to call O'Hare — he'd know what to do! She got up and without an explanation or apology was off and away, leaving the Sister open-mouthed, gaping after her like a fish out of water.

She was trying to think where the nearest public telephone would be. There was one over on the High Street, but that was blocks away. What a fool she was! Why hadn't she thought to call from the school? She was pushing herself like a racer, the lunchbox in her shopping bag banging against her legs, when she suddenly remembered she hadn't even thought to look in his room — maybe he'd overslept! She was sure she'd seen his breakfast dish in the sink, but he might have felt tired and gone back to bed again.

Her hands were trembling so she could hardly unlock the door and she was calling his name before she'd got in the hall. But his room was empty, the bed neatly made, as she'd taught him. She sat down on the bed to calm herself and gather her thoughts, trying to think what to tell O'Hare. She didn't even know what Timmy had been wearing that morning. She hunted through his drawers and figured it must be the brown corduroy trousers and the green sweater, then went to the phone and rang O'Hare's number. The line was busy but she kept trying. She was giving the operator the devil every few minutes for not putting her through faster on an emergency call, but the girl was snippy, saying, "Sorry, Madam, but the lines are tied up. There've been a few other emergencies in Dublin this morning, or haven't you heard?"

It was over half an hour before she finally got through and they told her O'Hare was out and probably wouldn't be back till late. Couldn't they please try to reach him, she said, it was very important. And would they please tell him to call Mrs. Agnes O'Connell right away — he knew the number. They said they'd try but they couldn't promise, and was there anyone else who could help her? She said yes, please, she wanted to report a missing child. The name? Timothy O'Connell she said; she was his mother.

After what seemed an hour, someone else got on the line. "Inspector John Riley," he said. By then she was so shaken she could hardly talk, but he seemed a gentle soft-spoken man and asked her for a description of the child.

She was struggling to be clear about the details. A boy just turned eight, she told him, with blond hair and deep blue eyes. Weight? Slim, about sixty pounds. Height? She thought around forty-eight inches, tall for his age. Well, she wasn't altogether sure about what he was wearing. Brown corduroys, she thought, and a green sweater. Did she have a picture? Yes, she did. He'd be sending over for it, but it might take a while. How long had the boy been missing? Since morning, he hadn't been to school at all that morning. No, he'd never played hooky before, but the thing was, the child had the diabetes and she was naturally worried. He needed to have his injection by late afternoon.

Riley said he'd get right on to it and would be calling her back the minute he had any news. It would be a good thing if she stayed close to the house, the boy might show up by himself. And would she be good enough to let them know, if that happened?

He never mentioned anything about the bank bombing, and she never asked him.

By two o'clock, she couldn't stay put another minute and, leaving the door open, ran next door to Jenny O'Flaherty's to find out if maybe she'd seen Tim that morning. Jenny was always out in her garden early and might have noticed him passing, or even talked to him. She rang the O'Flaherty's bell, keeping an eye on her house and scanning the neighborhood and, in exasperation, banged on the door, but it seemed there was no one at home.

Coming back, she saw Mrs. Finnegan walking along across the street and ran over to ask her if she'd seen Timmy anywhere. Kathleen Finnegan was fond of the boy. Tim and her son Mike were friends. She was troubled to hear that Timmy was missing, and full of expressions of concern and sympathy, but not much of a help. Though come to think of it, she said, she'd caught a glimpse of a boy who might have been Tim, standing outside Delehanty's not fifteen minutes ago. She hadn't stopped to greet him, thinking Tim would surely be in school at that hour and she must be mistaking some other child for him. She even offered to go round and see if she could spot him, but Aggie said would she mind just to wait in the house for a while, while she herself went to look—just in case the police might call back or Timmy come home, the while she was gone? She had to be doing something or she'd be going out of her mind. Kathleen kissed her and said sure and she'd be glad to, and Aggie must try not to worry herself sick, the boy would surely turn up safe and unharmed. Kids were always wanting to play hooky from school and scaring their parents half to death. He'd be home by the time school let out, wait and see, and feeling guilty as sin for all the trouble and fuss he'd caused.

The High Street was quiet, with most of the shops, including Delehanty's, shuttered and closed, and there were few passers-by. She stopped at the bus stand to ask if anyone had seen a small boy in a green sweater anywhere about, but no one had. She tried Madigan's — they had a Thursday closing — but there was no sign of him there. One of the salesgirls said there'd been a small boy who'd come in and spent quite a bit of time looking at the games, but that was around noon. She couldn't remember if he'd been wearing a green sweater, but yes, he was blond. A lovely-looking child, she said, she couldn't help but remember him. Aggie thanked her, half-laughing, half-crying, and hugged her — the salesgirl must have thought her a loon — and walked home feeling almost human again. They'd find him in time for sure, and it would be all right. He was safe. The salesgirl had seen him in Madigan's that noon! He hadn't been anywhere near the Bank of Ireland. And why she'd thought he might be hanging around there, she couldn't begin to imagine.

She was a block from home when she met Jenny O'Flaherty and her mother, all a fluster with the news. Had she heard? A second bomb had just gone off at Burghers' Quay near the O'Connell Bridge.

12

It was Kathleen Finnegan who answered the phone, speaking in such a queer wispy voice that O'Hare could hardly make out what she was saying. No, Agnes wasn't there. She'd gone off to hunt for Timmy. He'd been missing since early morning. Jenny O'Flaherty had come by and offered to stay till Agnes got back, but Mrs. Finnegan couldn't bring herself to leave till she knew the worst, and the two of them were waiting together. Yes, the gardai had been notified. But she'd been calling around to the hospitals herself, to see if the child had been identified yet. No, no one seemed to know anything, or if they did, they weren't giving out any information. And wasn't it an awful thing, everything in such a terrible state of chaos! And did he think there was anything else she could be doing to help?

He said thanks, no, he couldn't think of anything, but would she please tell Mrs. O'Connell—Agnes—if she came home to stay there, and he'd be calling again in a little while? He was sure everyone was doing everything they could, and would she mind seeing to it that no one tied up the phone so that he and the others could get through if they had any news?

He put through a call to the station to check on what was being done and Riley told him the hospitals had been given a description and that he'd contacted Paddy Morphy, who was alerting the force to look out for the child. O'Hare said thanks, that was good, and he'd be following through himself, explaining to Riley he was a friend of the family's. He hung up feeling worn and wasted, and sickened by the smell of his own sweaty fear.

When he got out of the car, he saw her almost at once at the far end of the bridge, arguing with two of his men, and he went over and spoke to them and took her arm and walked her away. She was pale and quiet, listening when he told her he'd spoken to Kathleen Finnegan and that he'd just talked to Riley, a good man. They'd put out a special call to all the squad cars with the description of Tim, and they had two men checking the hospitals. He told her he'd been at the bridge himself since just after the explosion, before the injured had been taken away, and lied, saying he'd surely have seen Tim if he'd been among them. The boy had probably just gotten an urge to play hooky from school—he'd done it himself often enough when he was a boy—and gone off on a lark for the day, maybe to the movies, planning on being home by school closing and no one the wiser—and then stayed through twice, forgetting the time. Lost kids were always turning up, none the worse for wear. Everyone in Dublin kept an eye out for children, and someone was sure to report seeing him. The best thing for her to do was to go straight home. He was sure to have some news for her soon, if Tim wasn't there already.

She never spoke a word all the while. The drizzle was letting up, but it was turning cold and she was shivering against the wind. He put her in a cab and gave the driver the address. As he was closing the door she gave a plaintive little cry and said, "Call soon, O'Hare!"

13

He was lying in bed and a man in a white coat was bending over him. There was something attached to his arm with a plastic pipe leading into a bottle hanging over his head. He suddenly saw O'Hare standing in front of the bed and for a minute thought he might be dreaming, but O'Hare was wearing his uniform and seemed very solid, and after a little while he figured he must be real. He tried to raise his other hand to wave at him, but the doctor said, "Hold still a minute there, like a good lad." He tried to smile at him, but his lips felt funny and stiff, and he wasn't sure if he was smiling or crying.

The doctor and O'Hare went away, and after a long time O'Hare came back and pulled up a chair, taking his hand and saying not to worry, the doctor said he was going to be fine, and he might even be going home by the weekend. He hadn't been hurt hardly at all in the bus crash, except for a couple of bruises, and in a way the accident had been lucky for him, because the minute the ambulance had picked him up they'd seen his medic-alert bracelet, and they'd known right away what to do for him.

O'Hare promised to visit again tomorrow with his mother, and to bring him the cops-and-robbers game he'd told him about from Madigan's. He thought sure O'Hare would say something about his playing hooky from school, but all he said was, "Listen Tim, me boyo, let's steer clear of too many of those sweets from Delehanty's, for a little while anyway. What do you say?" He remembered the kangaroo and wondered how O'Hare had found out about it right off. He was certainly a wizard detective.

He managed the smile for real then, and promised.

14

O'Hare called her from the hospital the minute he finished talking to the doctor, to give her the good news. Tim was safe and being cared for at Mercy Hospital. No, it was God's truth, he wasn't lying to her, the boy was all right. She'd be able to see him herself tomorrow. Yes, Tim was awake and had talked to him. He was leaving the hospital himself now, and would be with her in a little while.

Jenny O'Flaherty was still there with Aggie when he arrived, and reluctant to leave till she'd heard the story twice through, about how they'd found Tim, and about the bombing and the explosion at the bridge, and all the terrible events of the day. She hung around, hovering over O'Hare, saying he must be exhausted, and didn't he want a bite to eat or something to drink, and she'd be glad to fix him and Aggie some supper, they must both be starved.

Aggie got rid of her at last and brought out the bottle of whiskey and a plate of cold meat and some stout. They were too tired to eat but they drank quite a lot, hardly talking.

He kept thinking he was going to have it out with her about her and Timmy, but he knew now wasn't the time.

They took the last of the bottle up with them, leaving the food and dishes on the table, and finished it off before they undressed. He crawled into bed then, every bone in his body crying out for rest and peace. Thank God, he was drunk now and could sleep.

She seemed sodden too — though she hadn't had nearly half what he'd taken — befuddled with tiredness probably and the relief, as much as with the drink. Her movements, awkward and stumbling as she got out of her clothes, had a wanton appeal, and looking at her he felt a stir of anger and longing. She was standing at the mirror, arms upraised, swaying unsteadily, trying to brush her hair. The curve of her naked back, so soft and defenseless, struck him like a blow and he wanted to say something to hurt her.

She came into bed and put her arms around him, but he moved away and turned over, pulling the covers close around him so he couldn't feel her body touching him. He could hear her weeping softly, even hear the tears falling on the pillow. She let out a moan that was half a curse, and he thought of a woman he'd seen at the bridge, down on her knees, bending over her dead husband. He couldn't get the picture out of his mind, the hate in her face, and the stunned faces of the people gathering silently round her, the hush broken, as keening her grief she wailed, "Ah, look what the murderin' scum have done to you now!"

He turned back and said "Jesus! Stop sniveling!" and grabbed her, pulling her close, holding her tight by the buttocks and pressing her hard up against him. He knew it wasn't going to be any good, he was too tired and full of drink, and she was jumpy and worn out, and angry now, too. She was trying to push him away and caught him a cuff on the nose that stung so, he almost slugged her back.

He could feel the knot of pain and fury rising in him like some poison, the tension that had been building in him all day exploding into a rage of passion, and he pulled her down by the hair and held her, pinning her arms, pushing her face into his crotch. She was twisting her head every which way, gasping for breath, but in a minute she was taking him and they were at each other like a pair of wild rutting animals. He was into her now, but still fighting her all the way, trying to ride out the storm, a wind of misery and frustration howling around him like a banshee, speeding him on, until like a burst of thunder, he was gone, a great torrential wave pouring over him, dissolving the hate and the hurt, washing away all the sins of the world.

15

Everything had gone wrong that morning. She'd burned the bacon and scorched the eggs and had a fight with O'Hare and said she'd be damned if she'd fix him another breakfast after the things he'd been saying to her. Then to top it all, she'd stormed out of the house and gone off to give Delehanty a piece of her mind, and wound up making a fool of herself, crying and carrying on like a loony in front of that crowd of women.

She thought over the events of the morning and wondered why in God's name it had all turned so sour . . .

O'Hare had gotten up before her. She could hear him at the telephone when she came downstairs. She was feeling washed-out from all the running and the fright yesterday, groggy still from the stuff she'd drunk, not to mention their wild time in bed after. She sat down at the kitchen table trying to gather the strength to clear away the dishes from last night and fix some breakfast when he came out back to the kitchen to tell her he'd just spoken to the hospital and Tim's condition was reported as good. He'd checked in too with Riley to tell him he wouldn't be coming in till noon. The two of them could have the morning together. He'd promised Tim a cops-and-robbers game from Madigan's. They could pick it up on their way to the hospital and they might go out on the town in the evening, after he was through with work, if she felt up to it, to some posh restaurant or one of the singing pubs, if she preferred. There was something he wanted to talk to her about, but it would hold till then.

He made her a cup of tea, clearing the table, then sat down with her and said quietly, his face flushing, he hoped she could bring herself to forgive him for being so rough with her last night.

She put her hand on his lips saying "Shush now, there's nothing to forgive!" and that maybe it was she who ought to apologize, she'd been pretty rough with him herself. He grinned then and put his arms around her, kissing her face with soft little kisses, whispering in her ear, calling her "Agnus Dei," his own love, his own lamb, telling her she was the light of his life and he'd never known another woman like her . . .

There was no question about it, the man had a way with him — looks or no looks — that'd charm the skirts off the nuns in a nunnery, and she was beginning to feel a lot better, thinking surely he was ready at last to give her the word she'd been waiting for. She begged him to tell her what it was he was wanting to talk to her about till he finally gave in.

Well, she was far off the mark. What he had in mind that was so important was the way she was handling Timmy! He hoped she wouldn't take it amiss, but he felt things weren't right between her and the child, and he thought it might be a good idea if she maybe could see her way clear to making some changes or at least think about the possibility of what he was about to suggest . . .

She said sharply, "Changes? Like what?" Her disappointment and the sense of him sitting there in judgment on her, with his holier-than-thou air, while at the same time trying to spare her feelings with that mealy-mouthed speech, put her back up, and she got up and went to the stove and banged the skillet around, tossing the rasher into the pan and breaking the eggs into a bowl, making a great clatter of cooking.

"Like not being so quick-tempered, for instance," he said. "You're not the only one who's concerned for the boy."

"Is that so?" she said. "And who's concerned about me, and what I have to put up with?"

"I am," he said, "and you know it. Don't you think I know how hard it's been on you?"

"Then just what is it you're talking about?"

"It's hard on the boy too, don't you see that?"

"*I'm* hard on the boy, is that what you're trying to say? Why don't you say it straight out then? You think I'm a rotten mother!"

"Agnes," he said, "will you just listen!" He tossed the bag of caramels on the table. "It's this I'm talking about, things like this." The bag was torn and crumpled and had Delehanty's name stamped on it. "Would he be going around behind your back sneaking sweets, if you didn't keep hiding them around the house all the time? Yes, you're hard on the boy! Giving him the feeling that it's a sin for him to want something special once in a while, and that it's a sin and a shame he can't have it. Changing your mind every minute, taking away with the one hand and giving back with the other. In God's name, can't you see what you're doing?"

"I haven't had a caramel in the house all week!" she said.

"They were in Tim's pocket, when they undressed him at the hospital!"

"Well, he got them from Delehanty himself then!" she said. "And the man's a fool or a villain—he knows the child's not allowed any sweets!"

"He *is* allowed treats, on a sensible basis! He should have them! The doctor said so. And he ought to be allowed to go out and play with the other kids after school. You're blaming yourself and you're punishing Tim for something he can't help, out of your own anguish and despair. And that's what I'm talking about, Agnes. For God's sake, will you stop treating the boy like there's nothing left to his life except the injections and the special diet and sitting quiet alone by himself, while the rest of the world goes dancing by!"

"Mary, Mother of God! The child's a diabetic!"

"So he is. It's a sickness, and he can live through it with proper care. You make it sound like a crime!"

The bacon was sputtering on the stove and there was the smell of burnt eggs.

"The only crime I see is the way you're telling me what's right for my own child! You're not his father, and not likely to be it seems, and I'd be thankful to you if you'd keep your nose out of my affairs!"

O'Hare gave her a look then that turned her blood cold, but she couldn't stop. She said, "If you want some breakfast, you'd better fix it yourself. I'll be damned if I'll do it!"

She picked up the caramels and threw them clear across the room, left everything and went out of the house, slamming the door behind her.

★ ★ ★

When she got back from Delehanty's, O'Hare was gone. There was a note by the hall telephone telling her he'd be at the hospital till noon. She hadn't expected it. For a while there, she'd felt certain it was all over between them.

As she put the note down, she caught a glimpse of herself in the front hall mirror. She looked terrible, her hair wild, her face puffy with crying. She spent an hour trying to find a decent dress to put on and to fix herself up so she wouldn't look as miserable and beaten as she felt, but it was time wasted. By the time she got to the hospital, it was well past noon, and O'Hare was nowhere in sight, which didn't improve her mood.

Seeing Timmy with that intravenous thing plugged into him scared the life out of her. He was asleep most of the time she was there. The Sister could see how worried she was and kept assuring her Tim was all right and just needed the rest, but she was that distraught she couldn't think straight. And when the child finally woke up, all she could do was scold him for running off and giving her such a terrible fright, though she hadn't meant to, and was sorry the minute the words were out of her mouth. Luckily, he didn't seem to mind, or maybe he hadn't made out what she was saying, because he gave her a smile and a wave, then shut his eyes and went right back to sleep.

When she came out, she was surprised to find Paddy Morphy standing down the hall waiting for her. He'd come by to give her the message that O'Hare had to go off out of town — it was some business to do with the bombings — and would be in touch with her when he got back.

She had a rush of disappointment remembering their promised night out together. But worse, with his going off, she'd no way of straightening out their morning quarrel, of telling him how sorry she was. A grievance, like a thorn that was not removed promptly, could fester.

Paddy came back into the waiting room with her and told her how sorry he was to learn about Tim, but he'd heard from O'Hare the boy was doing well. He said he had the squad car downstairs and could he give her a lift somewhere? She said no thanks, she'd be staying around at the hospital for awhile yet. She asked did he know how long O'Hare would be gone? He said it might be a couple of days, or a week maybe, there was no way of telling, adding with a wink, no doubt O'Hare would be warning her himself when to expect him back. He took her hand then and held it, saying if she needed anything, not to hesitate to call on him, he'd be more than willing to oblige. And if she wanted some company that night or the next, she knew where to reach him.

She was sorry, in a way, to see him go.

She'd met Paddy at a dance one evening when she'd first moved to Clontarf, and had gone out with him a number of times. He called her often in those days, and though she really was taken with him, she started to make excuses about being busy. He was a lot younger than she was, and not much of a prospect for marriage, and when she started seeing O'Hare, Paddy gradually faded out of the picture.

He was as different from O'Hare as day from night, handsome as a movie actor, with green eyes and reddish blond hair, and brash as a new copper penny. Full of fun and lewd jokes he was, and a terrible flirt. Not to mention conceited. The first time he'd taken her out to a fancy restaurant, he'd leaned over and licked her ear and whispered, "When are you comin' to bed with me Aggie me luv?" And when, startled, she'd said "Never!" he'd laughed, saying "I'll lay odds on, you'll be begging me to before the night's out!" It had turned her straight off, but you couldn't really stay mad at him. With all his nerve, he was so engaging and lively, it seemed foolish to take offense. And the conceit was probably just the way he had of putting up a big front. He wasn't more than thirty and had never married, and for all his boasting, she was sure he wasn't nearly as experienced as he tried to make out. Still and all, he'd come close to making good on his wager, and if Timmy hadn't happened to wake after Paddy had brought her home that evening, she might have been tempted to let him stay . . .

Around four o'clock, the nurse came out to tell her Timmy was up. The child's color was good and he seemed cheerful, and she spent an hour with him playing the cops-and-robbers game O'Hare had brought. He kept asking after O'Hare and got very excited when he learned the man had gone off to track down the gang responsible for the bombings. He asked wasn't it a terrible dangerous mission? And she said she guessed it might be, but she was sure O'Hare could take care of himself. Actually, the idea of the danger hadn't occurred to her till Timmy mentioned it, and the thought made her anxious.

She got home from the hospital feeling depressed and lonely. The house seemed like a tomb without Timmy, and the prospect of O'Hare's being gone for maybe a week upset her. She'd been a fool to lose her temper with him when all the man wanted was to help her and the boy. If he called, *when* he called, she'd tell him how wrong she'd been, and how sorry she was.

She didn't know what had gotten into her lately. There'd been a desperate turbulence growing in her over the past few weeks that even O'Hare's sudden fierce lovemaking last night hadn't been able to still. She had this heartsick longing to be young and carefree again, to be the girl she once was, full of life and the joy of living, who'd been wooed by James Ward O'Connell and the fine young men in the great city of New York, like a princess in a fairy tale, with never a care or a worry in the world.

She hadn't eaten all day but was too tired to think of fixing herself a decent meal. The caramels were lying all over the floor where she'd thrown them, and she picked one up and started to chew it, but it sickened her and she had to spit it out.

She was dead on her feet and getting ready for bed when the doorbell rang. It was Jenny O'Flaherty, come over to inquire about Timmy and to bring her a plate of stew and some pudding old Mrs. O'Flaherty had made. She hadn't the strength to turn her away, and though Jenny saw she was in her nightgown, the

woman stayed to gossip as usual. Aggie picked at the food,
pretending to eat while Jenny rambled on about her and O'Hare
(feeling no doubt she had the right, since she was the one had
introduced them), saying what a great catch O'Hare was, and
how she was expecting to hear any day now they were posting the
banns, and that it looked like Agnes had won out over quite a few
of the other women the man had been carrying on with. There
was one in particular, a schoolteacher she was, young enough to
be O'Hare's daughter. Did Aggie know about her? A Protestant
by the name of Eileen Hackett, who'd come down from Belfast
some years back and was living over in Howth with her brother
and his wife and their two children. But Jenny didn't imagine he
was seeing much of the girl these days. She was sure Aggie held
first place in his heart. It was clear as day, you couldn't miss the
light in O'Hare's eyes whenever he looked at her! And wasn't it
wonderful the way the man was with Timmy?

It was the first time Aggie'd heard any mention of the woman
by name, though she'd known O'Hare had been seeing someone
before he met her.

She said coldly, it wasn't as though she and O'Hare were
engaged yet, and she certainly felt free herself to go out with
anybody else she liked, so why shouldn't he? Besides, it really
wasn't anyone's concern but their own.

Jenny O'Flaherty finally left looking miffed, and Aggie
crawled into bed exhausted. The sheets were still rumpled from
last night, and when she burrowed under the covers, the smell of
O'Hare seemed to fill her nostrils. Tired as she was, she couldn't
get to sleep but kept twisting and turning, hugging the pillow
he'd slept on, wondering where he was now and what he was
doing, thinking maybe it had all been a lie, an excuse to get rid of
her, sending Paddy to tell her he had to go out of town on police
business. He might be in bed making love with that young
schoolteacher from Howth this very minute . . .

*A Catholic child, interviewed by a reporter
from the United States about her father and
brother killed in the fighting in Derry, is
asked, "Doesn't it make you lose your faith
in God?"*

She replies, "No, in man."

1

Willie Connaught, traveler in linens for the Daintee Damask
Company, Ltd., home office in Belfast, North Ireland, was in
Howth at the time the bomb went off at the O'Connell Bridge.
He'd just returned from delivering a gift to the children of an old
friend who had moved down from the North and now lived near
the Head. He heard the news over the wireless at O'Halloran's
Pub, where he'd only just stopped for a pint but had stayed till
closing, talking loudly to strangers and saying some things that
might have been better left unsaid.

He woke the next morning in a bed at the Green Dragon Inn
without the least notion as to how he had got there. He had a
consuming thirst, an awful head, and a worse conscience, and
spent the rest of the day in the bar trying to ease all three with
little success, wondering what he should do. By five o'clock he
concluded that the only decent thing was to warn his friend that
some fool had been shooting his mouth off at O'Halloran's the

night before (the fool being Willie himself, but he saw no reason to mention that) and that it might be wise for his friend to disappear up North for a while, or get out of the country altogether. A stoolie, hungry for the reward of £100 sterling for information about the Dublin bombings, could be alerting the gardai that very minute.

What Willie didn't know was that he'd been under surveillance since the previous evening, when he'd pointed the finger straight at the man he was now trying to save.

He was back in O'Halloran's late that night, feeling relieved and pleased that he'd finally performed his good deed, when the police picked him up. Connaught wouldn't say a word under questioning except to swear he'd had nothing to do with setting the Dublin bombs. It was true; he hadn't. But they threw him in the lockup anyway. His sober conclusion, after he'd had a while to dry out and think things over, was that virtue wasn't always its own reward, and that doing a favor for a friend often didn't pay off.

The following day when he learned what had happened, he tore some strips from the blanket on the cot in his cell — they'd taken away his belt and boot laces — and hanged himself.

It was O'Hare, come to take him back to Dublin, who found him quite dead and helped the gaoler to cut him down.

2

The call came into the station at twelve twenty-five in the afternoon and was put through to Inspector John Riley. He listened a moment, then signaled O'Hare, who had just come in, to pick up on the extension.

A man by the name of O'Halloran who ran a pub in Howth said he had an interesting piece of information that might have something to do with yesterday's bombings, and he thought the Dublin police might be wanting to follow it up. Naturally, he felt it was his patriotic duty to report what he knew, but he was wondering if the offer of the £100 reward still held?

When Riley assured him it did, the publican explained at some length that of course everyone knew the O.F.F. had done the job, at least they'd claimed the credit, but he was sure he was on to something important. Under Riley's patient prodding, it turned out that the source of O'Halloran's anticipated windfall was a bibulous traveler in linens from Belfast who, he thought, might very well be a courier for one of the Northern extremist factions, maybe the O.F.F. The man was presently stopping at the Green Dragon in Howth. O'Halloran himself was calling from there now. No, the man hadn't named names exactly, but he'd let drop several broad hints that he might be in a position to collect the reward.

There was a breathy silence.

Riley shook his head wearily at O'Hare, who shrugged back in sympathy. On the basis of O'Halloran's report, Riley said, he felt the traveler should be given a slightly longer leash before being picked up for questioning. He suggested O'Halloran put the chief of the local gardai on to it at once. But under no circumstances was the person in question to be alerted to the fact that he was being watched.

O'Halloran replied he'd already taken care of that, not to worry. The traveler was well in his cups, and had been since the previous night. Sergeant Gilligan had already been notified — he was just finishing his lunch and would be coming over directly. But as Inspector Riley undoubtedly knew, the force in Howth consisted of two gardai and a couple of volunteers, one of them being himself, and while nothing was happening at the moment, the matter could turn into something bigger than the local constabulary could handle, and he thought it might be a good idea if Dublin could provide some back-up help. Just in case.

Riley agreed and thanked him, and said that he and his assistant, Detective O'Hare, would be out in Howth in under an hour.

★ ★ ★

O'Halloran, a fat fussy man, was waiting for them together with Sergeant Ginger Gilligan on the steps of the post office across from the pub. After the introductions, O'Halloran reported that it looked like the suspect wasn't about to move anywhere for a while yet. The man was on his sixth jar at the moment. Young Jamie Flanagan, the junior member of the local gardai, was in at the bar drinking with him, but someone had better replace Jamie soon, for as everyone knew, the poor lad had no head at all for the drink.

Gilligan, who had met Jamie back in the men's not ten minutes ago, confirmed this. The young garda had nothing new to report, but was suffering from a terrible case of the hiccups, and it was plain he wouldn't be able to hold up much longer.

Riley solved this dilemma with his usual tact and efficiency. He suggested that Jamie be relieved of further duty for the present and that Sergeant Gilligan return to the station and keep an eye out for the everyday needs of the citizens of Howth. O'Hare would take Jamie's place at the bar, and he himself would keep watch outside, spelling O'Hare in an hour or so if the traveler still hadn't made a move.

Loathe to terminate his moment of glory, O'Halloran proceeded to give them a long-winded description of the suspect, which in sum depicted a convivial, talkative man about fifty, balding, sporting a reddish moustache, tall, heavy-set but soft-looking. He was wearing a greenish tweed jacket with suede patches at the elbows, and had signed in at the inn's register under the name of Willie Connaught.

Riley thanked O'Halloran again for his help, and complimented Gilligan on his competence in running such an effective police operation with so small a force. In a few minutes, Jamie Flanagan received a discreet message that he was wanted at home and staggered out of the bar just as O'Hare entered. Officer Gilligan escorted the junior garda back to the station and put him to bed in one of the two cots in the only cell in the gaol, which fortunately was empty. He promptly collapsed and stayed knocked out till later that night when Willie Connaught was brought in.

3

Rory Hackett ran a fish bar in a cottage not far from Howth, renting out fishing boats to vacationing sportsmen as a sideline. It was a living, but something of a comedown for a graduate engineer with a degree in chemistry from the University of Belfast. His wife, Grace, did the cooking and helped out behind the bar. They lived behind and over the shop in four rooms with their two children, Haila and Ian, and Rory's sister, Eileen. Eileen held a position in a small Protestant school run by the Church of Ireland in Dun Laoghaire, a distance of some fifteen kilometers from Howth, which she traversed by bicycle twice daily in all weather.

Rory was a defector, a former activist in the Orange Freedom Party, a militant Protestant organization adamantly opposed to any and all offers of a coalition government. The members had pledged themselves to the establishment of the free and independent State of Ulster and the return of the three counties stolen from them by the South. Rory had joined the secret terrorist sector of the party, the Orange Freedom Fighters, straight out of university, providing the group with explosives he made himself, and doing his share of the fighting in the bloody street wars of the 1970s till the day his brother Billy, age sixteen, was killed by one of Rory's grenades. The mechanism had been faulty, or the boy had waited too long before tossing it. There'd been little enough of him left to bury. They'd had to weight his coffin with rocks so it wouldn't seem empty.

Rory's wife, Grace, threatened to leave him then, taking their two small children with her, if he didn't quit the party. Rory agreed to get out. He didn't need much persuading. He had seen Billy's head blown off and the boy's arms and legs, dismembered, go sailing through the air. The vision would stay with him the rest of his life.

The family planned to leave Belfast together, but Rory was forced to go first. Both the British and the I.R.A. Provos (the radical terrorist wing) were after him, and he ran with the help of the party (not yet aware of his decision to desert the cause) to Liverpool. He spent a miserable year there hiding out, then, without telling his comrades, moved on South to the Republic, where he was joined by Grace and the children and his younger sister Eileen, settling finally on the east coast near Howth. He felt safer close to the open sea.

Eileen had been supporting all of them till Rory got the idea of setting up the small food shop and boat rental business. It was a decent seasonal trade, catering to local sportsmen as well as to the tourists who came in the spring and summer to visit the Point, and make the grand tour of Howth Castle and the monasteries on the islands of Monkstown and Ireland's Eye.

When he'd left Liverpool, he'd changed his name. The true Rory Hackett, a former university classmate, was now safely away in Australia where he had a fine job with a big engineering firm and was not likely to return. Forged identity papers had not been difficult to arrange.

The business at Howth did well enough, but the new Rory was a bitter cankered man. His earlier political fervor and once fierce anti-Catholicism now seemed to him senseless in the light of what had happened to him and his family. Living under an assumed identity in the Republic, hiding from his former friends in the O.F.F., wanted by the Provos and the Brits, he was eaten up with pessimism about his chances of being allowed to live out his life in peace, tending his shop and renting his boats. His pessimism was not long unjustified. It was three years almost to the day since he'd run from Belfast, and a month before the Dublin bombings, when the O.F.F. found him.

That afternoon, a fisherman who'd rented a boat came in with a fine catch. He generously offered Hackett several of the bigger fish, which Rory accepted with thanks. As he was paying for the rental, the man dropped a hint to the effect that *Mr. Hackett* was in a unique position to do a small favor for some of his old pals in Belfast. Rory gave him his change and disappeared into the boathouse without saying a word. The man left quietly enough, but a few days later two visitors from the North stopped off at the boathouse. They took one of the boats and rowed out to the Point. Hackett accompanied them. They repeated the original suggestion. Hackett threatened to go to the police and name names. Though still amiable, they were extremely persuasive, pointing out what a mistake that would be. They begged him to reconsider, promising this would be the last job the party would ask of him, swearing once it was done, they'd never trouble him — or his family — again. The threat to his family convinced Rory he had little choice.

In despair, he agreed. He filled the order, with certain modifications, and delivered the merchandise, as instructed, to a storage locker at the Dublin airport, mailing the key to a box number c/o General Delivery at the Wexford post office.

The day of the Dublin bombings, Haila and Ian came home from school with a small package and a note addressed to their father some stranger had given them. The man said his name was Willie Connaught and that he was an old friend of the family, back in Belfast. Hackett took the package out of the boathouse and checked it carefully. It was a transistor radio. There was nothing to defuse, nothing planted inside. The accompanying note read simply, "A small gift for your children as a token of good faith. We knew we could depend on you."

He tore the note up and hid the radio under some tarpaulin at the back of the shed. He had no intention of letting his children have it. With some minor adjustments, it could be turned into something quite useful.

4

O'Hare slid onto the bar stool recently vacated by Jamie Flanagan. It was still warm.

The convivial, talkative Connaught of O'Halloran's description turned out to be a morose, silent hulk of a man who had, as accurately reported, a quite remarkable capacity for Guinness. It was clear that he had some heavy weight on his mind, but he seemed disinclined at the moment to disclose what it was to anyone at the bar. Except for sighing deeply and regularly between long draughts at his frequently replenished glass, and acting generally as if the sorrows and worries of the world were his alone to bear, he stayed silent as the tomb and entirely unresponsive to O'Hare's attempts to draw him into conversation.

At four o'clock, Connaught slumped over the bar and fell into a deep and sonorous sleep. O'Hare helped the barman put the traveler to bed and in a little while came out to report to Riley that he'd searched the room with Connaught snoring away and had found nothing of significance. The man's bona fides seemed legitimate. The only thing that was the least bit odd was the fact that he appeared to be representing two different, possibly competitive linen firms; one under the name Daintee Damask, the other called Fiona. While there was nothing illegal about that, it had given O'Hare something to think about, and might be worth checking into.

Cold and tired by this time, Riley said irritably, "The whole thing's a wild goose chase!"

"I'm not sure," O'Hare said.

"I am!" snorted Riley. "We make an offer of a reward for information, it's widely circulated on the wireless and telly, and in no time at all there's a flock of jackdaws calling in to tell us they're on to the bugger who did the bombing. There's nothing like the dream of snagging a hundred quid to stimulate the imagination."

"One of them might be right."

"Not this one! So far, all we know for sure is that O'Halloran said he heard Connaught bragging he *might* be in a position to collect the reward. That sort of boasting combined with the amount of drink the man's taken isn't hard-core evidence of anything except a loose lip and a desire to show off. It's my considered opinion, we're wasting our time."

"Maybe," O'Hare said. "But since we've come this far, why not give him a bit more rope? Let Connaught sleep for an hour, and if by this evening he hasn't tipped his hand, we'll take him in charge and see what we can get out of him."

"He's all yours!" said Riley. "What I want is some hot tea and a decent meal." And he stomped off to Mary McGonigle's Tearoom on the corner.

O'Hare stayed in the car keeping an eye on the entrance to the Green Dragon and Connaught's yellow cabriolet sitting in the car park next to the inn.

He was glad for a chance to be alone for a bit. He'd been uneasy and jumpy all morning and had driven recklessly on the way out to Howth, speeding up to pass a lorry with a cart coming up on the outside lane, then slowing to a crawl, till Riley had said they'd be lucky to get to Howth by Christmas, if at all. Embarrassed, he explained that he'd been on twenty-four-hour duty earlier that week and, what with the bombings and all, hadn't had much of a chance to catch up on his sleep. The truth was, his mind was on a million things other than the job, and he was desperate for a while to sit quiet and try to sort things out.

It was queer how he'd thought of Eileen Hackett with a pang the minute the call had come in from Howth, after hardly thinking of her at all these past several months. It was a short run from town to the Head, and he thought he really ought to go out there and see her. They'd never had an understanding, but they'd been going together on and off over the preceding year, and he felt he owed her some kind of an explanation for not being in touch with her this long while.

When they'd first met, he'd wondered about her brother, a soured man whom he'd seen only once. He'd thought Rory Hackett might have been involved in the Troubles in Belfast, before the family moved down to Howth. He'd even had Special Services check him out, but they'd given him a clean slate. According to their report, Hackett was "a strict moderate" — if you could put it that way — and even as a student at university had steered clear of politics. They'd watched him for a long time, but there'd been no whisper of a connection between him and the Belfast mob.

Eileen was nothing like Agnes. She was a gentle slip of a girl with a quiet disposition and a deep sense of moral values. A real Prod she was, but Irish to the core. Not a great beauty perhaps, but with her close-cropped curly black hair and her clear sea-green eyes, might easily have passed for one. There was an aura of sadness about her that moved him, and on the rare occasions when he could get her to smile, she'd give off a flash of radiance like the sudden sparkle of sun on a shadowy pool. What he liked best about her was her young freshness. She was a lot younger than him, still only in her twenties, and inclined to be idealistic.

They'd once talked about the Troubles, always a touchy subject, and for all her gentleness, she was fierce in her beliefs, convinced that given half a chance, the Catholics and Protestants could learn to live in peace together. When the three MacGuire children had been killed in Andersontown in '77, she'd marched with the Catholic women who'd taken to the streets in a great crowd, calling for an end to the senseless bloody strife. A number of Protestant parents at the school where she had taught were outraged at the idea of a "Pro-Catholic" teaching their children, and it wasn't long before she'd been ousted from her job.

During the time he was seeing her, she didn't seem keen on his coming out to the house. First off, there was their difference in faith. And besides, she was naturally leery of letting on to the family that they were lovers. They'd bedded down wherever they could that spring and summer, a couple of times in an old fallen-down shepherd's hut in the hills. But more often, when the weather was fine, they'd go out on the dunes to an abandoned part of the beach near the Point. After, when he thought of her, it was always with the sharp scent of heather and bracken, and the tang of salt air on his tongue. She was a decent straight girl, kind and natural, and easy to be with. Making love with her was like having a cool thirst-quenching drink of clear spring water when you were parched. Still, there'd been no grand passion in it — on her side either, he was sure.

Well, it seemed you didn't love someone for their virtues—maybe in spite of them, if you were lucky. He'd never fallen in love with Eileen, with all her good qualities.

He thought of Agnes slamming out of the house that morning, her sudden outbursts of temper, her small senseless deceits with Timmy, her selfishness, and her quick cruel mood changes with the child. And all he knew was that he wanted her. Ah, love, love, wotinhell was it all about? That longing, that itch in the crotch, that breast-swelling sense of nobility and exaltation! There was no rhyme or reason to it! He wondered was it her money he was after? She was rich by Dublin standards, and he'd no objection to the money, but he was sure he'd be after her if she hadn't a penny. He saw her naked back as she stood before the mirror, and remembered her walking along the street at his side the first day they'd met. Ah, the bloom on her! But if it was only that, he'd probably never bring himself to marry her. He'd bed her instead, as long as she'd let him, and steer clear of the altar. Maybe she didn't know it, but it was Timmy that weighted the balance. Tim needed a father, and he could do a lot for the boy. And that made all the other madness that went by the name of love—right—somehow.

The girl on the bicycle riding by gave him a startled look, braked abruptly, and almost lost her balance. Flushed and embarrassed, still straddling her bike, she said quietly, "Hello, Thomas. I wasn't sure it was you."

5

He wanted to get up, but he didn't think he could make it. You've got to do it, Willie, he thought. For your friend, good old friend, good old Donny . . .

He'd known Donny since childhood. They'd grown up next door to each other, though he hadn't seen him in years. He'd been on the road when that grenade had killed Donny's young brother, Billy, and he'd sent the family a condolence card.

He knew he'd been saying too much at O'Halloran's, though he couldn't recall what exactly. There'd been a lot of talk about the bombings in Dublin, and he'd let slip something about how he'd once known a man who had a fine hand with explosives and the job looked like it might have been his. He wasn't sure whether he'd mentioned that the man now lived a hop and a jump from Howth.

He had to get up. Not only for Donny's sake, and the sake of his own conscience, but for Grace and the kids. He was particularly fond of Grace. She'd always been decent to him, not a cold fish like her stuck-up sister-in-law. He'd once thought of courting Eileen, back in the old days, but she'd turned out too prim for his taste, and he'd given up after a couple of discouraging forays.

He'd known Donny had taken it on the lam, but only recently found out that the family had settled near Howth. He wanted to go out and pay them a visit, but the boys from Belfast said no, just deliver the package to the kids at school, and they'd given him the new name the family had taken.

He himself had never been an activist, and his connection with "the Firm" was purely commercial. As a traveling salesman he was useful for carrying messages from the North to the South and back, and his services as a courier brought him a small but pleasant additional income. His knowledge of the organization's affairs was minimal, a sensible precaution that provided satisfaction and security to all concerned. The messages he delivered were simple coded forms drawn up under the imprint of Fiona Linens, listing orders for napkins and tablecloths, or lengths of linen of various sizes and quantities. He had no notion of what the items or numbers stood for.

His head was swimming and he had this terrible need to go to the jakes. Never make it down the hall, he thought.

He managed to raise his head off the pillow and sit up, but moving anywhere seemed out of the question. He felt like the wrath of God, his head weighed a ton, his limbs were like lead, and his mouth was coated with fuzz. The pressure on his bladder made him feel like crying. There was no way he could resist the urgent message it was sending him.

He reached over carefully to the bedside table and picked up the bottle he'd left there. There was maybe half an inch left at the bottom. He took the last nip and felt a bit better, thinking the dog of the hair . . . no, the hair of the dog . . . He grinned. This was the first time in his life he ever remembered being glad to see a bottle empty.

He got his fly open, raised himself up on one buttock, and still sitting, inserted his pecker. It was a tight squeeze, the neck of the bottle was small, but the relief, once he got going, was lovely. He was impressed with the great quantity of liquid that kept pouring out of him, worrying a little that the bottle might not hold it all. But he was lucky; only a few drops dribbled onto the rag rug next to the bed.

What time was it anyway? He lifted his hand to his face to look at his watch, but the dial squirmed like an eel in front of his eyes. At that moment, the clock in the hall chimed the quarter hour. Not much help; he'd no way of guessing what the hour might be. He turned his head, a little at a time, to look out the window. Dusk was beginning to fall. Must be close to five, he figured. Late enough! If he could get in his car and drive out, he could be there in no time at all. But when he tried to stand, he knew he'd never be able to make it.

In Dublin, if you'd a drop too much taken, the gardai were very good about driving you where you needed to go. But you seldom if ever saw even a traffic guide on the main road in Howth. What a joke if he asked a garda to take him out to the Head! Assuming he could locate one. Well, it would be quicker, and smarter probably, to telephone.

Holding tight to the banister, he somehow managed the single flight of stairs to the lobby. He didn't have the number, but the girl at the desk could get it for him.

She was a fancied-up trollop, he thought. If he were sober, he'd give her a run for her money. He still had a way with the ladies.

"Darlin'," he said, steadying himself at the counter, "could you do a poor man a great favor and find him a phone number he's needin'?"

"Be happy to!" she said, crinkling her eyes at him. "Could I have the name?"

He coughed nervously, stalling for time, trying to recall the damned name, and gave her an apologetic wave of the hand. For the life of him he couldn't remember the alias Donald Henley had taken. Tears were flowing out of his eyes, and he found himself wheezing in earnest.

She came out from behind the counter and gave him a few hard whacks on the back. "That's a terrible hacking cough you've got there, Mr. Connaught," she said when he finally caught his breath. And went blithering on about how her grandmother had an awful cough too, just like his, and they'd found the only thing that would help her was a hot whiskey toddy. But he hardly heard her. For suddenly, like a spring, one of the words she'd said snapped his mind open, and the name he'd been hunting for leapt out at him.

6

A mist was rolling in from the sea and O'Hare could barely make out her face. She stopped in front of the car, got off the bike, and wheeling it over, leaned it against the side where he was sitting. He had a feeling of unreality, as though he'd been having a dream and waked to find the dream figure standing next to him. She seemed younger even than he remembered her, slim as a reed in her fisherman's sweater and tweed skirt.

"Éileen Hackett!" he said, opening the window all the way. "I was thinking of you this very minute."

"That's nice to hear."

"I've been meaning to call. How's things with the family?"

"The same," she said. "The kids are growing. Were you coming to see me," she asked, "or somebody else?" Her voice was light but he sensed the awkwardness in her.

Struggling for a tone to match her own, he said, "Who else would I be coming to see in Howth?"

"Then ask me into O'Halloran's for a drink."

"I wish I could. I'd be happy to, but I'm waiting for someone." No sense to mention the job.

"A woman, I hope."

"No, a man."

"Ah," she said, "a pity!" — then, dropping her bantering tone, said simply, "I've missed you, Thomas."

"You've been much on my mind too, these past few months," he said with a twinge, wanting to believe it.

"You're a sweet liar," she said. "But thank you for that."

They were both quiet a long moment.

He wished he could find something to say to ease the sad silence between them, and found he wanted to tell her the truth.

"The fact is," he said, "I've some news of my own," and before he could stop himself blurted it out. "I've been thinking of getting married." The minute the words were out of his mouth, he felt like a blithering idiot. What on earth had pushed him to tell her when he hadn't even asked Agnes yet!

"Well, that *is* good news! Good luck to you, Thomas!" she said and turned away.

He couldn't bear to leave it at that. "I'd have asked you first, but I knew you wouldn't have me."

"No," she said, "I don't think I would've."

"I wasn't lying when I said I've been thinking of you, Eileen. I keep wondering about us. We were good with each other."

"No need to wonder or worry," she said. "It wouldn't have worked. We were never in love . . . and there were a few other barriers."

"You mean the difference in our faith."

"That wouldn't have mattered to me."

"I'm a lot older than you."

"Your heart's young. She'll be getting a good man."

He reached over and took her hand. "Did I ever tell you you're a lovely girl?"

"Many times," she said, "and I used to believe you." She touched his face gently and gave him a smile then, but there was no glint of sunshine in it. She got back on her bike. He was about to say "Stay a minute" when out of the corner of his eye he caught sight of the man in the green tweed jacket, wavering in the doorway of the inn.

She pushed off and started to pedal away. "God bless!" she said, calling back over her shoulder.

The traveler staggered across the road and stopped drunkenly in front of the bike. O'Hare called "Watch it!" and was out of the car and sprinting toward them. Startled, Connaught grabbed hold of the handlebars for support and almost brought the girl and the bike down with him.

Struggling for balance, Eileen cried out, "Let go, you fool!"

"Are you hurt, Eileen?" O'Hare asked her. She seemed shaken but managed a rueful grin. "No harm done, he gave me a scare. I thought I'd run him down."

O'Hare took Connaught by the arm and tried to walk him away, but the man was glued to the spot. His head weaving back and forth, he looked first at O'Hare and then at Eileen, uncertainly. Shaking O'Hare off, he suddenly let go of the bike and threw his arms around her.

"Eileen, is it?" he said. "Eileen Henley! Me ol'darlin'! How are ya? And how's Grace and the kids? I just spoke to your dear brother, Donald. But you know Donny, getting him to talk is like trying to pry open an oyster."

Pale as a ghost, she pushed Connaught away. "Get off, you damned souse!" she said. "I don't know who in the world you're thinking I am!"

"Eileen Henley," Connaught said, "you can't have forgotten your old friend Willie? Willie Connaught!" He stared at her mournfully.

"The name's Hackett!"

"Hackett?" he said blankly. "Not Eileen Henley?" A light dawned. "Eileen Hackett, of course! So it is!"

She turned to O'Hare. A look between rage and despair passed over her face. "The man's daft with the drink!" she said. "Sod the bastard!"

He'd never heard her swear, nor seen her angry before. She'd always seemed so cool. But she was upset with good cause. The man had come near to knocking her off her bike, and had mauled her into the bargain.

He wondered if it was possible the traveler knew her? *Eileen Henley?* Maybe she'd been married once and hadn't wanted him to know. It didn't seem likely. He'd always found her to be straight as a die. Connaught must be mistaking her for some other Eileen. The man was that drunk he wouldn't have recognized his own mother. And she'd never mentioned a brother named Donny.

She straightened her sweater and skirt and, adjusting the bike seat, climbed on. "Good-bye, Thomas," she said, not looking at him, and took off with a swoosh of her wheels.

A cold chill prickled the back of his neck. *Henley,* he thought. Connaught had said — not just *Eileen,* but *Grace and the kids.* And *I just spoke to your brother Donald . . .*

It was not some husband she was hiding, it was "Rory," her brother. Her brother was the notorious, long-missing, still-wanted O.F.F. terrorist, *R. Donald Henley . . .*

7

He was in the shed just finishing the adjustments he was making on the radio when he heard the phone ringing. He pulled the canvas back over the worktable and loped across the path toward the house. He wanted to get to it before Grace started yelling for him. She was always at him these days about how she had more than enough work to do taking care of the kids, keeping the house, doing the cooking, and waiting on trade without having to be answering the phone as well. He knew that wasn't the reason. There weren't that many calls this time of the year, and only a few stragglers came by now to rent one of the boats or stop for a bite to eat, so she wasn't that busy. She hated answering the phone. She was always expecting the worst, certain it would be some angry Teague on the other end threatening their lives, or maybe someone from home calling to warn them it was time to run again.

Somehow, with the change of seasons, the days growing shorter and trade falling off, she'd begun to show signs of her old sickness. Nothing was right, doom and gloom all around. She didn't know about the visitors from Belfast, or the job he'd had to do for them, but she was jumpy as a cat just the same, mournful and suspicious and driving him crazy. He had enough to worry about without her nagging at him all the time to tell her "the truth."

Yesterday, when the kids had told her about the package they'd got from "a stranger," she'd nearly gone over the edge. Who was the stranger? What was it? she wanted to know. She wasn't a fool. He had to tell her something. He said it was nothing, a small radio, a gift from Willie Connaught, nothing to concern herself about. But she'd kept after him half the night with her questions.

"How come Willie knows where we are?" she'd asked.

"It's okay," he said. "I dropped him a line."

"Why on earth would you do that?"

"He comes down this way on business. I thought he might drop by. I trust him," he lied to her.

"If he knows, they'll all soon know. Trust him? You know how he talks."

"Will you quit worrying! He won't talk."

"Tell me the truth. What was in the package?"

There was no way he could quiet her, or his own frenzied thoughts, and he'd finally exploded. "Will you shut up already, and let a man sleep!" But she wouldn't leave off and he'd gotten up and gone downstairs where he'd tossed and turned on the old couch in the kitchen alone — thinking about his life and the grief he'd brought on his wife and family — with only the specter of Billy to keep him company. He'd spent the rest of the night wide awake, trying to plan out the things he still needed to do, wracking his brain to figure out where they could go, wishing to God he was in the real Rory Hackett's shoes now, far off in Australia, the family safe and away beside him . . .

Just as he picked up the receiver, she came out to the shop and stood there, hands on her hips, elbows akimbo, looking anxious and aggrieved. The voice on the phone gave him a shock and he thought, This time she's right.

He turned toward her, his hand over the mouthpiece, and said, "What are you waiting for? I thought you were busy?"

"I am," she said. "Who is it?"

He said, "Do me a favor and get back to your work."

She gave him a black look and went back to the kitchen, pushing the swing door hard before her, so it drummed back and forth angrily.

"Hackett here," he said into the phone. "Yes?" he said, "yes, I see," trying hard to keep his voice cool. He was sure she was standing behind the door listening.

"What makes you think that?" He listened to the voice gabbing away, thinking it was bound to come, he'd known all along it would. Only it was too soon.

"Get on with it, will you? I haven't all night." But he couldn't make head or tail of the story, except that he knew he had to get moving.

"Thanks for the information," he said finally, and hung up.

He grabbed his heavy mac off the hook near the door and went through to the kitchen. Grace was at the stove.

"Your supper's ready," she said.

"I can't stop for it. Something's come up."

"What is it?" she said, looking ready to cry.

"In God's name, don't start in. I've just got to go out for a while."

"For how long?"

"I'll let you know when I'm back."

He went swiftly upstairs and took his gun out of the place where he kept it. Except for the package in the shed, it was all he needed. He had some other gear stowed away where he was going.

When he came down, Haila was at the kitchen table doing her homework. He bent down and tousled her hair and asked, "Where's Ian?"

"Playing outside."

"It's getting late. Better call him in." She got up obediently and went through the shop. He could hear her thin piping voice calling her brother from the porch, but there was no answer.

He turned to his wife and said, "Take care," and feeling the weight of her woe gave her a peck on the cheek. "Don't worry," he said, "Eileen will be home soon."

He went out the back, closing the door softly behind him. When he got to the shed, Ian was there fooling around at the workbench. He said sharply, "You know you're not supposed to touch anything here," and pushed the boy away.

Ian said, "I was only just looking."

"It's supper time. Your mother's waiting."

He watched his son turn and walk off, and wished he could say a decent word to the boy.

His mind was racing as he made the final adjustments on the transistor. He couldn't figure out for sure what was behind the call. Why Connaught? He'd known Willie since they were kids together and knew that he sometimes ran errands for the party. But the stuff they gave him had always been carefully coded. Why had they told him where he was? Did they want him caught? Something was wrong.

He was just finishing and was lighting a fresh cigarette when he thought he heard a sound from the road. He put it out quickly and doused the light. He listened closely. It was not a motor, more like the sound of light wheels on gravel. It must be Eileen. He would have liked to talk to her. But there was no time. He still had to launch the dinghy.

8

It was close on five-thirty when the two detectives from Dublin came into the pub with Connaught. O'Hare steered the man to a place at the far end of the bar, while Mabel got him a Guinness. Riley took O'Halloran aside and told him they were depending on him and that Gilligan was coming to take the man in, it wouldn't be long now. Riley seemed in a great hurry. He signaled to O'Hare, and the two detectives left. O'Halloran could tell they were on to something big.

Dreams of glory and £100 notes danced in his head. When it was over there'd be a grand story to tell — how he'd contacted the cops in Dublin and given them the tip, taken the man in charge, and helped break the case, practically single-handed. Very likely, his picture would be in the papers.

He was keyed up and could feel himself sweating. The room was beginning to fill up, but there was no cause for worry. It was Mabel's shift; she'd come in at four. She was quick and handy and used to the rush, and from the look of him, Connaught wasn't likely to be giving him any trouble. Drunk as a lord he was, the traveler from Belfast, and seemed quite pleased with himself, a sly grin fixed on his face. Only once, for a moment, stirred by some troublesome thought, he frowned and blurted out, "Colder than a nun's ass!" Some of the men looked over angrily. O'Halloran took hold of him by the lapel and said flatly, "Now, none of that, Mr. Connaught!" and the man clammed up.

He kept watching the clock. The hands seemed hardly to move, and he couldn't believe it was less than five minutes ago that the detectives had left. He stood at the sink washing glasses for Mabel, while keeping his eyes on the traveler, who looked about ready to pass out again. Noticing the man's glass was empty, he dried his hands and picked it up. "Will you have another?" he asked.

The traveler seemed to perk up. "I will, Mr. O'Halloran," he mumbled thickly. "The Guinness again, if you please."

He'll be down in the Guinness Book of Records at this rate, O'Halloran thought, and grinned at his own wit.

He felt he deserved a drink himself. "Will you have a wee bit of Jameson's for a change of pace?" he asked Connaught. "On the house?"

He put out a pair of shot glasses and started to pour. His hand was none too steady and some of the precious stuff spilled onto the bar. He wiped it up and raised his glass.

"Slainté!" he said, with only a small twinge of conscience, and downed the whiskey. "Drink up!" he said. "Sure, 'tis the water of life!"

"Cheers!" said Connaught, obediently emptying his glass.

9

The distance from Howth to the house was usually a ten-minute run, but the trip tonight seemed to take forever.

She must have been mad to take up with O'Hare in the first place. A Catholic cop! She'd known from the start she was playing with fire. She had no one to blame but herself. But the man had something about him she found it impossible to resist, a kind of integrity, in spite of his job — and a gentleness, with all his big frame and burly tough looks, that had taken her by surprise. She'd come to care for him more than she was willing to admit. He gave her the feeling of being *tended,* befriended, the feeling that he wanted to take care of her. God knows what had given her that illusion; her own need, no doubt. He'd caught her off guard at a time when she'd been worn out with the struggle, drowning in the bog of cold misery and despair that had engulfed her these last hard years. And he'd raised her up. She'd been frozen with fear and loneliness. And he'd warmed her.

She had brooded about his silence these past months, and had finally given in to the impulse to call him at work. She'd called twice. He'd been out both times, and she'd refused to leave her name. She didn't know how to handle it. She'd never been jilted before. Well, it was over now. For good, it seemed. Everything gone, and now her brother's life endangered.

She turned off the road into the lane that led to the house, legs pumping hard, her heart jumping, her breath coming short.

What a fool she'd been! If only that drunken lout Willie hadn't happened along, just at that moment. And she'd handled the whole thing so badly, losing control, screaming like a tart, "Sod the bastard!" O'Hare must have known something was wrong.

Dear God, she thought, I've betrayed my own brother! God forgive me, she prayed, let him be safe!

She skidded past the shed, dumped the bike on the path, and ran for the house. There was a light on in the kitchen out back; the rest of the place was dark. The wind was skittering up and she had trouble getting the back door open.

Ian was standing in the entryway used as a larder, unpacking his schoolbooks.

"Where's your Da?" she asked, trying to keep the panic out of her voice.

"I dunno," he said. "Out in the shed, I think."

"Is that you?" Grace called out.

"It's me," she answered, wondering what she should tell her.

Her sister-in-law came out of the kitchen, wiping her hands on a towel.

How old and tired she looks, Eileen thought. Still a young woman, still only in her thirties—and once such a beauty! She turned away. "I'll be back in a minute," she said. "I need to see Rory."

"He's gone into the village, or out to the Point or somewhere. Someone telephoned him." She went on, her voice heavy with accumulated grievances, "He wouldn't say what about, just said he'd be back when I saw him." She sniffed angrily, adding a final complaint, "Wouldn't even stop for his tea."

"He didn't take the jalopy?"

"Did he not?"

"I think it's still in the shed."

"He's maybe not left yet."

Eileen said, "I'll just go and see."

Grace put out a hand to stop her.

Ian was standing there dawdling, watching the two women. "Da was angry," he said.

"Go into your supper, Ian!" his mother said sharply, pushing the boy through to the kitchen and shutting the door behind him. She looked at Eileen searchingly, "Something's gone wrong. What's wrong, Eileen?"

Eileen put her arms around her. She could feel her own heart beating and Grace's thin frame trembling against her. She thought, The woman's lived so long with disaster, she's like a trapped creature, waiting for the final blow. "It's all right," she said. "There's nothing. It's nothing at all."

Grace pushed her away. "You've no right to keep secrets from me! I'm his wife. I've a right to know. Tell me what's happening!" She took Eileen by the shoulder and shook her, as though the truth could be shook loose that way.

"Let me go, Grace," she said. "Let me see can I find him."

She'd broken away and was out through the door and close by the shed when the car coming fast took the turn toward the house, freezing her in its headlights.

10

O'Hare braked sharply. Riley said tersely, "Stay put," and got out of the car. "Miss Hackett?" he called.

She stood quiet a minute, then said, her voice lilting up, "Yes?" as Riley came toward her. Her eyes were half-closed, fighting the glare of the headlights. O'Hare was tempted to turn them off, but thought better of it. There was a taste of bile in his mouth. Ignoring Riley's order, he got out of the car, wondering whose side he was on. Certainly not his own.

She moved away a little and put her hand up to shade her eyes. "O'Hare, is that you?" she called out. "I didn't expect you so soon."

Riley interposed sharply. "I wonder if we could talk in the house, Miss Hackett?" He moved forward and took her by the arm. "I'm John Riley, Dublin police." He showed her his badge. "Just a few questions." He looked back and said, "Detective O'Hare won't mind waiting out here for a while."

"Of course," she said. "Come along." She turned back toward the house, stumbling over the two-wheeler on the path. Riley held her up, shoving the bike aside with his foot. "Easy there,"

Riley said. She bent down, freeing her arm from his hold. "I'll just put it out of the way in the shed," she said, "it's a hazard here."

"Later," said Riley. "It's really your brother I'd like to talk with."

"He's not home."

"May I come in? It's a bit cold talking out here."

"You're welcome to warm yourself by the fire. You may even search the house, if you like."

She's playing for time, O'Hare thought. He's away and long gone by now. Connaught put in the call an hour ago.

A light in the front of the house was switched on. Hackett's wife and the two kids stood framed in the doorway.

"Who is it, Eileen?" she called. "Is it Rory?"

"We've visitors from Dublin," Eileen called, her voice loud but easy, as though warning her sister-in-law to stay calm, or maybe warning her brother, if he was within earshot.

O'Hare could see Grace nervously smoothing her apron, the kids peering out curiously. She stepped back, shepherding the children before her as Eileen and Riley came up the steps and entered the house. The door shut behind them.

There was no sound but the steady lapping of the water. O'Hare got the electric torch out of the car and sent the light in a slow arc, circling the grounds around the house, them moving swiftly into the shed. The beam picked up some tools lying about on a workbench, and what looked like parts of the insides of a small wireless set. Inside the shed, the faint scent of tobacco hung in the air. I was wrong, he thought. He can't be long gone, or far.

He turned off the torch, came out, and looked down the beach toward the dock, dimly outlined in the shadows. One of the boats had lost its mooring and seemed to be floating free, but the tide was coming in and kept sending it back toward the shore. I could wade in and get it, he thought. At that moment, he heard a door open, then saw Ian and Haila come out of the house. They went toward the bike, picked it up, and began wheeling it over to the shed. As he turned back to the beach, he heard the metallic sound of an oarlock. He flipped on the torch and saw Hackett. He was standing in the water on the far side of the dock, trying awkwardly with one hand to maneuver the boat out of the shallows. In the other hand he held a small brown box.

"Hackett!" O'Hare called, standing very still. "Let's talk."

The man seemed not to have heard. He got into the boat slowly, placed the package carefully on the seat, picked up a cord, wound it around the spring starter, and pulled. The motor sputtered loudly, struggling to catch, then died. O'Hare's gun was in his right hand as he ran for the dinghy.

A door slammed and someone came running out of the house.

"Thomas!" Eileen screamed. "Don't shoot!"

The scene seemed to take on a strange slow-motion quality. He heard Eileen let out a muffled cry and Riley say in a loud voice, "Just stay very still, Miss Hackett!"

He was racing over the dunes, but the shoreline seemed to be receding and the sand and the sea-grass kept sucking at his feet. The motor turned over again but failed to catch. He saw Hackett pick up the box and throw it like a football, straight at his head. Hardly stopping, he caught it, fielding it like a pro, and tossed it in a long arc over his shoulder. It landed with a thud somewhere behind him.

"Ian, come back!" Grace was screaming. And suddenly, everything speeded up.

Ian was panting after him yelling, "That's my Da! Leave him alone!"

Hackett was out of the boat and wading ashore, shrieking like a madman, "Grace! Haila! Run!"

O'Hare, startled by the man's unexpected about-face, dropped his gun. Hackett was past him. He turned and tackled him. They went down in a heap with Ian jumping on top of them, pummeling O'Hare's head and shoulders, sobbing, "Leave him alone! Leave my Da be!"

Hackett, the breath knocked out of him, was struggling as if he were possessed. Face down in the sand and the rocks, he managed to get out a strangled plea, "In God's name, O'Hare!"

Riley picked Ian off O'Hare's back and tossed him aside.

There was the sound of an explosion and a great sheath of flames. A little girl's voice let out a high whimpering wail, "Mum! . . . Mum . . ."

The sound hung in the air for a moment but was soon drowned in the harsh rush of wings and the fierce cries of the outraged gulls.

Part
3

Show me a hero and I will write you a
tragedy.

F. SCOTT FITZGERALD

1

Starched skirts sailing, her coif slightly askew, Sister Bernadette,
the pretty young nurse, came bustling into his room. "Well,
Timmy!" she said, her eyes bright as berries, "I've a grand
surprise for you! Dr. Vogel says you're to be goin' home. And take
a look at this!" It was yesterday's paper.

HENLEY TAKEN, the black banner said. And there on the front
page of the *Irish Times* was a picture of O'Hare, looking stiff and
serious, his arm in a sling, standing next to a handcuffed
prisoner.

Sister Bernadette insisted on reading the whole account aloud
to him. She seemed even more excited than he was, though she'd
met O'Hare only the once, when he'd come by to visit the day
after the bombing, to bring the cops-and-robbers game from
Madigan's. And she'd hung around all that morning, talking a
blue streak and interrupting their game, acting like O'Hare was
her friend, like she owned him or something. Tim figured maybe
she was in love with him, the way she carried on, or maybe even

wanted to marry him, though he knew nuns weren't allowed to. They were all married to Christ when they took their vows. At least that's what his mother'd told him. He couldn't figure out how come Jesus was allowed to have so many wives. He'd have to ask her. She was coming by at noon to get him.

His heart gave a jump as he thought maybe O'Hare would be coming with her. He could hardly wait to see him and hear the whole story firsthand—how he'd tracked down the bomber, captured the man, and brought him in. Everybody in Dublin, in all of Ireland, maybe the whole world, must be talking and reading about O'Hare. He was a hero!

He was glad to be going home finally. He started collecting his things, taking the newspaper of course, and the cops-and-robbers game and the schoolbooks his mother thought he should have. He'd been out of school three whole days—a relief!—though the hospital wasn't exactly the place he'd have chosen for a holiday. Actually, the only thing he'd really minded was not seeing O'Hare and his friend Mike. But the whole class had sent him a long sheet of paper with get-well wishes, everyone signing their names, and Sister Mary Theresa had written her own special message at the bottom, saying, "Think of yourself as a soldier wounded in the fight to unite Ireland!" which gave him an odd feeling, as if he was some sort of a hero himself.

Maybe when he was older, he'd join the Provos and fight for the Republic. Some of the kids playing in the street marched about with big sticks over their shoulders pretending they were carrying guns, chanting

> *White, green*
> *Black, red*
> *We'll beat the Prods*
> *Until they're dead!*

Once when he'd joined them, his mother had called him in and given him what-for, and when he'd wanted to know why, she'd said fighting and killing was a sin. He didn't see the sense in it—they were only pretending! Besides, the Bible was full of killing, and no one blamed David for killing Goliath. Anyway, O'Hare had fought Henley and taken him, and O'Hare was a hero in everyone's eyes — except maybe some of the Prods in the North.

Maybe he'd join the force like O'Hare and become an officer in the *Gardai Siochana,* which meant "Protector of the Peace." That should please his mother! Though he'd heard plenty of cops got shot and killed, North and South. So how was that different?

His mother once told him that in America, where he'd been born, people thought the Prods were no better and no worse than the Catholics. And though almost everyone there was Protestant, they'd even once had a Catholic for a president. But he'd been shot and killed, too.

He was dressed and ready, and beginning to be impatient, when his mother finally showed up. She didn't seem nearly as thrilled as he was about O'Hare's being in all the papers, and when he asked had she heard from him, and when was he coming to see them, she said, "I haven't the least idea!" She sounded miffed, and said would he hurry please and finish up and get his sweater on.

He felt really let down that O'Hare hadn't come, but he guessed being a hero must be keeping him pretty busy these days.

2

It was Saturday week since she'd brought Timmy home from the hospital and ten days since she'd last seen O'Hare. Ten days since their terrible fight, nine since he'd captured the O.F.F. terrorist. He'd called but once in that long time, sounding as cold and remote as if he were in Alaska, saying he was busy, had some personal matter he had to attend to, would be in touch with her shortly.

Shortly. The word jarred. He might have been talking into a dictaphone, dictating a business letter.

Shortly? Meaning when?

When he could. Pretty soon.

He had barely asked about Timmy. When she'd said, "Tim's wild with excitement, he's dying to see you. Everyone says you're a hero!" he'd been silent as the grave.

"O'Hare?" she'd said. "Are you all right?"

"Take care . . . " he'd mumbled and rung off.

She'd called back to the O'Learys' where he lived, but there was no answer. She phoned the station and spoke to Riley. He told her O'Hare was away on leave.

Why? Was he sick or what?

"Just tired," Riley said, and asked after Timmy.

She told him the child was home now and fine. Did he know where O'Hare might be reached?

He said he was sorry, he couldn't help her.

She was sure he was lying. O'Hare must have told him not to tell.

The next day she went round to the O'Learys' and, flushed with embarrassment, thinking they must be thinking she was chasing after the man — which she was — inquired if he was at home. They were polite and told her they hadn't seen him in a while. He'd gone off and left no message. Not like him. But the man must be burdened with work these days. He might be up North collecting evidence. No doubt he'd be back soon; Henley's trial would be coming up before long.

"Speedy justice and a quick end!" Mr. O'Leary leered at her, pantomiming a hanging. "Too good for the villain!"

"They don't hang them now!" Mrs. O'Leary said. "He'll get sentenced for life."

"I know that!" answered O'Leary. "But it's a crying shame, and I'm sure there're plenty of others thinkin' the same!"

"Would you be wantin' to leave him a message?" Mrs. O'Leary asked.

"No, thank you," she said. Then walked home all the way talking to herself, railing at O'Hare.

Well, if that's the way you want it! Don't think I can't manage without you! . . . You ought to be glad he's back safe, she scolded herself. I am! I am! Then what in God's name do you want? Nothing! But her heart continued to rage. Back where? Holed up with some tart, God knows where!

People passing stared at her, giving her queer looks. She thought, *Mishe, mishe* — I am, I am! What is it I am? Looney in me loneness! . . .

To add to her torment, the newspapers the whole week were full of stories of him — the brave detective and his fearless capture of Henley alias Hackett, who'd been number one on the Ten Most Wanted List in the Republic as well as Britain and North Ireland. There he was on the front page of the *Times,* and all the papers were hailing him and Riley as heroes for apprehending the bomber who'd managed to evade the British C.I.D. and Special Services for over three years while hiding out under their very noses. In his desperate effort to escape, Henley had tossed a fire bomb at his pursuers, wildly aimed, and had ended up instead killing his wife and their little girl.

There was even a picture of her — the schoolteacher from Howth — the one she'd been so jealous of, that Jenny O'Flaherty had told her O'Hare had been going around with. She'd been stunned to discover the woman was Henley-Hackett's sister, and she couldn't help wondering if O'Hare had been tracking down the brother all the time the poor woman thought he was courting her. In a way, she hated to think that might be true. It would make O'Hare out to be an awful stinker! In the picture, dressed in black, Eileen Henley was standing with her nephew, a child no older than Timmy. And looking at them now, all she felt was the terrible waste, and a great pity for the two of them.

She got through her days somehow in a passion of cleaning. The house was as bright as a shiny new penny, the furniture gleaming, the windows and curtains streaming with light. She cooked mountains of food, but couldn't eat any — not even a sweet.

At night, she walked upstairs and down and all through the house, pacing the floors, trying to decipher the conundrum of O'Hare's desertion. Her thoughts were like acrobats turning flip-flops, twisting first one way, then the other.

He was mad at her still for the terrible way she'd told him off and had slammed out of the house that last morning when they'd had that terrible fight over Timmy.

Nonsense! He was a lovely decent tolerant man. He was just busy or worn out and needed a rest. He'd be back any day now.

Everyone knew he was sick with love for her!

He was fickle as the weather! A seducer, had never truly cared for her. All that concern about Timmy was just a ruse — his clever way of pushing her into bed.

She thought of their last wild night together and felt crazed with missing him.

She was a fool to think he might be sparing her a moment's thought, now that he was such a paladin!

Well, he was mistaken if he believed all she'd do was sit home waiting for him to call her!

She longed for the sight of his plain ugly mug, the touch of his hands, yes, admit it, the sweet man-smell of him close in bed with her . . .

If — *when* — he came back, she'd slam the door in his face! She never wanted to see him again.

But what if she got her wish, and he never came back? Well, there were dozens of others who'd suit her as well — even better!

The man had toyed with her, lied to her — just as he had to that poor gullible schoolteacher in Howth.

Out of old habit, she started to recite the Confiteor and found herself saying, *"Oh, My Love,* I am heartily sorry for all my sins . . ."* and was startled by the blasphemy.

"Thom darlin'," she prayed, "I'll be what you want, whatever you want me to be. I can do it if I try. I'll be soft and thoughtful with you, gentle and loving with Timmy . . . give up sweets — not only for Lent, but forever . . . cage my temper like it was a tiger . . . only come back . . ."

She tried the Aspiration against Anger, but it failed her.

The one thing to preserve the little sanity she had left was Tim. She couldn't get over the difference in the child since she'd brought him home. He looked marvelous. It was hard to believe he'd ever been sick a day in his life. The roses had come back to his cheeks, his eyes were bright as two sapphire stars, and he'd even put on some weight. He actually looked sturdy. When she tested his urine each morning, the color was perfect, and she got this high-flying feeling he'd finally got rid of the dreadful disease that so darkened her life — both their lives — and was cured for good! It was a blessed miracle. She couldn't wait to tell O'Hare the good news.

She called Dr. Vogel and made an appointment to bring the child in for an extra checkup. Vogel was pleased as could be with Timmy's improvement but brought her hopes down a bit, cautioning her that childhood diabetes was, in 99.9 percent of all cases, a lifetime condition, and Tim was simply having something called a "remission" — not uncommon, but unfortunately temporary. Still, she dreamed Tim might turn out to be in the blessed .1 percent — the miraculous exception!

He was in such good spirits, too, that ordinarily he would have helped to raise hers. The boy was beside himself with excitement over O'Hare and his capture of Henley, culling the newspapers every day, clipping all the accounts and pasting them up in a special notebook. And he never stopped talking about him, how brave he was! What a grand hero! How cleverly he'd tracked down the O.F.F. terrorist! And he'd gotten a citation and been promoted to the rank of captain! It was O'Hare this and O'Hare that, every minute of the livelong day. When was he coming? And why was he so long away? It got on her nerves finally, till she was ready to scream. She was grateful when she could get him to bed and be by herself. But then, her thoughts became so troublesome, she was almost tempted to wake him.

The nights were growing colder. The wind came whistling down the chimney. There must be something wrong with the damper. O'Hare would have known how to fix it. She built herself a fire, but there was no warmth in it, and she shivered — less from the chill than from the hounds of conscience howling in her breast. O'Hare was too good for her. She didn't deserve him and she knew it.

When the phone rang that Saturday noon, it turned out to be not O'Hare, but Paddy Morphy asking her coaxingly would she consider coming out with him that night. She thought t'hell with O'Hare and said "Yes!" so loud she almost shattered the phone, adding, "Why not? I'd love to!" her voice clattering back at her through the receiver.

Paddy laughed and said, "Fine! I'll come by to pick you up then around seven."

She didn't want Jenny O'Flaherty sitting with Timmy — though the old maid had done it before, and was always offering to — but ran over to Kathleen Finnegan's instead, and asked her could Timmy spend the night over there. Kathleen said "Of course!" and that Mike would be wild with delight.

3

O'Hare lay in the bed in the little dark room that felt like a coffin. A half-empty bottle stood on the table next to the bed, his second or third since he'd come here — he couldn't remember exactly — and when he couldn't stand the dragon clawing away inside him, he'd take a good swig, hoping to numb it, to make it let go. But the creature was an obdurate monster, not to be drowned so easily, and it hung on.

He had no idea how long he'd been lying there, or even what day of the week it was. The long bristles of his beard were rough and scratchy when he turned his face into the pillow, so it might be two or three days. What day would that make it? At least he knew where he was. He was inside the Green Dragon with a slimy green serpent inside him, tearing away at his gut.

He'd taken the same room Connaught had. A small penance perhaps. But it seemed fitting somehow that they should share something in common, that dumb stoolie and him.

When they'd booked Henley, gotten the confession, and finished the paper work, Riley told him he'd done a great job, then put his arm around O'Hare's shoulder and said he looked worn out, and ought to go off somewhere, take a week's leave;

there'd be plenty of time yet before he was needed for the trial. He'd protested at first, but Riley insisted and he finally agreed.

Clearing his desk, he thought he ought to give Agnes a call, and maybe stop by and see Timmy before going home and falling into bed. He was dead-tired. He made the call from the station, but found himself tongue-tied, and could hardly get out a word. He decided he was in no mood to see them. Or to be more exact, for them to see him, the shape he was in. He went home then to his two small rooms upstairs from the O'Learys', but he couldn't stay put. The place seemed so empty and shabby and cold. He needed to get away, go somewhere where nobody would know him. He got in the car and just drove in a kind of a daze and found himself back in Howth. He wasn't surprised somehow; it was the place he needed to be. He thought of going up to the monastery on the hill and making a retreat, but he'd long ago given up observance of any kind and couldn't face the falseness of seeking relief without belief. Besides, he didn't feel he deserved the glib solace it might offer.

Now he lay in the bed in a little dark room, drinking and thinking. He hadn't moved except a few times to go to the bathroom down the hall. Once, the girl who worked as a clerk at the desk, Daisy Clooney of the orange-petal hair—she looked like a day-glo picture of her name—had come up and knocked at his door, saying, "It's Daisy, Mr. O'Hare. Are you sure you're feelin' all right? Is there anything at all I could get you?"

He'd muttered, "No, nothing," not opening the door to her. She'd said wasn't he hungry? She'd be glad to get him something to eat. But he hadn't answered and she'd finally gone away down the hall, her high heels clicking over the linoleum.

He knew there was to be a service for the mother and child. He'd seen the announcement in the death notices:

Grace Henley, 34, wife of R. D. Henley, and daughter, Haila, age 6, murdered in the cause of freedom.

> *Gone are the ones we loved so dear*
> *Silent the voices we loved to hear*

Special service, Church of Ireland, Dun Laoghaire, Friday, September 26, 12:00 noon.

If he went, what would he say? Sincere condolences?

Died in the cause of freedom? Whose? What did it all mean?

There was life and there was death, and all that went on in between was the miserable struggle to escape the stench of evil.

He'd have to come to a decision soon . . . Perhaps not.

He could lay here and rot forever, for all the difference it would make. It's all so small, he thought. All the petty vanities and concerns cluttering up your life suddenly falling away, leaving you shrunken and naked.

He needed an answer—some answer to a question he couldn't put into words. What was it he wanted? What was he looking for? Peace, he thought, a bit of peace. A mind that was clear and easy with itself, that knew what was right, what was wrong. In the old days, it all seemed so simple. You did what you had to and took the consequences. But that was before. He'd never killed a woman and a child before.

A black rage rose up in him. It was an *accident!* But he should have thought, should have known! In the end, it was his hand that so mindlessly threw the thing that did the murders.

Three deaths in one day to his credit, if you included Connaught's. Might as well. His guilt was big enough to swallow another victim—though the man was involved, and the O.F.F. or the Provos would probably have gotten him anyway.

If he believed in the doctrine of Original Sin, would it let him off the hook? Agh, what he'd done was done, and nothing he did now could change it. There was no way he could wipe it out.

He knew suddenly what the question was. *How was he going to live with it?* The black guilt gnawing away inside him would never be stilled till he could find forgiveness. He wept, longing for his lost childhood faith, his young innocence in the days when he believed God's love and mercy would be there for him always.

But who was there could absolve him now? Not himself! Not God! Eileen? If there were some way she could bring herself to forgive him, he might be able to forgive himself. He might even learn to forgive God.

In the early days of the Church, the priests had sold indulgences, granting exculpation. What forfeit would he not offer now, to be free of the torment, the pain that had exploded like a bomb in his chest, leaving his heart in fragments? He could still hear the sound of the child crying with her dying breath for her dead mother.

The bottle was empty. He looked out the window and was surprised to find it snowing. Snow in Howth in September? Dies Irae . . . and the angels weeping crystal tears? He wanted to go out and kneel in it. Like King Henry at Canossa, who knelt in the snow to be shriven, and had risen up pure and clean again.

He got up and washed his face. He looked at the stranger in the mirror over the washstand. The strange man there looked out of his mind. He put on his hat and coat. He knew he had to go out to the Point. He had to find Eileen and talk to her.

4

Trying to get through the mob at Clancy's on Saturday night was like running the obstacle course at Baldoyle. If you could manage the early hurdles at the front bar and were still up and going, you might make it for the prize of a glorious time in the big hall at the back. The night was still young and the real entertainment would not be starting till later, but the place was already brimful of people let out of work, rushing to celebrate their Saturday night freedom.

A blue haze of smoke hung in the air, and what with the crush of bodies pressing all around her and the fumes from the whiskey and beer, she was feeling half-drunk herself, flushed with expectation and the kind of dizzying excitement she'd felt as a girl when she used to go partying. Well, she was having her promised night out after all, her night on the town — only not with O'Hare. And whose fault was that? Anyway, she was wearing the diamond drop earrings Timmy's father had given her for their tenth anniversary, and the darling new dress she'd gone out and bought this afternoon, and she couldn't help notice the men's eyes following her as she and Paddy pushed through the crowd.

The big room in the back when they finally got there was as jam-packed as the front, except for a small space that had been kept clear for the dancing, and the laughter and chatter rose up in a wave to greet them. There was a group of men squeezed into a booth against the far wall, and one of them called out to her, "There's plenty of room here for a lovely lass!" and another said, "Come sit with us, darlin'!" There were four of them, all about her age or older. A great hulk of a man, Gavin his name was, stood up and gave her his place, and asked her and Paddy what he could get them. She asked for a gin and lime, and Paddy said he'd have a black and tan. There were first-name introductions all around. The men were in high fettle, and in no time at all paying her wild compliments and flirting outrageously with her.

One of the men, Frank, asked if she and Paddy were married. She said, "No, just friends." Paddy leaned down and kissed her on the cheek saying, "But we might be engaged any day now," and the men cheered, and Frank turned to her with a grin and said, "I figured as much. The poor man can't seem to keep his hands off—not that I blame him."

It was true. All the while he was standing there next to her, waiting for the drinks, Paddy'd kept touching her, little gestures of affection or possession, taking her hand, running his fingers along her arm, and once even stroking her back and shoulders inside the back of her dress. She thought he might be jealous of the attention the men were paying her, and wanted to make it clear they hadn't a chance, or maybe he was feeling outnumbered and not part of the group, with all of them sitting around her. Whatever the reason, he seemed to her suddenly vulnerable and unsure of himself—she'd always thought him so cocky—and the young hunger and uncertainty in him stirred her.

"Which brings to mind the story of another Paddy," the perky little man with the moustache was saying. "Now stop me, if you've heard this one. It seems Brigid and Paddy'd been goin' around together for more than ten years and Brigid was beginning to think he was never going to pop the question. One day, exasperated, she said finally to him, 'Paddy, we're neither of us gettin' any younger. Don't you think it's time we got married?' 'Ah, shure now, Brigid, that's a foine idea! But who in the world would have us?'"

She'd heard the old chestnut a dozen times but it still made her laugh. Gavin came back with the drinks, doubles for everyone, and there was a round of toasts. Sean, the gentle slim poetic-looking man — he seemed the softest of the lot — said, "To a united Ireland and an end to the Troubles!" and everyone drank solemnly, and that started the talk of politics and the bombings that took place last week. Frank said angrily, "I'd just love the chance to pay out those Orange bastards who go around killin' and maimin' innocent people!"

"Och! Come on with ya, Frank! You know it's not only the Orangemen that are doin' the killin'," said Sean. "More violence ain't the answer."

"Maybe not," said Frank, "but can you think of a better?"

"Yes, where's the alternative?" chimed in the perky little man whose name she couldn't seem to remember.

"In '49," Frank went on, "when we ran up the flag of the Republic, we thought we'd totally finished with the bloody fightin' and murderin'. But in the last couple of years there've been more people killed than in all the decades since the Easter Rising. It seems there's no end to it."

"It's hard to make sense of it," said Sean. "My mother lives in Derry and she wrote me a letter the other day tellin' me about a Catholic woman who was hit by a stray bullet in an IRA raid, fallin' dead on the pavement in front of her four-year-old child. That very same week on the same street, a baby less than a year old, bein' wheeled by her ten-year-old brother, was run down by a British lorry. The driver'd just been shot by a young Provo — a kid barely fifteen! Can you make any sense out of that?"

"Both sides killin' each other, and their own people as well," the perky little man said with a sad smile. "And all in the name of religion!"

Aggie said, "Ah, if only the British would get out and stay out, I'm sure the North Irish could work out their own salvation."

And everyone agreed, except Gavin, who said that it might be a start, but it wouldn't stop the extremists from killing each other. It turned out he was a professor at Queen's College, and the others listened to him with some respect.

"As I see it," he said, "the problem's basically economic. The truth is there's nothing like an empty belly to make a terrorist out of a man. And there are hungry Protestants up North, as well as hungry Catholics. The day they discover they've a common cause, they may just stop killing each other."

"Well," said Frank doubtfully, "but it's the Catholics that're the poorest. And right now they're the ones who're bein' thrown in jail, or gettin' themselves killed."

"Ach, it's the curse of the downtrodden everywhere . . ." the perky little man — Brian his name was — said piously.

A waiter came by with a tray full of drinks for a neighboring table, and they grabbed hold of him and gave him their orders.

"The women could stop it," Agnes said. "They could put an end to all the killing. When the Catholic and Protestant women marched together — after the MacGuire children were murdered — there was peace for a month, with not a single shot fired, or any fighting in all of the North."

"Yes," said Frank, "but the Peace Women's kids got beaten up in school by the other kids, and in no time a'tall it all started up again. It'll take more than the Nobel Peace Prize and a few women marching, to put a stop to it."

The drinks arrived in record time, and everyone seemed to cool down.

Aggie told them her little boy Timmy had been on the bus that just escaped the explosion at the O'Connell Bridge. He'd been bruised a bit, but was fine now, and they all commiserated with her and said how lucky she was, and how glad they were that the child was safe. She shivered and thought, I *am* lucky. I should be thanking my stars every minute, instead of brooding about O'Hare!

The music, soft in the background till now, broke out in a loud jig, and people started clapping and jumping up to cheer the performers. There was a group of young men sitting nearby, with beards and boots, dressed in denim jeans and bright shirts, tourists most likely. Some of them had guitars and they joined in with the music, strumming and hooting and stamping. Between their contribution, the noise of the crowd, and the sounds of the fiddles soaring, pipes jangling, and spoons clacking away, the din drowned out all possibility of further talk.

Paddy, apparently feeling more confident about his acceptance by the group, deemed it safe to leave her, and went off to pick up another round of drinks. When the set was over, the band started up with a waltz, and Gavin pulled her out of her seat and onto the dance floor. One of the musicians gave her a wink and a grin of approval as she swung by, and she tossed her head at him as if to say, "Better steer clear, I'm spoken for." Gavin saw the bit of play, and tightened his hold on her waist, pulling her close up against him. She didn't protest, only looked up at him quizzically, and he made a small moue of apology with his lips and his eyes, and loosened his hold just a bit. And she thought how funny it was that so much could be said—a whole little drama played out, its meaning quite clear, without anyone's saying a word.

Gavin led her back to the table, but before she had a chance to draw breath again, the M.C. announced a rigadoon, and the crowd roared and the music started up. All of the men wanted her for a partner, and she took turns dancing with each of them. Frank kept putting the "Come 'ither" on her, and Sean whirled her around till she was dizzy, and Gavin kept after her for her address, but she said she didn't feel free at the moment to give it to him. He said, "I hope it's not Paddy you're thinking of tying the knot with? He's not nearly man enough for you."

And she said, "Now, how would you know that?"

Even poor Brian made his try, saying he was married, but now that he'd met her, he wished that he wasn't.

Paddy came back with the drinks, and Brian, out of guilt probably, offered him his place in the booth.

A hush fell on the crowd when the ballad singer came on. The music was soft and lovely, and everyone turned teary-eyed and sentimental. After the show, the M.C. announced anyone was welcome to come up and do a song, and the men kept pushing her to go up. She said, "But I've no voice at all!" Still, they kept pressing her and she finally went over to the M.C. and said she would sing "When Irish Eyes Are Smiling." She started off shy but gained confidence as she went along. In the middle, she noticed a man with a face that reminded her of O'Hare and her heart missed a beat. She thought, Oh luv, luv, why aren't you with me now! and her voice quavered, but she held on. When she reached "Sure, they'll steal your heart away . . ." her last notes, clear and limpid, seemed to hang in the air. Everyone was still for a moment, then broke out in a roar followed by a thunder of applause. She'd done her party piece and made a great hit.

Paddy, looking at once pleased and troubled, was beside her and leading her back to the table, helping her on with her coat and saying it was time to go. There were hugs and kisses from the men, with Gavin whispering in her ear that his name was Rafferty, and he was listed on the Dublin exchange, if ever she wanted to reach him.

It was after two when they got back to Clontarf, Paddy strangely quiet, not trying anything funny, although he'd kept his arm around her all the way. When they reached the house, he kissed her softly, with such pitiful importunity, she felt it only fair to kiss him back, saying, "It was a lovely time, Paddy. I did so enjoy it!"

She started out of the cab and Paddy got out with her, saying, "Won't you let me come in with you? Just for a moment?"

"It's late," she answered with some regret. "Maybe another time."

"Just for a nightcap—one for the road?" he begged. "I won't stay long," and before she could stop him, he'd paid off the cabbie.

"Now how will you get home?"

"I'll fly all the way!" he said, and that started them laughing.

"You've got to be quiet," she admonished, "Tim's asleep!" but suddenly remembered the child wasn't there at all, he was over at Kathleen Finnegan's.

Inside, she kicked off her shoes and took her earrings off and laid them on the coffee table. Paddy found the bottle and the glasses and poured out the whiskey. Somehow they never got around to drinking it. She was lying on the couch, with him kneeling at her feet, his coat still on, and he put his head in her lap and said, "Oh Aggie . . . Aggie darlin'!" his voice so rough with longing it made her tremble. She could feel his breath warm on her thigh through the silk of her dress as she petted his head, his curly hair soft as a child's under her hand. He seemed so young and defenseless, so sad and so sweet.

5

Mrs. Finnegan kept popping in and out of the bedroom to find out if they were all right. Had they washed properly and remembered to go to the bathroom so they wouldn't have to be getting up in the middle of the night? Were they warm enough, or too cold? Should she shut the window altogether? Or maybe get them another blanket? He and Mike answered yes to everything she asked them, which seemed to confuse her entirely. They snuggled down together in the narrow bed with their heads under the covers to muffle their hoots and guffaws each time she left the room, but in a minute she was back with her "Now this is the last time!" admonishing them to stop giggling and talking, it was late and they needed their sleep, and she'd have no excuses about their being too tired in the morning to attend mass! His nose stung and his belly hurt from trying to hold back the laughter, but she finally left them alone.

He couldn't believe his good luck, his mother letting him have a sleepover at Mike's. They hadn't had a chance to be alone together in ages, and there was something special he wanted to talk over with him, a grand idea that had come to him while he was in the hospital. Actually, he'd had the notion for some time, but it had only just begun to take shape in the last few days. What he'd been thinking of was to set up a *real* cops-and-robbers scam, in which he'd be the robber and O'Hare would have to try to track him down. But what he needed was to work out some solid scheme, if he expected to fool O'Hare. Maybe Mike could help come up with a plan.

Mike was thunderstruck at the idea, but the more they talked about it, the more excited he got, and pretty soon he was begging Tim to let him come in on the deal. Tim told him about the nine-year-old kid in New York he'd read about in the papers, who'd robbed a bank, slipping a note to the teller and getting away with $300! He'd spent most of it before they'd finally caught up with him.

"Jesus!" said Mike. "Maybe the two of us could try that! One of us could be the lookout."

"A bank's pretty risky," Tim said cautiously. He was suddenly not sure he wanted Mike to share in the glory. "God knows what would happen, if we got caught!"

"My Da would certainly kill me! Maybe you're right about the bank . . . How's about holding up one of the shops, like Delehanty's?"

"He's already been robbed," Tim said. "He says he's prepared, he's got a rifle stacked and ready, on a shelf in the back —"

"So what! He's little enough. We could take him together."

"Maybe . . ." He still felt doubtful about letting Mike come along. It would spoil the excitement, if two of them were caught. But he didn't know how he could get out of it. He'd have to wait and see. "We'd have to go disguised, of course! All Hallow's Eve's coming up in a couple of weeks. That's the target date!"

"Agreed! That would give us the time to work out the details and get ready! It'll be a cinch! With all the other kids roamin' around in their costumes that night, wearin' masks, who'll ever guess who we are? Good thinking! What would you say to doing Madigan's? Think of the toys we could pinch!"

"Too big. Too many people around. Besides, cash is the ticket, isn't it?"

"Right!" said Mike loudly.

Mrs. Finnegan banged on the wall, yelling, "Will you quit the jabberin', the two of you!" and they looked at each other comically and got down under the covers. They were quiet for a little while and pretty soon they could hear the sound of the bedsprings creaking from the next room.

"It's their Saturday night," Mike whispered. "They do it Saturday night."

"Do what?"

"You know. He's fucking her."

"How does he do that?"

"He sticks his pizzle, when it gets big and stiff, into the place she pees out of. It's just like the dogs."

"You're lyin'! Where'd you hear that?"

"Jimmy Scanlon. You know, the big kid who delivers for O'Rourke, the greengrocer? He told me about it. I didn't believe him at first either, but he crossed his heart and said 'Hope to die!' if it's not true."

"That's disgusting!"

"It is, isn't it? But he said it feels good, and when you grow up you get to like it."

"O'Hare would never do that to my Mum."

"Of course not, they're not married. Only married people are supposed to do it. It's the way they get babies."

"You're a liar!"

"So help me! Jimmy Scanlon swears it's the truth."

"How does he know?"

"He said he tried it once."

"Och, he's not married! He's no more than fourteen!"

"All I know is he said he did it once and the priest told him it's a sin, unless you're married."

They were both silent a while, thinking of Jimmy Scanlon sinning.

"Mine gets stiff sometimes when I'm having a bath, or if I rub up against something," Mike told him.

"Father Malachy says it's a sin to touch it."

"Listen, you have to hold it when you pee. Otherwise, you'd be spoutin' all over the place!"

They snickered at the thought.

"I wonder who he did it with?"

"Who?"

"Scanlon."

"He didn't say," Mike said yawning and turned over, curling up into him.

They fit together like a pair of nesting chairs, Mike's backside in his lap, and his own knees fitting neat under Mike's legs.

"Would you ever marry a Prod?" he whispered into Mike's back.

"I might, if she was pretty enough."

There was a moon high in the heavens shining through the lace curtains. A bird was calling *"Tu whit, tu whoo . . . tu whit, tu woo . . ."* It lulled him. Mike was asleep already, he could hear him snoring softly, feel his back rising and falling against his chest. It was lovely having someone to share a bed with. But he'd never do that dirty thing, if ever he got married.

The house was quiet, not a sound now from the other bedroom. He snuggled his chin into Mike's shoulder. There was hardly any other person in the whole world he'd rather be with this minute than Mike . . . except maybe . . .

He was just falling off when he heard one of the birds twittering *"Wish't was you . . . Wish't was you . . ."* and another answering, calling, *"Who . . . who . . . who?"*

* * *

They were up early Sunday morning, clowning about, doing somersaults in bed, sometimes landing on the floor with a thump. Mrs. Finnegan was bustling about getting ready for church, scolding to hurry them along. Mr. Finnegan wasn't attending mass and remained in his bed. Mike and his mother didn't eat any breakfast, but he was allowed a biscuit and a cup of tea because he hadn't been to confession and wouldn't be taking communion, and besides he was supposed to eat something first thing in the morning.

At St. Anne's he looked around to see if his mother might be there, but there was no sign of her. She didn't go every Sunday. After the service, Mike and Mrs. Finnegan walked him home and he remembered to say, "Thanks, Mrs. Finnegan, for a lovely time," and punched Mike on the arm, saying "See you in school tomorrow!"

He opened the door with his key and went in quietly, thinking his mother might still be asleep. Her diamond drop earrings were on the coffee table, and when he picked one up to admire it, he noticed a man's coat lying on the floor near the couch. His heart leapt in his throat at the sight. *O'Hare's back!* he thought, and was running up the stairs calling, "Hi, Mum! I'm home!"

6

When he turned the car onto the lane, he saw the hearse standing in front of the house. Two cars were parked near the shed. He pulled up alongside them and shut off the motor. He sat in the car waiting, wondering how he could face her, trying to think what he could say.

A little man got out of the hearse and walked toward him. A dress coat with a velvet collar was slung over his shoulders and he wore a tall black top hat and gloves. O'Hare rolled down the window. I should get out, he thought, but he wasn't sure his legs would hold him.

The man leaned over to talk to him. "Ferguson's the name," he said introducing himself, waiting for O'Hare to do the same, then proffered a card. O'Hare looked at it.

> *Funeral Arrangements*
> *Executed*
> *With Tasteful Care*
> *Reasonable Cost*
>
> *John Ferguson, Owner-Director*

O'Hare said "Excuse me," and opened the door and got out. He shivered against the wind and buttoned his coat. He could barely stand.

"A terrible sad business. You've come to pay your respects, I suppose. A friend of the family?"

O'Hare coughed and spat up some phlegm. He wiped his mouth on a soiled handkerchief.

Ferguson shook his head, looking concerned. "It's the grief that does it," he said. "They'll be leavin' in a little while, but you're welcome to join the mourners."

O'Hare stood there. The man looked at him puzzled and said, "This way . . ." pointing up the path, and started ahead, expecting him to follow.

O'Hare said, "Hold on a minute. Could you just take a message?"

The man turned back frowning. "What is it?"

"Could you ask Eileen—Miss Henley—if I could see her alone, just for a minute? I know it's a poor time, but it's important."

"Who shall I say? Are you friend, or family?"

"Just tell her Thomas." Not a friend, he thought, her enemy. "Never mind," he said, "I'll come back another time."

The man shrugged and went back up the path to the hearse. O'Hare stood there watching the gulls wheeling soundlessly over the water. The soft susurrus of the sea, the snow falling soft all about, held him suspended in some timeless frozen space.

The door of the house opened and several men came out carrying the coffins. A small group followed and stood on the porch quietly, watching as the two boxes, one large and one small, were placed side by side in the hearse. Eileen came down the steps holding her nephew by the hand. She lifted her veil and he could see her face, pale but unweeping.

He walked slowly toward her, feeling the eyes of the group turning to watch him. He stopped when he came close and said her name, then just stood there not knowing how to go on. When she looked up and saw who it was, she let go of the child's hand and turned away with a cry. Then turning back, she slapped him, a hard stinging blow across the face. Two of the men grabbed him, shoving him aside, holding him as though they thought he might hit her back.

One of the women said in an angry voice, "It's him! The garda that killed them!"

"The nerve!" another said, her voice strident with shock, with outrage.

He said quietly, "You can hit me again, as much as you like. I need to talk to you."

She said, "Have you come to arrest me too?"

He looked at her but said nothing.

"Leave him alone," she said to the men. "I want to know why he's come."

The men let go of his arms but stood nearby, alert, protective.

"Will you listen to what I have to say? Give me one minute alone!" he said, feeling shamed in front of the group, hating the way his voice sounded begging.

She stood silent a moment, then said to the others, "Go on ahead." One of the men started to protest, but she cut him off. "It's all right," she said. She turned to the woman beside her. "Will you take the child with you?" She touched the boy's face, saying, "Don't worry Ian, I'll be along in a minute."

The woman took the boy's hand and the group moved off slowly toward the cars, their black silhouettes fading away in the swirling snow. Mr. Ferguson stayed beside the black coach, watchful.

Eileen walked a little way over the dunes out of view of the hearse, and stood looking down at the sea. He followed, wanting to take her arm, to help her over the rocks and sand, wet and slippery with the snow. He came up and stood next to her, watching the silent flakes fall, thousands and thousands of white crystal stars drifting down through the air, disappearing in a moment as they touched the surface of the glassy green water.

Staring down at the sea, she said, "I haven't much time, so get on with it, whatever it is you've such a great need to say to me." He looked at her angry face. His heart was a lump of ice in his breast. He said hopelessly, "I know there's no way you can bring yourself to forgive me."

"If it's me you've come to for absolution, I've none to give you! You must go to your priests for that!"

"I'm not asking it. I just want you to know . . . if there's anything I can do for you and the boy, anything at all, you've only to tell me."

"How generous!" she said. "Did you think you could knit up our lives like an old raveled sweater?"

He took her hard by the arm and shook her. "Don't you know I'd give my life to undo it!"

She stumbled against him, and he put his arm out to hold her, to steady her.

"It's too late," she said.

"I know I can't bring them back!" he cried out in despair. "But there must be something! I'll testify for him at the trial. Did you know your brother was being blackmailed? The men from Belfast kept threatening him. He was worried to death about the family. But he swears the bomb he delivered to the airport was a dud, and he never planted the ones at the bank or the bridge. If he's telling the truth, I could get his sentence lightened. Tell me what more I can do!"

He put his arm around her. He could feel her trembling beside him, the soft curl of her hair brushing his cheek.

"It wasn't your fault," she said. "I know in my heart it wasn't. It all started a long time ago, long before the two of us met. We lost my brother Billy at sixteen, the same way. It seems there's no end to it. The blame isn't yours."

"Maybe not. But the guilt is. I can't seem to live with it."

She straightened up and moved away from him.

He stared at her hopelessly. She put out a hand and touched his face. "I shouldn't have struck you. I'm sorry. That was wrong."

"I didn't mind," he said. "It felt like a kiss."

She wept then, tears as soft and silent as the snow that fell all around him. He put his arms around her and held her.

He could feel the salt taste of her tears on his lips, and he thought of the other times, the sweet summer days when they'd been alone together and he'd tasted the salt of the sea on her skin.

"Oh Thomas!" she cried out, "why did it have to happen?"

There was no answer he could give her.

*Nothing is secret that shall not be made
manifest.*

THE BIBLE, LUKE, 8:17

1

She hasn't been mucked about so royally first thing on waking in
ages. It gives her a lovely feeling. O yes, he is her darlin', her
darlin', her darlin', Paddy is her darlin', the young grenadier . . .

" 'Tis a great boon to the health of a mornin'," he'd said
piously, which made her laugh. But she agrees entirely. It makes
the whole world seem right, everything bright and sweet, and at
the same time somehow comical.

She feels she loves everyone. *A touch of sin makes the whole world
kin* — which isn't exactly how it goes, she knows, but it sounds to
her as good, better maybe, than the original. Turning over in the
bed, leaning on her elbow, she looks at him. He lies there, eyes
closed, his skin warm and fragrant, his damp curly hair a bright
flame against the white pillow. She can't bring herself to disturb
him just yet, but she will have to get him out soon. The street
will be filling up in a little while with the neighbors, the
churchgoers coming home. She sees them exchanging looks, lips
tight, eyebrows raised as they watch him, the handsome young

brute sneaking out of the widow's house — that one from America. Has she no shame? And at this hour of a Sunday morning!
With a clear brow she will tell Jenny O'Flaherty that Mr. Morphy
has just stopped by for a minute with a message from her good
friend O'Hare. Jenny simpers knowingly. Och! She brushes the
image away. She will not let herself be put in the position of
having to make explanations to anyone, certainly not to
O'Flaherty.

A pang of guilt sets up a faint alarm as she thinks of him —
Thomas Francis O'Hare — my first true love since O'Connell.
It's not adultery, only fornication — a sin certainly, but she's committed the same with O'Hare. Yet it was different. Every lovely
tomcat is different, each with his own special charms to offer.
And at least she can't be accused of being *unfaithful* — what a
dumb word that is — since O'Hare never once promised to marry
her.

Why can't a woman love two men? Or at least love one and
enjoy another? Isn't it cruel to make it a sin and at the same time
such a terrible temptation, so delicious? So impossible to resist!

I have been unfaithful to thee, Thomas, in my fashion — I
thought of you almost all the time I was making love with him.

What would happen if O'Hare were to find out? No need to
worry. Who'd ever tell him? She wouldn't. And Paddy surely
would never let on.

The last time she'd gone to confession, it was three Novenas
and a Hail Mary, let off easy considering the joy she'd had of
O'Hare.

"Oh, let me Aggie-Maggie," he's awake whispering. "Just this
once — just the one more time," he begs, tickling her ever so
lightly.

She says no and no and no, certain she means it, saying she wants
him out of the bed and out of the house and out of there — right
now and stop it this minute before it's too late till she's gasping for
breath, falling, drowning, dying with terror and delight, crying O
my luv, my luv, when she hears the child calling out to her from
downstairs, letting her know that he's home.

"Get dressed, for God's sake!" she says, flying out of the bed.

"I could hide in the closet and wait till nightfall," he tells her. "Wouldn't you like that?"

"Shush, will you now! Be quiet!" He must know she's upset.

He sighs sadly, throws off the covers, and sitting naked, lazily starts to put on his socks.

Standing with her back against the door, she calls, "I'll be down in a minute. Put the kettle on, will you, luv?" as the telephone rings shrilly.

2

He is bathed and shaved and is wearing his Sunday best suit, carrying a bunch of Michaelmas daisies, which vie shyly with the pinks and the bluebells, coming to call on his lush ladylove to ask for her not-quite-dainty hand in marriage. He moves swiftly along, surprisingly, laden as he is with the posies in one hand and with the other wheeling the junior-size bicycle for her son — soon, if all goes as planned, please God, to be his as well. He feels fresh and free from taint, his heart aflame yet brushed with a faint tinge of melancholy, as befits so solemn an occasion — Eileen's pardon, his ablutions, and the renewed decision to get on with his life and marry Agnes having combined to cleanse him of the heavy detritus of doubt and misery that had so darkened his soul and beclouded his vision this long hard week.

He is also slightly drunk, that is to say not unmanageably, just enough to cushion him with the courage he needs to face up to the impending, drastic change in his life — much for the better, he assures himself, but still slightly unsettling — which settling down to becoming a husband again, *and* a father, will inevitably entail.

When he telephoned — can it be less than half an hour ago — it was Timmy who answered, shouting "O'Hare!" on hearing his voice. And before he'd a chance to greet him properly, the child was abruptly displaced by the mother, her voice cool, her tone a bit prickly — understandably — his silence and unexplained absence undoubtedly troubling her. But she accepts his apologies and his promise to explain all, and seems finally truly pleased to hear from him, suggesting only that he delay his arrival for say, half an hour? Time to fix herself up, he figures. Hence the time spent belting a few at Moriarity's, where the flowers and the bike proved a source of much joshing and merriment, a minor, not unpleasant, embarrassment. For word gets around quickly in Dublin, even quicker in Clontarf, and the news of his proposal and her swift joyous acceptance — of this he has comfortably little doubt — will be all over the town, give or take an hour or two.

Impatient, he is a bit early still. He hesitates before ringing the bell, hearing raised voices within — angry, arguing, the boy and his mother at it hammer and tongs, the child shouting defiance, voice quavering, high-pitched, "I won't! You can't make me!" and her thunderous command, "Get back in your room and stay there!" A door slamming. A whispering silence ensues. He rings the bell quickly, longing to rescue them, the two people he cares about most in the world, from this untoward tempest of tempers on this beautiful sunny celebrant Sunday. Surely St. Patrick is smiling down on him from that azure sky, so miraculously clear after Friday's unseasonal snow.

A long wait. He rings again, rehearsing his lines. "Marry me Agnes, my love, my own. I'll adopt the boy, give him my name if you agree. Tell me you love me, say you'll be mine," though not necessarily in that order.

When she opens the door, she looks distraught, slightly disheveled, though radiant. With anger? With anticipation? She is wearing a new dress and seems to him, in her flustered disarray, more beautiful than ever.

His heart awash in a sea of love, he proffers the flowers. She takes them with a tremulous smile, ushering him gravely over the threshold. The shiny red bike stands between them but he reaches for her with his free arm, embracing her passionately, pressing her and the bouquet to his bosom.

"Will you have me, Aggie?" he blurts out, burying his face in the flowers, forgetting the words so artfully prepared. "Say yes! Say you will!"

3

In the state known as bliss she watches as, led out of his room by
O'Hare with laughter and shouts and the assurance his mum
says it's okay — his sentence commuted — her son follows head
down, sulky, to be confronted by the shiny new bike and the
news: It is his! And his mother has said she will marry O'Hare.
The brand new two-wheeler a gift to him to celebrate their
connubial commitment. And he's to call O'Hare "Dad" now or
soon!

Her moist happiness is mirrored obliquely in the child's eyes,
his lashes still beaded with tears, in the astonished oval of his
mouth, slightly swollen, expressing disbelief at promised joy.
"Mine? For me?" And as she and O'Hare, confirming it is,
embrace him, he makes the swift leap from despair to sweet
ecstasy. "Can I ride it? Right now?"

Rubenesque, titian-haired, she stands in the doorway on this
lustrous Sunday afternoon, breathing in the fresh Clontarf air
with only the faintest flutter of apprehension as her gold-haloed
son, astride his red charger, pedals off down the street, his mount
veering uncertainly, her soon-to-be husband running alongside,
hand holding tight to the underbrace, a lever for balance. And in
three or four trials, O'Hare has let go, and breathless with effort
and pride is shouting encouragement, "Not too fast — that's it.
Keep it steady, Tim! It's all in the forward motion!" as the child
rides off and away on his own, into the glittering sunlight.

O happy day! Caloo, calay . . . What can happen to mar the
perfection of this exquisite moment? She is certain it will stand
fixed, enshrined in her memory forever.

Circling back skillfully he returns, flushed and triumphant,
her errant child-knight on his fiery steed, trumpets sounding,
bike bell beeping, to smile up at his Mum and her consort,
standing arms entwined as they beam down at him in royal
approval. O'Hare, tossing him onto his shoulders, bears the

conquering hero into the house; she, wheeling the bike toward
the rear, calls out, "O'Hare! Be careful!" as Tim's tender head,
swiftly ducking, grazes the low lintel. But he is unhurt. And all is
still sunshine and roses.

She enters through the kitchen door and is assailed by a
lingering scent of danger, an uneasy whiff of memory, recalling
as if in a dream she dreamed long ago, this morning's hectic
imbroglio . . .

O'Hare's longed-for untimely phone call . . . Paddy's whispering voice complaining, "I can't find my tie!" Her frantic
response, "Will you be still for God's sake, and just go!"
. . . Tim's inopportune presence – the child a possible witness? . . . His defiance, her rage, his furious disappointment as
she banishes him to his room, punishing her son for her sins . . .

A frisson of terror. Shuddering, she shuts her eyes, struggling
to consign to oblivion the memory of those final frenetic
moments when – with the doorbell ringing, the rebellious child
weeping – the tardy lover, shoes in hand, makes his hasty exit
through her kitchen door, just in the nick . . .

Calls, shrieks, and wild laughter – Tim and O'Hare playing
hide-and-seek. The demonic image is shattered, swiftly displaced by maternal concern. She is sure the excitement is too
much for the child, but is reluctant to interrupt their festive
hilarity. O Lord! In this whirligig of a day she has completely
forgotten to feed him, check his urine. Remission or not, he still
needs watching. "Dinner in a little while," she calls out, and sits
down on a kitchen chair to still her flamboyant heart, offering
meanwhile a swift prayer for her undeserved good fortune.
O'Hare loves her! Loves the boy. And Tim loves him. And God
knows how deeply, how truly, how long she has longed for this
numinous moment!

Scampering footsteps overhead. O'Hare's voice booming out
"Eight! Nine! *Ten!*" burbling with threat. "Ready or not! Here I
come!"

Deep silence. Sudden clattering sounds resound through the
house; a rush down the stairs.

"Home free!" screams Timmy, as safe and breathless he hurls himself into his mother's sheltering arms.

"I didn't tell," he whispers, nuzzling her happily.

"Tell? About what?" she asks sharply, heart sinking, pushing him off.

"You know . . ." her son says, unable to meet her accusing eyes, kissing her cheek, anxiously seeking a return to her warm embrace. "It'll be okay, Mum. Don't worry. I promise!"

4

He is trying to get to sleep. Tomorrow is a school day and his mother's always after him about how he needs his rest. Only he can't stop thinking about all the things that have been happening to him this day. His own two-wheeler! And O'Hare coming into his room to let him out of solitary. And asking him if it's all right with him if he marries his Mum!

"Your mother said yes, but I'd like to know how you feel about it, Tim." He'd been crying and had this big fight with her, and was so shook with the news he hardly knew how to answer.

"I'd like it fine," he said finally. "I'll be havin' a father then, just like the other kids."

O'Hare gave him that great grin and took his hand and said, "Come on out, I've a surprise for you!" And there was the new red bike! He's already learned to ride it, with just a little help from O'Hare. And won't the kids at school be dying of envy when he comes flying into the yard riding high off the seat, pedaling away like a racer!

He is tired but restless and can't seem to settle down. And now that he's alone, can't stop thinking, worrying about how it will turn out.

What about his Mum? Will she be the better or the worse now that she's got O'Hare? What if O'Hare cares more about her— more than he does for him? Maybe once they're married, he'll be on her side, and it'll be the two of them against him.

He wonders if O'Hare will be doing it to her, the same Saturday thing Mr. Finnegan does to Mike's mother. Yuck! The thought makes him squirm. And suppose he does and they have a kid of their own, or maybe even a bunch of them. Where would that leave him?

> *Up the spout*
> *Down the spout*
> *In and out*
> *O-U-T spells*
> *You-are-out!*

When he'd swung him up on his shoulders to carry him into the house, O'Hare said, "Well, me fine boyo, and how are ya these days?"

"Great! I've got a remission. It means I'm not spilling sugar now."

"That's wonderful! Your mother told me."

"It might last. I might even outgrow it."

"Well, let's hope for the best. Whatever happens, we'll work it out. You'll be fine!"

His backside is sore, maybe from riding the bike, maybe from the injection she gave him. He noticed her hand shaking before she put the needle in. What was she doing upstairs in her bedroom with that guy, when he'd come home from church? And who was he anyhow? He'd only caught a glimpse of him, before she'd made him get back in his room.

He punches the pillow and kicks the covers off.

Lying is a sin, he knows. But he didn't say "Cross my heart and hope to die," only crossed his fingers when he lied about the tie. It was black with a gray and red stripe and got snagged on a rough snarl in his sweater when O'Hare caught him upstairs under the bed during hide-and-seek. And when he came crawling out, there it was hanging on to him.

O'Hare looked at it puzzled, laughing, and said to him, "Well, what's this?"

"It's mine," he said crumpling it up and stuffing it into his pocket.

"Since when have you taken to wearing ties?"

"I do sometimes now," he answered. "Anyway it was a present. It's your turn to hide."

O'Hare gave him a funny look, but he just turned away, covered his eyes, and started to count.

Maybe if he counts sheep backward now, he can get to sleep.

A hundred, ninety-nine, ninety-eight . . . They leap over the stile in skittish procession. But suddenly they are hurrying, falling, legs all askew, one atop another until they are all piled up in a great white mountain and he is on top of them.

His heart is racing. He is racing downhill at breakneck speed. Someone on another bike is coming down fast behind him. Is it O'Hare? His mother is waiting for him at the bottom, calling anxiously, "Be careful! Be careful!" He tries to slow down but brakes too abruptly. And there he goes, sailing head over heels over the handlebars. O'Hare, for it *is* him, catches him in mid-air, and is holding him safe and sound in his arms. But the bike runs over his mother. He cries out "Mum!" and wakes with a thump.

O'Hare is really here, saying, "What, not asleep yet?"

"I was. I had a dream."

"Shall I sit with you awhile?"

His mum has come in too, and stands hovering in the doorway.

"I'm all right," he says, turning away, pulling the covers around him.

"There's nought to worry about, Tim, you know? I'll be a good father to you."

"I know."

"You can have my name if you want it."

"I'm kind of used to O'Connell."

"Well, think about it."

O'Hare runs a hand through his hair, and pats his back gently "I'll sit with him, Thom," his mother says.

O'Hare puts his hand out and draws her close. "Why not the both of us?"

They sit there, his mum on the rocker, O'Hare on the bed, watching over him. He wishes they'd get out and leave him alone. He shuts his eyes and breathes slowly, pretending to be asleep.

"He's off now," his mother whispers. Her new silk dress gives off a rustling sound. The bed bounces as O'Hare gets up. He is saying something, talking about a tie?

Jesus Christ! What a dope! He's gone and left the tie on the bureau!

"What tie?" she asks, her voice crackly.

"This one. Tim said it was a present." O'Hare says softly.

"Oh," she says, "I've never seen it. I guess from Mr. Finnegan, Mike's dad. Tim spent last night over there. Maybe Kate Finnegan wanted him to wear a tie to church."

O'Hare chuckles. "It must have come down to his knees."

"Come along out now, before you wake him," she hisses. The door closes softly behind them.

He is glad they're gone, thinking with small comfort, *I'm not the only one in this house who's a liar!* before escaping into sleep.

5

P.A. hears it from Jenny O'Flaherty, all about the disgraceful goings-on at her next-door neighbor's, not mentioning any names, but specifying the address — 123 Crompton Road — lest he think it may be her neighbor on the other side she is talking about; whispering how the woman — has she no shame at all? — is worse than a you-know-what, carrying on with two men at one and the same time, the regular coming in at the front door, the other sneaking out through the rear. As everyone knows, she's the last one to gossip or cast stones, but the truth is bound to leak out sooner or later. A pity! Just the one careless word and — poof! — in a flash, an end to that fine lady's grand dreams of marriage!

But it turns out the old maid is mistaken or exaggerating (a habit she has) or at the very least premature in her dire predictions. For the very next day here is Mrs. Agnes O'Connell coming into his shop, looking like she's just won the sweepstakes, to announce all starry-eyed her betrothal to the newly promoted Captain Thomas Francis O'Hare — the same one who rescued him that awful night of the robbery and is known now as the hero who captured the infamous Henley — saying she wants P.A. to be among the very first to hear her good news, and asking please will he help her plan the menu for their engagement party? Could he possibly consider catering the affair? And he says right off he'd be proud to.

About twenty people, she says, only her close friends and O'Hare's. A buffet supper, something filling but elegant, with a great cake, or maybe his famous chocolate mousse for dessert?

Delighted at their restored friendship, excited by the challenge, he leads her into the back room where they can talk privately, to discuss details. He suggests *boeuf en croute,* a delicate blend of braised beef and vegetables covered with a flaky pastry, as the main dish. With smoked salmon for a start, and a salad of fruits and greens. And of course there will be the whiskey and beer. And champagne to toast the happy couple. And perhaps a few bottles of a modest French wine for the ladies, those who may be delicate drinkers? She agrees entirely, and they will have it all — both the mousse and the cake as dessert, plus the modest French wine. And the menu is perfect! She thinks she can borrow the extra dishes and silverware from Kathleen Finnegan or Jenny O'Flaherty. And if it isn't too much to ask, could he give her some estimate of what it might all come to?

Taking pencil and paper, he figures quickly, and says he can do it all at a quite reasonable price, say, six pounds per head, including the liquid refreshment.

"You're a wonder, P.A.!" she exclaims. "Then it's settled!" And bending down to kiss him, whispers, "And what do you think? He plans to adopt Timmy!"

Struck by a swift barb of envy as he pictures O'Hare in full charge of the child, he somehow manages the appropriate response. "Now isn't that grand!" She hugs him impulsively, saying, "Oh, P.A., I've never been happier in my life!" and goes dancing out of the shop, her feet barely touching the ground.

He sits quiet a moment thinking. The chocolate mousse and the cake are all well and good for the grown-ups, but what about the boy? He will have to make something special for Timmy, and it comes to him in a flash what it will be. The very thing the darling has been hankering after, had asked for so plaintively the last time he came into the shop. Pierced with longing, P.A. remembers with his lips the yielding softness of the child's sweet mouth as, holding him close, helping him down from the high stool, they kissed.

Driven by the memory, he sets about without delay to work out the ingredients he will need to substitute for the original recipe. It won't be easy. He will have to experiment with carob instead of chocolate and use a sugar substitute, but he is sure he can do it. And it will be well worth the effort. He can already see the child's enchanting smile, those angelic violet-blue eyes widening with wonder and delight as P.A. presents his latest chef-d'oeuvre, card enclosed — *To Timmy with love* . . .

6

"Do you like it?" O'Hare asks anxiously.

"I love it! And the match is perfect!" He watches as she compares it with one of her diamond earrings. She seems to have lost or mislaid the other, but he finds she is surprisingly unworried. Perhaps not surprisingly, for the earrings are insured and she has already reported the mysterious loss to the insurance company.

"Are you sure now?" he presses her. "There's plenty of others to choose from."

The square-cut diamond gleams on her finger as she holds it up to the light. "It's this one I want. Oh, Thom! It's beautiful!" Her eyes glisten like the diamond.

"'Tis a great investment," the salesman says solemnly, man-to-man with O'Hare. "She's making a fine choice. Why, in no time at all, 'twill be worth twice the price you're payin' for it now."

"I've no intention of giving it up, now or ever!"

"Of course, of course not!" the salesman reassures her, patting her hand warmly, his fingers lingering. "Don't I know, don't we all, that the ring's value in cold cash could never measure up to its dear worth, its true meaning to the two of you?"

"You'll have to give it up just for now," O'Hare tells her. "There's something needs to be written inside."

Smiling tremulously, she agrees, and they leave the ring to be inscribed, the message his and the salesman's secret, for the nonce.

It has been a busy time for them. He's called Riley to tell him he'd like a few more days, is it all right? Riley says, "Do it! And come back ready to pitch in, there's plenty of work waiting." She has already arranged for the party (he has agreed they both want) to celebrate their engagement. He has even promised to go to confession and to take communion with her. They have paid a visit to Father Malachy to announce their intentions and are scheduled to meet with him three times in the next month to receive instructions for their upcoming nuptials.

The Father, a gnome of a man in a spotted soutane, looks up at them over his wire-rimmed spectacles as he jots down the dates. "Sure and you'll be needin' little in the way of counseling, since you've both been once wed," he says, his eyes twinkling. "But you wouldn't want to be deprivin' an old priest of the pleasure of expatiatin' on the responsibilities, the trials and tribulations, and of course the joys of the blissful *martial* state, now would you?" They nod nimbly, numbly.

The Father covers his mouth in a gesture of impish dismay. "Now, how in the world did I come to say that? A Freudian slip! I meant *marital,* of course!" They smile and shake hands, exiting hastily.

They have only to finish packing, pick Timmy up at school and be on their way. They are off to visit O'Hare's children.

Children? he thinks, picturing Kaitlin, the first-born, now with a tyke of her own; and Jamie, always pushing to get ahead, the father *in statu* of five-year-old twins, his wife Della's children by a former marriage. Aggie will be a grandmother, if only by proxy, but looks like a bride. Ah, the bloom on her!

They are driving the West road on their way up to Galway, Timmy riding in front between the two of them, cheeks rosy, eyes bright with excitement. "Two days off from school? Without excuse?" he'd asked incredulously, when they'd told him. And has insisted on taking along his new bike, packed tidily now atop the car.

The three of them have been playing games — Traveler's Alphabet, I Spy, I Packed My Bag with . . . — the boy coming up winners at all of them. A kid's memory! Defies adult competition. At home, when they'd played Concentration one rainy Sunday, he'd been amazed, embarrassed in fact, at how much sharper Tim was at remembering every one of the turned-down cards. He couldn't have beaten him if he'd wanted to, though at one point, piqued, he'd actually tried.

Aggie, looking pleased with her son's success, hugs Timmy and reaches across to touch O'Hare's face. He kisses the palm of her hand, nuzzling it gently. They skim along, stopping to admire the scenic wonders, the misty wilds of Connemara, the jagged grandeur of the Cliffs of Moher. He loves the freedom, feeling a kind of weightless buoyancy, like swimming under water. He thinks of her in bed with him. She seems shy to him since his return, almost virginal, as though the promise of marriage has cloaked her passion with a new purity. He is touched by her girlish reticence, titillated by the change. Their lovemaking, altered he feels by their new commitment, promising as it does respectability, plus the assumption of serious new responsibilities, climaxes on her part in a gust of tears, on his, in a sweeping tenderness, enveloping them both with a sweet and poignant melancholy, strangely more binding than their earlier feverish excitement.

They have reached journey's end and are turning in to the long driveway that leads to Jamie and Della's house. The road is lined with showy autumn blooms, great blobs of yellow and gold chrysanthemums basking in the sudden sunlit twilight. O'Hare honks the horn lightly signaling their arrival, only to discover the family ready and waiting outdoors to receive them. Kaitlin and Connor, who live on the other side of Salthill, have come by with their two year old to join the welcoming party, and the seven of them are lined up like a photo in the rotogravure, posed to greet the old man and his bride-to-be. He has a momentary sense of awkwardness about his renegade role as lover-cum-husband, quickly dispelled by the shy excitement of the children and the warm feeling of being accepted still as paterfamilias.

Hugs and handshakes all around. Aggie, hanging back, is swept into the fold and turns pinkly radiant as she is sweetly embraced by Kaitlin and Della. Even Sheila and Shaemus, the twins, coached by their mother, essay a buss on "the pretty lady's cheek" before dragging Tim off with the promise of a ride on one of their Shetland ponies. Connor, answering Aggie's maternal questioning look, volunteers to go along to supervise.

Jamie has done well for himself. He has married a Protestant divorcée, an heiress, and their estate, seventy-five acres, boasts stables, a greenhouse, an old millhouse, and several outbuildings in addition to their fine stone cottage. Jamie, proud lord of the manor, is clearly taken with Agnes and offers to show her around the grounds. Della protests. They must be worn out and hungry after their long drive. Let them settle in first and have tea. But Jamie insists at least on taking her on a tour of the house, and sails blithely forth, Aggie in tow, O'Hare following behind holding Kaitlin's babe, exclaiming on her great weight and size (he hasn't seen her since her christening almost two years before), as Della and Kaitlin repair to the kitchen to prepare the evening meal.

It is a bucolic holiday. They go for long rambles and picnic outdoors. O'Hare takes Tim and the twins fishing in the burbling stream behind the house. Tim, who has landed the first trout and is blown up with pride, remains undeflated by Shaemus's claim that he'd gotten a much bigger one last week.

"It's the biggest anyone's caught today," O'Hare says mildly, and Timmy grins as he unhooks and bags his catch.

At lunch, Sheila asks Agnes, "Is it true when you and Grandpa O'Hare are married, you'll be our grandmum?" Agnes hesitates, looking to Della for help.

"She will," O'Hare answers promptly. "And what's more, Tim here will be your uncle."

Tim, astonished at the idea, lets out a guffaw.

"Gow on," Shaemus says, "you're joshin' us. He's too young."

"No, he's not!" Sheila protests hotly. "He's older than we are!" She is already more than half in love with Timmy, who has helped bait her hook and has been teaching her to ride his two-wheeler. Then adds quickly to cover her tracks, "But Mrs. O'Connell doesn't look anything like Granny Nell. She doesn't wear glasses or have white hair."

"Grannies come in all shapes and sizes," says Jamie, brightly eyeing his promised stepmother.

The last night of their visit, they are gathered around the large open hearth in the main room, the grown-ups drinking mulled wine, Kaitlin's baby long since put to bed, Timmy and the twins stretched out on the sheepskin rug, drowsing before the fire. All are pleasantly tired after the day's activities. They have been sailing in the bay, played croquet, driven to Salthill to shop and buy gifts, and are now sweetly silent, lulled by the fire, the drink, and the ample dinner Della has served.

"Tell us how you got on to Henley," Jamie asks lazily.

O'Hare is quiet a long minute. "There's not much to tell."

"It was a shock reading about it in the papers, seeing you with your arm in a sling. We were that worried about you!" Kaitlin complains. "When we called your office they said they didn't know where you were. You never gave us a call at all, till the day you broke the glad news about you and Agnes!"

"It must have been a busy time for you," says Connor. "When's the trial coming up?"

"In a few weeks."

"He'll get life, of course," says Jamie.

"It's likely," O'Hare answers, wishing they'd get off the subject.

"Of course he will," says Della. "Unless they lynch him first. Can you imagine an Orangeman getting a fair trial in Dublin?"

"I can," says Kaitlin. "Now up North, they'd let him off scot-free and probably give him a medal!"

Connor interposes smoothly, "Sam Johnson was right. He said 'The Irish are a fair people. They never have anything good to say of each other.'"

"Come on, Kaitlin! It's the Provos that get away with bloody murder every time, and you know it!" says Della.

"Not true," Jamie says. "The extremists on both sides are mostly tried and punished, as they should be."

"That's a joke!" Della glares at her husband. "Did the ones who did in Lord Mountbatten and his family ever get caught even? And if they had, the IRA in their hoods and masks would have spirited them off quick enough."

Kaitlin's face flushes a bright red. "It wasn't the Provos in their hoods and masks that tried to kill Bernadette Devlin!"

"They're only giving as good as they get! They've learned the hard way, the only answer to the IRA diehards is to give them a taste of their own medicine. And I for one don't fault them for that."

Aggie in a flurry says, "That's easy enough when you've not been touched by it. Timmy was almost killed when the bomb went off at the O'Connell Bridge."

"What a terrible fright for you!" says Jamie. "Leave off, Della, will you?"

"I can't. I'm sorry, Agnes, it's awful, I know. But the North is entitled to be a free and independent nation! Don't you think the majority has the right to self-determination?"

"Not at the price of children's lives. Or anyone's, for that matter," Connor says softly.

"Try to tell that to the Provos! They're the ones started it."

"We've Protestants here in Eire and they've no cause for complaint," Kaitlin says bitterly. "Would that the Catholics in Belfast had the same deal!"

"It's plain there's plenty of anti-Protestant prejudice here!"
Della says hotly.

"Enough!" says O'Hare, angry more at himself than at the
arguers.

Has he ever taken a clear stand? Publicly he is opposed to
terrorism; in his heart, secretly sympathetic with the IRA. He is
deeply troubled by the rising tide of victims on both sides but
has done nothing to help stop the carnage. He feels he has been
shilly-shallying all his life, and is still fiddling while Ireland
burns. *Which side do you take when you feel both are equally wronged?*

"My apologies," Della says sharply. "I've been a poor hostess."

He is truly fond of Della, feels his son's marriage is a good one.
But why did Jamie have to marry an ardent loyalist?

"It's all right, Della," he says, "you're a fine hostess."

Turning away, she taps Shaemus on the head. "Time for bed,
children! Upstairs!"

Shaemus, who has been yawning prodigiously all evening, is
suddenly wide awake and rebellious. "Aw Mum! Can't we stay?
It's early yet!"

"It's after ten! Well past your bedtime!"

"When I'm grown, I'm going to stay up all night!"

"Fine," says Jamie, "but you've a bit of a way to go yet."

"I'll tuck them in," O'Hare says, picking sleepy Sheila up
from the rug. "Come along Tim, Shaemus." He tousles
Shaemus's hair and asks, "And what are you going to be when
you're all grown up and staying up nights?"

"President of a united Ireland, I hope," his father answers.

"Over my dead body!" says Della.

"Then Sheila, perhaps," says Jamie lightly. He takes Sheila
from O'Hare. "I'll give you a hand, Dad."

The high-hearted holiday spirit has flown off and left him
feeling miserable and uncertain. He sleeps poorly that night,
twisting and turning, toting up all his failures, thinking of Eileen
and the promise he made her. He will fail there too. He wishes to
God he'd never caught Henley.

They leave the next day in a blistering downpour. He drives
abstractedly, his glum mood matching the weather. The roads are

slippery. Skidding around a sharp curve, he has a sudden feeling that the car is in charge, racing them all toward disaster while he sits idly by, playing with the controls, pretending to drive. He prods the brakes lightly and is relieved as the car responds.

They arrive home late. Timmy is asleep. He carries the child into the house, tucking him in, sending Aggie, who is worn out, upstairs to bed. Untying Tim's bike from the top of the car, he wheels it around to the back of the house to store it in the small shed next to the scullery. The path is dark. Tim's bike has a lamp and he switches it on to light the way. Swearing under his breath, he stares at the shed door. Emblazoned in white paint in letters a foot high is the single word: WHORE.

The graffiti artist, inexperienced or careless, has allowed the letters to drip so that the jagged effect seems to add a further touch of evil to the malignant intent.

Storing the bike, he hunts on the shelves for the can of green paint he left there last spring when he put up and painted the shed. The container is almost empty, and the only brush he can find is stiff as a board, but it will have to serve. He finishes the job quickly and goes up to bed. He sleeps fitfully again, but rises early and is ready and dressed in time for church Sunday morning.

7

Skewered with shock, Jenny O'Flaherty discovers the banns have already been posted and trembles as she hears them read out at St. Anne's by Bishop Burke in the rolling tones and reverberating cadence of his rich baritone voice.

Agnes Moira O'Connell, widow, and Thomas Francis O'Hare, widower, do this day declare their sacred intention to be bound in Holy Matrimony on Sunday, January 15th of this coming year. If there be any who know of just cause why these two should not be joined in wedlock, let them come forward herewith.

A quick hum of interest from the congregation rises like a hymn to the echoing dome. Then silence.

Is it possible that no voice will be raised to protest this unholy alliance? Not Jenny O'Flaherty's own, despite her righteous indignation?

Not the Woman's, naturally, for she is bent on concealing her reckless duplicity.

Nor her Confessor's, for it is unlikely that she has confided in him, and in any event, he would unfortunately be bound by the privacy of the confessional.

Not Thomas Francis O'Hare's, for he, apparently still blissful in his blind ignorance, sits close between the woman and her spawn, looking flushed with happiness.

And not the Other Man's. Which stands to reason, since he is not present, though he might have been the most likely candidate.

But surely, she thinks desperately, there must be someone here, among all these devoted churchgoing members, with enough decency, sense of propriety, religious fervor — at least one righteous soul staunch enough to stand up and decry this frightful mis-marriage! To announce clearly, boldly to the world what everyone must surely know by now — that this woman is shameless, a fornicating adulteress, at least twice over. An unrepentant sinner. Unfit — in fact, proscribed by papal law from taking the vows of that Blessed Sacrament.

In the curious waiting, Jenny's voice too, to her shame, remains silent. The image of herself rising solo to trumpet forth her clarion concern before this hushed assemblage sends shivers quivering up and down her spine. Never mind, her mind is already busy, abuzz with alternate possibilities.

The proper course, of course, would be to approach O'Hare discreetly, to meet privately with that poor, decent, deceived man whom she so admires, to warn him before it is too late. And yet . . .

The thought of so brash, so direct a confrontation is somehow unnerving. Perhaps not without reason. For it is well known, throughout history and folklore, that the bearer of ill tidings, however nobly motivated, is often severely punished. Sometimes by death! And has she not already performed her duty? Sadly, she is not at all certain that that small hybrid Frenchman to whom she confided her dreadful scandalous news can be depended upon. So far as she knows, he has not yet proven himself a worthy ally. And the message she left on Agnes O'Connell's door has been, if not ignored, already painted over.

Which leaves her, it seems, little choice.

Bishop Burke is offering up a doleful eulogy in commemoration of the innocent souls who have lost their lives in the wake of the recent bombings, and extends tender commiserations to the bereaved families. Taking as his text for the day's sermon the second great commandment, he extrapolates political as well as personal enjoinders on his flock to adhere to God's injunction to love their neighbors as themselves, exhorting them to lay aside their anger and their pain, and to seek forgiveness in their hearts for themselves and their enemies.

"Let us pursue," he begs them, "the paths of peace and love. For with love and God's mercy, the ferment and the violence will cease, the North and the South will become one—joined together as in holy wedlock." He is well launched into "the merits of true neighborliness" (Proverbs 17:4), but Jenny is barely listening as, soothed by the rumble of his declamatory eloquence, she begins to compose in her head the letter she feels it her Christian duty to send to the heroic Thomas Francis O'Hare.

My dear Captain O'Hare,

It is my belief—I believe that—you should be made privy to—I feel it is my unpleasant—my painfully unpleasant duty—to have to inform you of the recent carnal carryings-on—the terrible sinful acts—which have taken place—behind your back at 123 Crompton Road.

While you were away—carrying out your recent, courageous, police mission—your presumed—your erstwhile—fiancée has been dallying with—entertaining—did spend the night with—has been copulating—

with a former friend and colleague of yours — who — shall for the moment — remain nameless.

Needless to say — difficult as this is for me — deeply concerned as I am — I have only your best interests — your dear welfare — at heart. My heart shares your pain.

Should you feel impelled to — if you are in need of — or desire — further confirming details — I am entirely at your disposal.

You may contact me.

I can be reached — c/o Post Box (   ), the Main Post Office, Dublin.

I am yours — Ever Faithfully — A Loving Friend . . . (?) One Who Cares . . .

8

He'd known, of course, everyone knew she was going around with O'Hare. Only he never thought it was serious. Anyway, how could he, in good conscience, have turned down the chance at a bit of nookie, with no one the wiser? And it wasn't as though he'd forced her. After all, it takes two to tango, and she wasn't exactly unwilling.

When O'Hare comes into the central room this Monday morning, half the men are jumping up and gathering around him, thumping him on the back and shoulders, pumping his hand, crying, "Welcome back!" "Good to see you!"

"All hail, Caesar!" he says, looking up from his desk as O'Hare comes over. "When'd you get back?" As if he doesn't know.

O'Hare shakes his hand and says, "Thanks for looking after Aggie. She mentioned you took her to Clancy's."

"My pleasure," he answers with great sincerity.

Hearing the racket, Riley comes out of his office. "So you're back finally," he says. "I must say you look a hundred percent better."

"I feel a hundred percent better," says O'Hare, and turning to the group announces, "and in case any of you haven't heard yet, I'm getting married."

Hoots and calls from the men. "Hitched, is it?" "Tyin' the knot!" "Poor fella!"

"Mrs. O'Connell, I gather?" Riley says.

"Right!"

"My sincere felicitations. I'll take you to lunch to celebrate. And to catch you up on Henley. One o'clock?"

"Thanks," says O'Hare.

The jade! Paddy thinks. Jumps out of bed with me and straight back in with O'Hare! So they're getting spliced. Well, good luck to them. Though it's too bad in a way. She's such a blaze of a woman, even if she is a bit older than me. Not that there's anything wrong with that, he muses. Actually, he prefers older women. Experienced, always wanting to take care of you. None of that giggling school-girl stuff. Don't touch me. Ooh, not that way! Besides, he feels being younger gives him a bit of an edge.

Of course, there's always the possibility that marriage won't interfere with anything. Add a little spice even. Could she handle two men in her life? With her lusty hunger, probably half a dozen. It's true, he's never been keen on playing second fiddle. Still, better the lover than the husband. Besides, he's sure he could take her away from that old buck any day. If he wanted to. The man must be pushing fifty!

Riley's past sixty and should be retiring soon. O'Hare's next in line and doubtless will get the promotion — he'll be the Big Boss then, wearing the horns Paddy Morphy's put on him.

It's past noon, and he isn't getting much work done. She's gotten under his skin. He's been thinking about her all the week, remembering the sweet woman smell of her, the lovely soft feel to her skin. Great tone it has, silky smooth, yet firm. No sag there yet. He has this fierce longing to see her. That lush bosom. Makes his mouth water.

He'd tried calling her that same night, after his hasty early departure, but O'Hare had picked up and he'd cut the connection, dropping the phone like it was a hot coal. He'd even rung several times during the week, but there'd been no answer. He figured they must have gone off somewhere together, and when he'd asked after O'Hare, Riley told him he wouldn't be back till Monday — today. He'd wanted to call her again last night, but thought better not.

He's tempted to try her right now. At least he's sure O'Hare won't be there to pick up. What excuse? He's left his tie. Would it be a terrible bother for her to bring it to him? If it was, he could always ask O'Hare to fetch it. That should bring her.

He grins, lifting the phone, and dials her number.

9

Waking late, she turns over drowsily, pressing her lips into his pillow, wishing it was him, then opens one eye to look at the clock. Almost noon — she ought to be up, up and about. She stretches deliciously, feeling herself rising over the bed suspended in air like the lady in the magic act she saw once as a child, at a carnival come to Kilkenny.

Light as a feather, still half-asleep, still in her nightgown, she levitates over the carpet and down the stairs to put on the kettle, waiting dreamily for the first fragrant sip of her morning tea, remembering this whole lovely past week with O'Hare, the happiest week of her life . . .

"Don't fly too high, Miss!" she hears her mother's voice warning her over the hiss of the steam in the kettle. "For if you do, you're bound for a fall!" She'd heard that lesson, God knows, a hundred times over the years, and still believes it is true. Runaway joy gallops off with you, your heart singing, the wind caressing you like a lover, and suddenly there you are, the breath knocked out of you, down on the ground, bruised and battered, with no one about to pick you up or to patch your wounds. Only this time, please God, it has turned out just the opposite! She's risen from the depths — a whole week of heaven and still flying high!

After the rotten time she'd had with O'Hare gone and no word from him, and the terrible scare with his sudden return (not to mention the sorry business with Tim and the tie), she'd felt numbed to the bone, certain she'd never know another moment's peace or happiness but would be paying for her sins, mortal and venial, all the rest of her days. But in this last lovely week the haze of fear has vanished, been banished, burnt off by the sweet heat of love's promise.

To Aggie, Ever Thine, Thomas, the ring is inscribed.

"Will you have me Aggie?" he'd begged her. "Say yes! Say you will!" standing in her doorway looking flushed and anxious, crushing her in his arms, the flowers between them. And has hardly left her side in all the time since, except when he'd gone home to pick up some clothes for their trip while she'd stopped off to Delehanty's to ask would he cater their engagement party. He'd taken her to Eigen's to pick out the ring, and they'd gone together to see Father Malachy. On the way home she'd mentioned casually that Paddy Morphy had taken her out to Clancy's Saturday, and he'd said, "I'm glad. Did you have a good time?" and she'd answered, without flinching, "Not bad." He'd seemed reluctant to talk about Henley, or to say what he'd been doing the long while he was away. When she'd asked, he'd said, "I just needed to clear up some business," looking so grim she'd decided it would be wiser not to press him. She never mentioned anything about having heard he'd been going around for a while with Henley's sister, though it was a sore temptation. So she'd talked instead about their future, and they'd made love and planned their itinerary, and Wednesday afternoon, packed and ready, they picked Timmy up at school and took off, driving across the country to see the sights and to visit his children in Galway.

She'd been a bit anxious about meeting his family, but they seemed to like her, and she liked them, and they were all so sweet with Timmy. Jamie, acting the gallant, had even pretended to flirt with her.

"Bring her into the garden, Dad," he'd said. "I want my roses to see her." She'd flushed laughing, saying she was a country girl born and bred, and knew the roses would be gone this time of year. But she was mistaken. Jamie, a botanist and landscape architect, actually had a bower of white alpine roses budding wildly, and there were great beds of scarlet and blue anemones in full bloom. She told him the anemone was her favorite flower, and he said, "See the poor things, they're drooping their heads in envy, just looking at you!"

She'd fallen in love with their house; a white-walled stone cottage, it was a marvel with its slate roof and huge beams and great open hearth. The main room was furnished with cane chairs and a few fine antique pieces. The gleaming wide-planked floor was hand-pegged and covered with a scatter of sheepskin rugs. The kitchen was modern with all sorts of appliances, and upstairs there were two large bedrooms and even a playroom under the rafters, with a grand view of the bay. There were stables and greenhouses and an old mill that Jamie had converted into a potting shed, with two small bedrooms and a tiled bath upstairs for guests.

She hadn't expected anything half so posh. Kaitlin told her later that the entire estate was a wedding present from Della's family, wealthy Prods who lived up North. And Jamie was able to keep the place up, though he'd only made a fair living until recently, since he was getting more commissions now than he could handle, through contacts his in-laws provided.

Timmy was invited to stay in the main house with the twins, and she and O'Hare were put up in the mill. They used only one of the bedrooms, but she hung her clothes in the closet of the other and slyly rumpled the bed there, a discreet gesture toward propriety.

She hadn't ridden since she was a girl, and then only an old broken-down mare, but she learned fast—"Takes to it like she was born in the saddle!" Jamie said—and she'd felt wild as a gypsy as she flew through the woods, over the fields, and down to the bay on their early morning run, Jamie on one side of her, O'Hare on the other.

Della had a royal touch with food and served a sumptuous table, stuffing her guests with Galway prawns, lobster, and tender lamb, home-baked bread, fresh farm butter and eggs, and fruit and vegetables out of the gardens. And there were lovely desserts, pies and puddings and fresh-picked berries served with mounds of clotted cream. With all the rich food, she needed to keep a sharp eye out on Tim, though she made sure not to embarrass him in front of the others. Luckily, he'd been good as gold about sticking with a proper diet, or at least staying within limits, and his remission seemed to be holding on. Which, added to everything else, kept her happy as a lark.

All in all, it was a wondrous holiday, and she hated the idea of leaving. But the whole family said they'd be up to Dublin for the wedding, and Della even invited them back to spend a few weeks in the spring or summer, adding as an inducement, "We're that fond of Tim. He and the twins, especially Sheila, get on so well, it would make a lovely time for us all."

Their last night there'd been a bit of a shindy between Kaitlin and Della over politics, which made her uneasy and seemed to upset O'Hare, but it all wound up peaceably enough.

They left the next day in a drenching downpour, but arrived safe and sound. She was dead-tired, and O'Hare said he'd put Timmy to sleep, sending her upstairs to bed. Just before she fell off she thought she heard him puttering around down near the shed and wondered what he was doing, but in the morning they were in such a rush to get to St. Anne's she forgot to ask him.

They managed to get to the church on time and O'Hare squeezed her arm as Bishop Burke read out their banns in his great booming voice. After the service, quite a few of the neighbors came over to shake hands and offer good wishes. She noticed Jenny O'Flaherty with her mother at the edge of the crowd, but they passed by without giving her so much as a nod. Not that she gave a tinker's! The poor dried-out old maid must be dying of envy.

The clock in the hall strikes the half-hour, and here she is, past noon of a Monday, Tim off at school, O'Hare gone back to work, herself lazing about the house blowsy with happiness, drinking her third cup of morning tea, dreaming great dreams of her future as Agnes Moira O'Hare, bride-wife, risen like the phoenix to a new life, never again Agnes O'Connell, widow, poor thing . . . She says it aloud, loving the sound of it, savoring the sweet taste of it in her mouth, "Mrs. Thomas Francis O'Hare . . ."

In her vision, radiant, she moves down the aisle in her silken gown, flowers and music all about, hears the *Oohs* and the *Ahhs* of the assembled crowd. In front of the altar she pledges her troth to the one she loves. The bells ring out in a paean of joy. Taking her in his arms, he kisses her with a kiss that bears them aloft, higher and higher up to the clouds, far from the madding crowd, now laughing and cheering wildly below. Up, up, up they go, flying off in their golden coach to the carillon of the trilling bells.

Still in her dream, she floats rapturously to answer the phone as it rings — O'Hare calling to say how much he loves her, how he hates being a moment without her . . .

But she is wrong, and her mother is right, and the runaway horse is bolting again. "No," she says, "no, I can't. It's out of the question!" And listening, goes plummeting from heaven to hell in one swift moment.

10

His desk is covered with papers, the in-basket a mountain of forms and memos waiting to be answered, filled out, signed, filed. Wading through the stuff is like trying to climb out of a bog, every step taken makes him feel he's only sinking in deeper.

It's too early in the day for him to be feeling this tired, but he slept poorly again last night, the graffito on the shed door troubling his mind. He feels he has been irresponsible, careless of Aggie's reputation. He ought not to have stayed over so often. Leaving the car outside the house overnight was a bad mistake.

He needs to clear his head. He ought to see Henley, set up a time soon. Go through the record. There may be some clue he's overlooked. Henley swore he never planted the bombs that went off at the bank and the O'Connell Bridge. Then who had? He also insisted that the men who'd come down from the North to threaten him were strangers to him. Was he telling the truth? If he was, and O'Hare could prove Henley was being blackmailed, there was a good chance he could establish mitigating circumstances. Not that Riley or Ted Garrity, in charge of the prosecution, would be exactly sympathetic with any attempt to get Henley off the hook. Except maybe if he could net them some bigger fish.

He ought to go up to Belfast. They've an informer there who plays both sides using two names, John White and Jonny Black, depending on where he's at the moment. The man's schizy, an actor who loves to dramatize everything, but he's a good source. Contacting him seems the likeliest possibility.

The promise of a reward, still pending, for information leading to the arrest and conviction of Henley's co-conspirators, has set off a barrage of crackpot calls and letters. He finds a few phone reports clipped together with a memo from Riley. "We've had maybe fifty of these altogether, and have weeded out most of the chaff. (See file on HENLEY — REWARD.) These came in Saturday and should be checked out." He leafs through them. There's no way of knowing where they may lead. In the file on HENLEY— REWARD, he notes that O'Halloran, the publican from Howth, has been calling regularly to find out when he's due to collect his £100 for putting them on to Connaught, who'd led them to Henley. Riley has marked it: "Keep telling him he'll have to wait till after the trial."

He decides to put through a call to the number he has for his contact up North. He lets the phone ring through three times, as per protocol, then hangs up and calls again. The phone is answered on the second ring.

"Top o' the morning," a voice says.

"Sean Connery," he answers, wincing. He hates playing this game.

"Ah!" comes the answer, "The very man I've been waiting to hear from! I've just the thing you've been looking for. How does Tuesday night suit you?"

"Fine."

"The same place, eight o'clock? Beyond the Pale, as we put it."

"Very good. I'll be there."

"See you then. Take care."

"Do my best," O'Hare says, feeling foolish, but better.

At one, his desk still a shambles, but his mind somewhat clearer, he answers as Riley buzzes to remind him of their lunch date, asking does he mind if Ted Garrity comes along. He says, "Fine."

Dinty Noonan, the ancient office boy, shuffles over as he's getting into his coat and hands him a letter. "Hand-delivered by a lady," Noonan sniffs. He adds reproachfully, "It's marked personal," as if that were a sin. The handwriting's not familiar. He shoves it into his jacket pocket and runs down the stairs.

Riley has outdone himself with extravagance, but the lunch isn't exactly celebrant in spite of the smoked trout, the claret, the great ribs of beef, the strawberries drowning in rich cream. O'Hare and Garrity argue fiercely throughout the meal. Looking like a bantam cock, feathers ruffled, Garrity crows hoarsely when O'Hare suggests Henley may not have been directly responsible for the bombings.

"Are you out of your ever-lovin' mind, man? He's confessed! We've got it on tape!"

"He's confessed that he was blackmailed, his family threatened. He says he deliberately made the bomb he planted at the airport a dud."

"We've only Henley's word. Who'll take that?"

"I'm only saying we know there were others involved. We know Henley ran from Belfast. He tried to get out, took a new name."

"That's not hard evidence. It could have been a ploy."

"The bomb at the airport never went off. Henley's counsel will make much of that."

"Forget it, O'Hare. It's not in our interest. If we don't get him on criminal conspiracy, we'll have him on murder. He killed his wife and the child."

O'Hare is quiet a moment, then says softly, "You could charge me with that. He threw it at me. I tossed it at them."

"We've every intention of charging him as well with the attempted murder of a police officer! You're playing the fool, O'Hare. He's a known terrorist!"

"I want the men behind him."

"Get him to talk!"

"He swears they sent strangers to him. He hasn't been with the O.F.F. for years!"

"Once in, never out. It's the same on both sides."

Riley, who has been sitting patiently by, says sharply, "Cut it! If you've a lead on the others, O'Hare, follow it up. When you've something solid, let me know."

"I'm working on it."

"You haven't much time. Henley's up for the Assizes on the thirtieth."

"That's almost a month."

The waiter brings brandy and coffee. Riley and Garrity raise their glasses in a convivial toast, wishing him luck on his forthcoming marriage. He manages to smile his thanks, his stomach churning irritably, and downs the brandy in a gulp.

Walking back with Riley along Grafton Street, he catches a glimpse of Paddy Morphy standing close to a woman in the entranceway to Daly's across the street. They seem to be arguing. Paddy's back is blocking his view. He stops for a moment, startled. It's impossible to make out the woman's face, but he has an uncanny feeling it's Agnes.

Riley is talking to him. "Are you serious about going up North?"

"I am," he says and moves quickly along, hoping Riley hasn't noticed, as he goes on talking distractedly. "The O.F.F.'s been boasting. They're claiming the credit."

"They may want the credit, but not what goes with it, once they're caught. Do you think you've a chance in the world of finding the ones responsible? And if you do, how will you get them to testify? You know how they stick together."

O'Hare shrugs. "I can try."

"You've about as much chance as Sisyphus, rolling a stone up a mountain only to have it come crashing down on you again. Be satisfied we've got Henley."

"I want the real culprits."

"Don't we all?"

Back at the office he pulls out and runs the taped record of his several interviews with Henley. There's little enough to go on. Henley freely admits his former connection with the O.F.F., his attempt to hide, to cut himself free. There seems no way to prove he wasn't responsible for the Dublin bombings. Except his word. Not good enough. Garrity could be right. The dud bomb at the airport might not have been deliberate, but a freak accident. For all O'Hare knows, Henley himself could have planted the bombs at the bank and the O'Connell Bridge . . .

Was it really Agnes he saw with Paddy Morphy? . . .

What in the world's come over him? Doesn't he trust her? Suppose she'd had lunch with Morphy? What would be wrong with that? There could be some simple explanation. He could be mistaken. It might have been some other woman. He'll call and ask her.

Vexed at himself, at her, he sits motionless, trying to rid himself of the uneasy feeling that has been nagging at him since this morning . . . something about the way Morphy had greeted him that made him squirm. Something in that smirking look that still galls him.

Getting up restlessly, he takes off his jacket, tossing it over the back of his chair. The letter falls out onto the floor. He'd forgotten all about it. He picks it up, and lifting the phone, dials Aggie's number. He hears the ring-through, but there's no answer. She's out marketing probably, or picking up Timmy from school. He dials again and while waiting idly flips open the letter. He is perusing its contents when Morphy barges in.

"Not busy, I hope," Morphy says grinning, surveying the welter of papers.

"It's all right," he says, hanging up but finding it difficult to tear himself away from the droll but absorbing account some idiot — "deeply concerned" and with only his "best interests" at heart — has concocted about Aggie and "a colleague" of his.

"Finish your letter. I can wait."

He shoves the letter in a drawer and gives Paddy his undivided attention. "What's up?"

"Riley says you're planning on taking a trip to Belfast. He thinks you may need some help. In case you do, I'm it."

Morphy is wearing an open-necked shirt. He takes a tie out of his pocket, buttons the shirt, and turns up the collar, looping the tie, black with a gray and red stripe, around his neck. He is pulling the knot up under his collar, smiling ingratiatingly, saying "When do we leave?" as O'Hare gets up, walks deliberately around the desk, and without thinking twice, fells Paddy Morphy with a great clout on the mouth.

11

She has given Timmy his dinner and is waiting for O'Hare. It's late. She hasn't had a word from him all day, though he might have tried to reach her while she was out . . .

When she'd gone to see Paddy that noon to give him the tie, he'd sworn to her he'd be still as a tomb.

"Why would I want to spoil things?" he'd said. "You've been lovely to me," implying she might be again.

"It's different now," she'd told him. "I'm to be married. You wouldn't want to ruin my chance for true happiness now Paddy, would you?"

He'd said, "I wouldn't do that." Then, like a petulant child, added, "But what of my happiness?"

She'd tried to laugh. "Och! You're young and good-looking, you're sure to find the right girl for you any day now!"

"You're perfect for me!"

"I'm too old for you," she'd protested, only half-meaning it. Truth to tell, she loved his wanting her at the same time it scared her half to death. "Swear to me you'll keep our secret!"

"I'll never love anyone but you." He sighed sadly. "I'll do whatever you want." Then wheedling, pressed her, "Couldn't you find it in your heart for us to be together sometimes? At least one more time, Aggie?"

She'd turned her back on him then and walked off, her hope snuffed out like a candle, but he came after her saying, "I promise, Aggie. Silent as the grave, I swear!" — taking her hand, kissing it, saying, "Trust me, luv."

She knew it was a terrible wild gamble, banking her happiness with O'Hare on his word, but she'd wanted to believe him.

She sits now at the kitchen table with Tim, helping him with his lessons. He has a lot to catch up with because of their holiday. She is smoking one cigarette after another, and has this terrible urge for a sweet. Only there's none in the house. She's kept her promise to give them up if O'Hare came back to her, and has not bought so much as sixpenny's worth since, but has taken up smoking instead. It offers her some relief, but is not the same.

"Say the six times table, once more," she says. She loves his sweet earnest look, his face the picture of concentration as he recites for her. He is up to six times seven when the doorbell rings. She is sure it's O'Hare, but why would he ring the bell when he has his own key now? She takes it as a bad omen. Tim jumps up and runs to the door. She lets him go, her intermediary, and hears O'Hare saying, "Up this late, are you? Isn't it past your bedtime?"

"I'm just finishing my schoolwork."

"Welcome," she says, getting up as he comes into the kitchen. "I missed you." He looks tired. She kisses him. "Can I fix you some supper?"

"No thanks." He stands there uncertain, then says, "Could you put the boy to bed? I'd like to talk to you."

Tim looks startled. "I'm almost through. Do you want me to finish up in my room?"

"Sorry," O'Hare says, "I didn't mean to be putting you out. But yes, I would like to talk to your mother."

She helps Tim collect his books, her skin prickling. "I'll be in soon, luv," she tells the child as he closes the door.

"Could we talk in the other room?" O'Hare says to her.

"It's cold in there. I'll fix a fire."

"I'm warm enough," he says, "no need to bother."

She walks into the parlor thinking, "That bastard Paddy! He's done it," and sits down primly in the straight-back chair. O'Hare stands facing the windows as though he doesn't want to look at her.

"I hate being lied to," he says finally, turning to face her. "I hear you've been taking Paddy Morphy into your bed. Is it true?"

Her voice mimicking his defiantly, she says, "I have *not* been taking Paddy Morphy into my bed. If he told you that, he's a liar!"

"Are you saying he never spent the night here with you?"

"The night we got back from Clancy's?" she parries, trying to control her breathless heart. "Yes, he stayed over. But not *with* me. Not in the way you're thinking."

"It was Morphy's tie, wasn't it, Tim brought out from under your bed?"

"Yes," she says unblinking, looking straight at him, thinking, So it was the tie after all, not Paddy broadcasting the news, that was bringing her down. Because of a tie found, a kingdom lost . . .

"Why did Tim say it was his?"

"I don't know. Maybe he wanted it." She feels he is cross-examining her as he would a prisoner in the lockup.

"You've not only deceived me, you've corrupted the child, made him into a liar!"

"I never said a word to him about the tie!" That at least was the truth. "I meant to talk to him about it, why he lied, but we were so busy and happy, so rushed all the week what with the trip and all, it slipped my mind entirely."

"Yet when I asked, it was you who told me Kate Finnegan must have given it to him. Why?"

"I was afraid you'd be thinking just what you're thinking this minute."

"It's no use, Aggie. I can't see us living with lies."

Her heart lurches violently in her breast. She says, "I love you, Thom, God knows I do. That's the truth."

As though he hasn't heard her, he goes on. "I can understand the temptation. I left on a bad note and was gone when you needed me. I knew how worried you were with Tim in the hospital, and how troubled you must have been about us. But once I got back, you could have trusted me enough to tell me the truth."

"I'm telling you the truth!" she shouts. "Will you listen to me now?" And goes on in a gusty bluster, "When we got back from Clancy's it was late. Morphy was drunk and dead-tired. He took off his tie and fell asleep on the couch. I dozed in the chair. When he woke, I won't deny it, he did make a try. But he wasn't hard to put off, and I sent him packing. It was near daylight by then. When I noticed that he'd left the tie, I took it upstairs, thinking that way I'd remember to return it."

He looks at her with a look between contempt and pity. "If it was all that innocent, why did you feel you had to lie to me?"

Is the lying worse than the fornication? she wonders. "It's no use talking to you! If I'd told you the worst, that he'd spent the night here, but that nothing had happened, would you have believed me? Would you have felt better then about us?"

He is silent a long moment. "I need some time. I've got to go off again on police business."

"Are you telling me you're breaking our engagement?"

The question, like a slap, lies stinging between them.

"I don't know," he says finally.

She doesn't slam out of the house this time, or hit him in the face, or collapse weeping, but says quietly, "Perhaps we both need some time," then stands and walks to the front door.

Holding it open, she says, "Call me if you feel like it, when you get back," and watches him as he walks down the path. She closes the door softly and leans against it, shivering. Tim calls her. She takes a sweater off the peg in the hall and goes out back to his room.

Tim is lying on the bed fully clothed and looks up at her anxiously. "How come O'Hare's gone?" he asks and, when she doesn't answer, says, "He never said good-night. He seems mad at me."

"He's not," she says and adds sharply, "Why aren't you in your pajamas?"

It's not O'Hare who is angry with the child but herself—
unreasonably, she knows. It's not his fault he found the tie,
brought it out from under the bed. But if not for that, none of
this would be happening now.

"Don't you want to look at my homework?"

"It's too late. I'll do it in the morning."

He searches her face mournfully, then sits up sighing, legs
dangling. He stays there like a lump, not moving. She tries to
control the sudden rush of rage, but it is beyond her. She hears
her voice rasping shrilly, "Will you stop lallygagging about, and
get ready for bed!"

He gets up, avoiding her eyes, and goes into the lavatory,
shutting the door.

She calls through to him, "Tim? I'm sorry, Timmy, I didn't
mean to be short with you. Just get undressed and I'll give you
your shot."

Her hand is shaking as she prepares the injection. She hates
having to do it. After all these months, it still makes her queasy.
And what if she doesn't push all the air out? Dr. Vogel has
warned her how dangerous it could be.

She shudders, rubbing her arms through the sweater. In God's
name, what is she thinking?

Timmy comes out in his pajamas and lies down obediently,
dropping the pants. She is trembling as she pinches the soft
round flesh of his backside and plunges the needle in.

The child cries out, "Ouch! That hurt!"

Pulling the needle out swiftly, she throws it down on the
bureau, then runs into the bathroom to retch.

Nothing except a battle lost can be half so
melancholy as a battle won.

DUKE OF WELLINGTON

1

They picked her up early that morning in Belfast as she was
coming across Hardcastle Road on her way home from the
marketing. The meat and vegetables she'd bought were scattered
all over the street as she tried to fight them off. The few passing
pedestrians, two young women talking busily as they pushed
their prams and an older matron carrying her string totebag and
clutching an umbrella as though her life depended on it, seemed
too stunned to cry out, though one of the younger women did
finally call, "In God's name, what are you doing!" and the older
woman suddenly came to life. Dropping her bag, she began to
hit out at the two masked men with her brolly, but by then it was
too late. Brushing the old lady off as though she were a troublesome insect, they shoved Eileen into the car and took off, turning
left at Donegal Street, speeding off to God knew where. She
couldn't tell the direction because by this time they'd blind-
folded her. She was bruised and frightened, but mostly furious at
herself. Why hadn't she run or screamed? If she'd managed to

fend them off even for a little while longer, someone might have come by to help. A false hope probably, since she knew people mostly stood by looking on helplessly or tried to fade off unnoticed, whenever "an incident" took place.

They never said a word during the ride, nor did she. It was as though she'd lost the power of speech, been struck dumb. She tried to keep track of the time, but her heart was still beating too fast and she couldn't tell how long it took. Ten minutes? Maybe half an hour, but it seemed like forever until they were pulling her out of the car and pushing her down a flight of stone steps. She heard a heavy door squealing open, then banging shut behind them, and the clanging sound of a heavy bolt being dropped into its socket.

When they took the blindfold off she saw there were three of them, all masked. They were in some kind of a root cellar, with a bare earthen floor and stone walls, mildewed and chill, that was hardly high enough to stand up in. There was a bed in the corner, and a chair and a table next to it with a fancy new shiny red touch-tone telephone on the table. It looked so incongruous there, she almost wanted to laugh.

One arm pinioned behind her back, the gun at her head, she held the receiver after Kelsey Owens — she knew it was him in spite of the mask and the effort he made to disguise his voice — put through the call from Belfast to Dublin. Covering the mouthpiece, he said, "Just this and no more. Don't make a mistake." The message was printed in clear block letters on a piece of cardboard held by one of the others.

She'd no idea how they knew about her and O'Hare. Maybe one of them had been told of his coming to see her in Howth the day she was taking Grace and Haila back home to be buried. She heard the dear familiar voice saying "O'Hare here" and tried to think of a decent ruse that would warn him.

Keeping the tone of her voice dead, she read as from rote, hoping he'd guess she was under duress. "It's Eileen Henley. I need to see you. I can't explain now. Will you call back at 247 44 26 in an hour?" and dropped the phone nervously to cover the fact that she'd read the number wrong. But Kelsey caught it and grabbed the back of her neck squeezing hard, so she had to correct it.

"Sorry, Thomas," she said. "It's 44 28." And the connection was broken as Kelsey quickly depressed the button. She continued to stand there holding the phone, trying to look defiant but feeling like a battered rag doll as he struck her across the face twice, knocking her down on the bed.

"No need of that," one of the men said softly. He brought her some tea poured out of a thermos. She wondered if it was drugged. Her lip was bleeding and made the tea taste funny anyway.

She must have dozed off, but the ring of the telephone roused her. She kept her eyes closed and heard Kelsey talking briefly. He hung up with a shout, announcing triumphantly, "That was Leech! O'Hare's bitten! The bastard'll be there ten Wednesday morning!"

2

Tuesday early, O'Hare went to see Henley at Strathmore, where he was being held pending arraignment. The man looked as though he had aged maybe ten years in the few weeks since he'd been brought in. Ellis Meighan, his counsel, was there with another lawyer. O'Hare and Meighan had known each other for some time and were friendly, but greeted each other with appropriate formality. Meighan introduced him to James McNaughton, Henley's solicitor, and they shook hands.

O'Hare asked Henley how he was feeling. Sitting there in his gray prison garb, Henley stared at O'Hare out of bloodshot eyes and said nothing. His hands were trembling and he put them behind him.

O'Hare said, "I spoke to your sister before she went back to Belfast," and went on in a comforting tone, "I'm sure she'll be here to see you before the trial" (which was only half a lie since he presumed it likely). "I promised her I'd do what I could to get you a lighter sentence" (which was true), "but I can't do that without your help. If you cooperate, give me some names, I'm sure the judge will take a recommendation of clemency under favorable consideration."

Henley turned to look at Meighan, who sighed, "I think Mr. Henley will be glad to cooperate if we can get a guarantee of that. I take it you are speaking officially for the state prosecutor?"

"Naturally," O'Hare said glibly, "we all want the actual perpetrators. If we knew who they were and could bring them to justice, both sides would benefit. It would satisfy the state and at the same time considerably bolster Mr. Henley's defense."

"Well, if we've your word on that, we will advise our client to try to see if he can help you."

Sod Garrity! he thought. "You have my word," he said solemnly.

Henley spoke up angrily, "I told you over and over! I don't know the men they sent down to me!"

"I'm aware of that," O'Hare said. "But you were good enough to give us some excellent descriptions. Unfortunately, it appears they were only intermediaries — messengers. And while we might bring them up on charges of threatening you, it's not likely we could get a conviction on your word alone. The question now is: can you tell us who in the O.F.F. was likely to have carried out the Dublin bombings?"

Henley, frowning, shook his head in exasperation. "You know it's been over three years since I left!"

"I know that. But party personnel are usually quite loyal, wouldn't you say?" O'Hare continued indelicately. "And if not lost by attrition, still likely to be carrying on with their assignments?"

"There's no way I have of knowing if the same ones are still operating!"

"I'm not asking you to prove anything, Mr. Henley, just to help us and yourself. It's our job, as you know, to discover and establish proof, if we can."

Henley threw up his hands and looked again to his counsel. Meighan pursed his lips thoughtfully and tapped the fingertips of both hands together. He held a whispered consultation with McNaughton. Turning back, he smiled encouragingly. "We would not be averse to your giving Mr. O'Hare any information that might prove useful to him in this matter. Our defense will be based on the fact that you are not guilty of the actual bombings. Certainly, if the state is able to place responsibility squarely on the shoulders of the party or parties who *were* involved, it would considerably strengthen our brief."

It was a tedious session. Reluctantly, Henley came up with some information. The head of the bomb squad used to be a man called simply the Wizard, famed for his skill in designing insidiously effective explosives. So far as Henley knew, no one in his sector had ever met him, or heard him referred to except by that name. The actual plot would have been, in all likelihood, carried out by John Peel and Kelsey Owens, two of the top gunmen in the O.F.F. Peel was small and skinny, quick and deadly; Owens, a lumbering giant of a man with red hair and hands as big as hams, feared and respected for his remarkable feats of strength.

That was all he could get. Not much to go on, he thought, but it was a start. Maybe Jonny Black would be able to help fill in details.

As he was about to leave, Henley stood up and took his solicitor aside. He seemed to be asking a series of questions. McNaughton nodded rapidly and said, "Of course," then turning to O'Hare said, "Would it be possible, do you think, Mr. O'Hare, for you to arrange for round-the-clock guards for Mr. Henley? He is being threatened by some of the other prisoners. We would like to be certain no harm comes to him."

O'Hare promised to see to it and stopped off to talk to the warden to ask that full security precautions be taken to protect the prisoner.

"I don't suppose you're aware," the warden said condescendingly, "that our staff has been cut almost in half this last year? I'm sorry, we just don't have enough men to provide twenty-four-hour guard duty. We'll do what we can, of course, keep an eye out, but—"

"I'm afraid that's not good enough!" O'Hare snapped back savagely, and was startled at his own short fuse. "If you can't make suitable arrangements for the safety of the prisoner, please let me know, and I'll arrange for some special duty officers to be assigned."

The warden busied himself shuffling through the papers on his desk and without looking up said, "My staff will do its best, you may be sure."

He'd had no breakfast that morning and stopped off for a bite to eat at Bridey Murray's small tearoom just off Merrian Square. It was crowded at this hour and he shared a table with a young mother and her small son. The woman was impatient with the little boy, who was picking at his food, and when he accidentally turned over his glass of milk, she cuffed him sharply across the face. The child didn't cry but stared dumbly at his mother with a look of such raw pain in his eyes that O'Hare could hardly bear to look at him. Bridey came over in a minute and cleared up the mess saying, "Not to worry, dearie, I'll have this right in a second. And I'll bring you another glass of milk, shall I?" But the woman said no and rose and stalked off, the child — head hanging — stumbling blindly behind her.

The tyranny of grown-ups! he thought. How do children survive it?

An image of Tim flashed through his mind and his heart clenched as he remembered the startled hurt look the boy had given him last night. Was it only last night — it seemed such eons ago — when he'd spoken to him so coldly, telling him to leave so he could talk to his mother alone. What was he going to do about Timmy? What was he going to do about Agnes? He tried not to think of what had happened between them, but the pictures unrolled on the screen of his mind, clicking over and over — of Agnes rubbing her arms against the cold, crying out, "It's you I love, Thom! That's the truth!" Of her standing in the doorway as he walked out of the house, the door closing slowly, inexorably behind him. Of the three of them skimming along on the two bikes on their way to Phoenix Park in earlier, happier days.

Bridey came over and asked, "Something wrong with the shepherd pie?"

He looked up startled and said, "No, it's lovely. I'm just not as hungry as I thought I was."

When he got back to the office, Dinty Noonan came over to say, "Himself wants you." Noonan thought of Riley as God and, like the Israelites, forbidden to pronounce Jehovah's true name, never referred to the chief except by indirection. O'Hare said thanks and made for Riley's office.

Riley wasted no time. Leaning forward on his swivel throne, he pinned O'Hare with his steel-gray eyes. "Close the door," he said abruptly. "What's all this between you and Morphy?"

"I'm afraid it's a private matter."

"No breach of discipline is a private matter!"

"Sorry."

"Is that all you have to say?"

O'Hare shrugged. "It won't happen again. The whole thing was my fault. I'm willing to apologize."

Riley growled, "And that's supposed to settle it? What about Belfast?"

O'Hare hesitated a minute. "If Morphy's not willing to come along, I'll take Donovan. He's a good man and more experienced."

"I can't spare Donovan. He's on another assignment."

"I'll go alone."

"Not on your life! You know that's out of the question!"

"Has Morphy said he wants out?"

"He's as obstinate and hardheaded as you are. He won't say a thing except he'll go if I order him to."

"Well then?"

Riley exploded. "How can I trust the two of you not to be tangling again?"

"You've my word," he said. It was the second time today he was making a promise he wasn't sure he could live up to.

"I hope you can keep it! And your temper as well!" Riley got up and went to the door grumbling, "Let's have him in then and see can we work out a truce."

Summoned by Noonan, Morphy came in looking like a small boy caught with his hand in the till, at once sheepish and defiant, sporting the red welt on his cheek and the swollen lip as though they were medals of honor.

O'Hare had a momentary surge of shame tinged with anger, as he fumbled an apology. "I'm sorrier than I can say, Paddy. I've been on edge lately. I know that's not much of an excuse, I only hope you'll be big enough to accept it."

Avoiding his eye, Paddy said coolly, "No sweat, O'Hare." Then turning, spoke to Riley, "I'm willing to forgive and forget, if he is."

O'Hare could feel his gorge rising.

"Well, shake hands then," Riley said and, sensing their tension, essayed a small joke. "But don't come out fighting!"

They touched hands like two boxers ready to square off.

The bell rang.

Riley picked up the phone. "Just a moment," he said and handed it to O'Hare. "It's for you, someone from Belfast."

"O'Hare here," he said. He listened intently, jotted down a number. "Yes, I have it," he said, listened a moment, then scratched out a digit and wrote in another. "Is there something wrong?" he asked softly. "Can't you talk now?" But the line had already gone dead.

Riley, who'd been talking to Morphy, turned to him. "Who was it?" he asked.

"Nothing important," he answered. He wasn't about to tell him it was Eileen Henley. "Someone just left a number for me to call later."

Back in his office he worked for an hour, then put through the call to the number she'd given him.

"Rafferty's Café," a man's voice answered.

He asked if Miss Henley was there. Could he speak with her?

"Och, too bad!" the man said. "She's just this minute gone off. Left a message though. Who is it calling?"

O'Hare told him.

"The very one!" he said cheerfully. "She said could you meet her here early tomorrow. Say ten o'clock? At Rafferty's Café,

6 Potter's Lane. Just turn left at the end of Corn Market Street and you're here. You can't miss it."

"I've got it," O'Hare said. "Will you let her know I'll be there?"

"You've got the place then? And the time? Wednesday, ten o'clock. Right?"

"Right, thanks," he said and hung up.

Uneasy, he checked the Belfast directory for the number of Rafferty's Café. The address was correct but the phone number was another one altogether. He tried it anyway, it might be an alternate listing, and asked for Miss Henley. The woman who answered said she'd never heard of her, and when he asked about the other number, said snippily, "We've only the one phone, and Lord knows, this one keeps me busy enough!"

He tried the first number again. It rang a long time but the ring was peculiar, and no one answered. When he checked with the operator, she told him the line was out of order. With a little prodding, she found that the number was listed for a public phone box on Queen Street. The public boxes were always going out of order, she said, and it was no wonder, with all the vandals seeing could they get a few pence out of them!

He thanked her and asked to be connected with the head supervisor. When the supervisor came on the line, he identified himself and said he hated to trouble her, but could she please put a tracer on a call made from Belfast to him at this number in Dublin around twelve noon? It took her over an hour to get back to him.

"Sorry to be so long, sir," she said, "but there seems to be some confusion in our records. We have a note of a call made to you from Belfast, but the number it was charged to is not a working number."

How was that possible? he asked. He'd gotten the call just a couple of hours ago. She was as puzzled as he was, couldn't explain it. Operator error, perhaps. She asked could he give her the name of the party who'd made the call? It might help her trace the proper number.

That was just it, he told her. He wasn't sure who'd made the call. It was what he was hoping to find out.

She was sorry, she said. Without further information there seemed no way of straightening out the confusion. "Would you like me to check the old listing for you anyway, sir?"

He said please.

She was back to him promptly this time to tell him the number he'd requested information about had been listed under the name of a Mr. William Connaught at 41 Amboy Street, Belfast, but had been disconnected two weeks ago.

"I hope that's some help to you, sir?"

It was, he said, and he thanked her.

But truth to tell, it wasn't much help. All he knew now for sure was that Eileen — or someone — had been able to make a bypass connection to reach him. He hadn't the least notion as to how they'd been able to do it, and only a faint glimmering as to why.

He put through a final call to his old pal O'Meara at the Royal Ulster Constabulary in Belfast. They talked for a long while and when he hung up, he felt somewhat easier.

He worked till late, missing supper, bringing his paperwork up to date, and at six-thirty, his desk cleared, buzzed Morphy to tell him it was time they were leaving to keep the appointment with Black. He had just got his coat on when Riley called saying he wanted to see him and Morphy before they took off.

3

It was well past seven and growing dark when they finally pulled out of Dublin, leaving them little enough time to get to where they were going. They took the shorter coast road heading toward Dundalk, O'Hare doing the driving.

Riley'd had them in for a briefing — something of a misnomer, since he'd held them up for over an hour with his longiloquence, spouting away like a steam kettle — about the delicacy of the operation, the need to proceed with the utmost circumspection, the importance of working closely together. Cooperation was the keynote, he kept cautioning them. The success of the mission, their very lives would depend on it . . . and so on and on, drenching them with every cliché in the roster, before he let them take off.

"And one final word," he wound up finally. "I don't give a tinker's damn wotinhell your argument was about. That's your business. I only hope it's over and buried. When you're out in the field, you've got to work as a team — that's an order!" Then linking hands with the two of them, he said, "Good luck!" and called out as they left, "Remember now — keep in touch! I expect constant close contact!"

Well, Paddy Morphy was all for close contact and teamwork, wasn't he? But all he'd got for his efforts so far was a split lip and a swollen cheek. No, in all fairness, not all. There'd been some rare sweet moments of pleasure in it for him, not to mention the joy of a job well done. Only the fracas that followed hadn't exactly improved his team spirit.

Still and all, he was pleased to be going along. It was his first big job and he could feel the excitement of it rising inside him, racing along with the deep hum of the motor and the steady thrum of the tires clicking over the seams in the road. They sped along in the dark. There were only a few cars on the road, but they passed them by in a wink. He didn't mind speeding when he was in the driver's seat, but hated it when he was the passenger.

The speedometer was up to seventy-five. O'Hare trying to make up for the time lost, he figured. He glanced at his partner intent on the road, and touched his sore lip gingerly. The spell of her lingered still . . . the silky feel of her skin, her soft hot mouth . . . He wondered where she was and what she was doing this minute.

O'Hare said, "What time is it?"

"Quarter past eight," he answered, checking his watch. Time stood still on the clock on the panel, stuck at ten after two.

"We're late," O'Hare said, pushing the needle up to ninety.

A bit nervous, he asked, "What's on for tomorrow?"

"I've an early morning appointment in Belfast. After that, we'll see. It depends on what Black can tell me."

"Who's the appointment with?"

"You can take it easy. I'll be going alone."

Angry, he said, "I thought Riley said no solos!"

"I think you can leave the planning to me."

They were both silent a moment.

O'Hare said, "Don't worry. You can play back-up. Should the need arise."

"You said you'd be filling me in!" He could feel the welt on his cheek pulsing hotly.

"Don't worry. There's plenty of time. Once I see Black, we'll have the whole night ahead of us."

He turned away from O'Hare and stared at the road. Bloody bastard, he thought, pulling rank!

They passed Fairways, a converted-mansion hotel, mostly for tourists. Aglow with light. Once, when he'd won a packet at the Curragh, he'd stayed overnight there with a girl, Katie Callahan her name was, an airline hostess. Nice, but nothing compared with Mrs. Agnes O'Connell. They flew past a roadside sign that said "Dundalk, 5 miles." He could make out the dim outline of the round Hills of Monaghan and Slieve Beagh off to the north.

As they approached the town, O'Hare slowed down for the turnoff. They went bumping along for half a mile over a cobbled road, then pulled in beside a small old stone building. The beam of the headlights picked up a wooden sign over the entrance, swaying in the wind. He managed to make out the picture of a bullock with a cock perched on its head; its neck extended, the cock seemed to be crowing lustily.

O'Hare doused the lights and said, "I'll go in first, find a place toward the rear. You follow in a few minutes, but stay at the bar. Black's not keen on company, he's inclined to be jumpy." He got out of the car and said, "Don't drink too much."

Two men in a van backed recklessly out of the parking area. They seemed to be in a rush, and took off with a great grinding of gears, narrowly missing O'Hare.

Morphy looked at his watch. It was close to nine. He waited a few minutes, then went in. A jet of steam rose up to greet him. The room was long and low, with smoke-blackened rafters and a peat fire smoldering in the rear. There were maybe a dozen men in the place, no women. He saw O'Hare sitting alone in a booth near the fireplace, and went over to the bar.

"Welcome to the Cock'n'Bull," the bartender greeted him. "What's to your taste?"

"A Guinness dark, thanks," he said. The barkeep set a foaming tankard before him. He put some coins on the counter and said, "Have one for yourself." The man nodded his thanks. "Stranger, are you?"

"I am," he said.

"You won't be for long. We're a friendly bunch here. Joe Tanner," he said. They shook hands. "Paddy Morphy," he answered, wondering if he should have used a fake name.

He drank half the pint thirstily, lit a cigarette, and glanced around, hoping to see a man fitting the description O'Hare had given him of Jonny Black. "Not the sort of a man you'd pick out in a crowd. Ordinary-looking, medium height, sandy hair, generally wears workclothes. Sports a moustache and a beard, sometimes. Rarely looks the same twice." It wasn't much help. At least half the men in the place were of medium build and wore workclothes. He noticed a man in a soiled anorak, with paint-spattered pants and shoes, move toward the back and stop near O'Hare. He seemed to be asking to join him. O'Hare said something and the man moved off to stand near the fire. Could that one be Black? If he was, why didn't O'Hare invite him to sit? Or were they being cautious? He felt like a kid playing I Spy.

He was hungry. He'd skipped lunch, they hadn't had time to stop for supper, and his stomach was growling away. He shifted his weight from one foot to the other, embarrassed, hoping none of the men crowded around him could hear it. He finished the pint, thinking he ought to pace himself, but decided wotthehell, and ordered a second. He looked at his watch again. Almost nine-thirty. Maybe Black had come and gone. They'd been over an hour late. He hated this waiting game.

Nothing seemed to be happening. O'Hare was still sitting alone, nursing his drink. Tanner bought a round and said, "Drink hearty, m'lad!" He wasn't sure he should have it, but he needed something to fill his complaining belly.

He drank the third pint slowly, knowing he'd have to empty his bladder soon. Was it okay for him to go to the jakes, or was he supposed to stay put? He decided to try to hold off for another ten minutes. He finished his drink and looked at his watch. Only nine-thirty-five. He decided he'd better not wait.

As he got up, O'Hare glanced over at him. He made a slight gesture with his head toward the men's and made for the door. It was locked. He stood there awhile, then tried knocking. Tanner looked up from drawing a beer, and shouted over the din, "It sticks. It's caught, maybe. Just give it a shove!" He shoved, but the door didn't budge. Tanner came out from behind the counter and tried it. He looked puzzled.

"There's no bolt on the inside," he said. They pushed together hard, and the door gave. A piece of wood, wedged between the floor and the jamb, flew out. Tanner said, "Somebody's been playing tricks," and went back behind the bar.

He went in. There were two urinals and a cubby with a swing door. A window in the back was open, its small soiled curtain billowing in the wind. He used the urinal and looked in the mirror as he was relieving himself. His face looked flushed and his eyes sleepy, his lip and cheek still swollen and discolored. A man came in and did his business quickly, and left without washing his hands, giving him a quirky look as he went out. He wasn't sure if it was because of his bruised face, or because he was still pissing away. He finished finally, washed his hands, and wanted to dry them, but there were no towels. He pushed open the lavatory door to get some toilet paper. A man sat slumped over on the toilet. Embarrassed, he said, "Sorry!" and quickly let the door swing to.

He wondered if something was wrong. The guy hadn't stirred. Maybe he was sick.

He noticed the soles of his shoes were sticky. He must have stepped onto something messy. He stood there a moment debating what to do, then opened the door slowly and stared at the man. A knife handle was sticking out of his throat. Blood had dripped from the wound onto the floor. That was what had got onto his shoes. There were some words chalked on the back wall.

He backed out suddenly, his stomach heaving, the Guinness flying up in his throat. He drew several deep breaths trying to quell his nausea, but the air was so foul it only made him feel worse. He splashed some water on his face, then forced himself to go back to look at the message on the wall.

Printed like a child's scrawl, it read:

TWO BIRDS WITH ONE STONE
COURTESY
THE IRA

He wondered why they'd said "stone" when they'd used a knife.

He was drying his hands and face on his shirttails, struggling still to quiet his stomach, when the outer door opened and O'Hare came in, saying, "What's taking you so long?"

Embarrassed, he tried to tuck his damp shirt into his pants.

O'Hare looked at him and said sharply, "Are you all right?"

"I was just coming out to tell you."

"Tell me what?" O'Hare asked. "We've wasted the night. Black never showed. Or if he did, he didn't wait."

He managed to say, "He showed up all right," pointing to the toilet door, "and he's still waiting," before he started to heave again.

4

They got to Corn Market Street before nine Wednesday morning. O'Hare parked the car near the intersection leading to Potter's Lane. Corn Market was busy with people going to work. Two small tinker's kids stood at the corner begging.

Morphy, lying down in the back, had slept most of the way. He stirred sluggishly and opened one startled eye. "Are we here then?" he asked.

He'd been up sick half the night and looked terrible. Experiencing an unwanted tug of compassion, O'Hare told him, "You'll feel better after you've had some breakfast."

"I'm all right," Paddy said tightly. "What's on the agenda?"

"I'm due at Rafferty's Café at ten o'clock, just up ahead on Potter's Lane. It's early yet, but I want to take a look around. Why don't you get yourself a bite to eat somewhere nearby, and I'll meet you back here after."

Morphy's face flamed as red as his hair. "I don't suppose I've the right to know who it is you're meeting or what it's about! I thought we were supposed to be working together!"

O'Hare said dryly, "Riley'd mark you ten for team spirit," and was instantly ashamed. Why did he keep baiting the boy, pushing him out? Was he still feeling vengeful? It was all over between himself and Agnes, wasn't it? And if there was anyone to blame, it was her or himself, not this stripling!

"Sorry," he said. "Of course you've a right to know. It's Eileen Henley."

Paddy's eyebrows shot up like two arrows. He stared at O'Hare. "Do you trust her? It could be a trap."

"It might be. But I don't think so. I think she just wants to help her brother. Maybe she knows something she wants to tell me. Anyway, we'll be taking every precaution."

"Like what?"

"I've a friend in the R.U.C. who's been alerted. And you can keep watch from the car. We'll be covered."

"Does Riley know you're meeting her?"

O'Hare could feel his irritation mounting again but managed to say smoothly, "Not yet. I'll be phoning him soon."

Paddy shrugged, "Okay, it's your cup of tea," got out of the car, and without looking back joined the flow of pedestrian traffic.

O'Hare sat in the car awhile trying to assuage his guilt. He should have told Morphy the truth, admitted the chances were a hundred to one on the rendezvous being a set-up. But Morphy was new at the game, inexperienced. Finding Black dead in the men's last night had made him nervy enough. There was no sense scaring him half to death in advance. And, green as he was, hadn't he raised the question himself that the meeting could be a trap? He was smart enough to be cautious.

He knew he was rationalizing. He was certain Eileen had been forced to make the call to him. He should have discussed the situation more openly, prepped Paddy more fully. The meeting smelled of danger.

T'hell with it all! When you joined the force, you knew you had to take your chances. And what guarantees were there against a bomb or a sniper's bullet?

He got out of the car, slammed the door, and walked the few paces to the phone box on the corner. He put through a call to Riley and, speaking quickly, gave him the news about Black, explaining where they were but not why, telling him only that he had another lead and wanted to follow it up.

"We'll likely be back by tonight," he said and added to distract him, "Incidentally, the police in Dundalk were very cooperative, even found us a place to sleep."

"Superintendent Hurley's a friend of mine there," Riley said. "Did you meet him?"

"We did," O'Hare said. "He mentioned he knew you." And changing his tack abruptly said, "Sorry, I've got to get off now. We'll be seeing you soon."

"Wait a minute!" Riley barked. "What's your lead? I want to know what you're doing and where you'll be if I need to reach you."

Avoiding the first question, he gave him the number on the pay phone and said, "We'll be here for the next hour or so. After that, I'm not sure. But don't worry, we'll keep in close touch," and hung up on Riley sputtering away, "Damn it, O'Hare! Wait a minute—"

Riley would probably try calling him back to bawl him out. He grinned at the thought. Riling Riley made him feel better.

He dialed a local number and when somebody answered gave his name and asked for Captain Meyer O'Meara. He and

O'Meara had trained as rookies together in Dublin some twenty years back, and had become good friends. O'Meara's mother was Jewish and his father Irish Catholic and Meyer had grown up speaking English and Gaelic with an East European accent—and Hebrew and Yiddish, so O'Hare was told, with a thick brogue. O'Meara's polyglot confusion caused considerable amusement among the men on the force and they'd nicknamed him "the Mayor"—a play on his name and an allusion to Robert Briscoe, the former Jewish mayor of Dublin. O'Meara insisted he was one of the rare true sons of Erin—he was convinced that the Celts were a lost tribe of Israel—and that his antecedents on both sides confirmed the fact. In '79 he'd married a Protestant girl, moved to Belfast, and joined the Royal Ulster Constabulary, but he and O'Hare still managed to see each other a half-dozen times a year.

The familiar rough voice on the phone boomed, "O'Hare! Where are you? I've been up all the night waiting to hear from you. Peg got the spare room ready. We thought you'd be staying over."

"Sorry. I got held up till too late and didn't want to disturb you. I'm in Belfast. Around the corner from Rafferty's."

"Good. I can be there in ten minutes."

"Don't come in uniform."

"I said I wouldn't. But I still think a small show of officialdom wouldn't hurt. And if the O.F.F. is involved as you suspect, we ought to call in the Brits."

"I'm not about to call in the whole bloomin' army! Whoever's behind it, I don't want them warned off."

"Hey! This is my territory!"

"Okay! But it's my case!"

"Calm down! You know I want to do what I can to help. I only thought if push comes to ambush, the two of us might not be able to handle it." O'Meara's sudden laugh crackled over the wire. "What am I saying? I know your answer. The two of us can handle anything!"

"We're three. I've got Paddy Morphy with me. He'll be in the Rover parked near the corner."

"Very reassuring. Isn't he the redhead, the young Lothario who came in just before I left Dublin? Let's hope he doesn't get distracted by the Belfast lassies."

There was a lull.

"Are you there, O'Hare?"

"I'm here," he said.

"I was just kidding. Don't worry, we'll be fine. I'll be there, in fancy dress, leave my flat feet at home. You don't even have to say hello."

"Thanks, Meyer," he said and hung up.

Potter's Lane, not much more than an alley, was quieter than Corn Market Street. He spotted Rafferty's a few doors from the corner. It looked like a hole in the wall, dark and dingy. He continued to stroll casually on the opposite side, stopping to peer in at a travel agency, not yet open, with brightly colored posters in the window advertising trips to Paris and Amsterdam and even to Africa, the last one jungle-green, with giraffes and lions and monkeys beckoning him to join them on a safari to Kenya. A sharp wind blew from the north, threatening rain. Africa was a temptation, or maybe the south of France. The clock inside said nine-thirty. He still had half an hour. He turned in at the tobacconist's next door and picked up a *Belfast Courier* and a tin of pipe tobacco, and asked the proprietor if he knew when the travel agency was likely to open.

"Hard to say," the man told him. "I wouldn't want to set my watch by it. The young woman who runs the place is new here, not long from Poland, and she seems a mite confused about Belfast time. It might be anywhere between nine and noon — in Warsaw!"

O'Hare laughed, pretending a humor he didn't feel, and keeping an eye on the street listened while the man chatted away, and when a customer came in, he left discreetly. He walked to the corner, buffeted by the wind. His back felt naked. He knew suddenly he wasn't going to go into Rafferty's and wait there like a sitting duck. It would make more sense for him to watch for Eileen on the street and take her somewhere else. He turned back. The travel agency was still closed. The clock inside said nine-fifty-five. He turned up his collar, lit his pipe in the shelter of the entranceway, and stood there waiting.

The rain came suddenly, flooding the gutters. He watched a lean priest, umbrella blowing in the wind, lifting his skirts to avoid the puddles, slosh hastily across the avenue and duck into Rafferty's. He opened his newspaper, pretending to read. A headline caught his eye: IRA BOMB KILLS 37 IN NEWRY.

It was after ten and there was still no sign of her. He wondered if he could have missed her. Maybe she'd come early and gone inside while he was still in at the tobacconist's. Not likely. He'd had a clear view of Rafferty's the whole time. He would have seen her. She might be late, held up by the downpour. Maybe she'd called and left a message for him. The thought made him uneasy. If that were true, there was nothing for it, he'd have to go in.

He started across the street and saw the two tinker's kids that he'd noticed earlier, wet and bedraggled, racing toward him from the corner. They got to Rafferty's at the same time. He stopped at the door, wanting to send them away, but they got the door open, pushed past him, and ran in ahead. Once inside, they stood shaking themselves like two puppies, dripping pools of water onto the lino.

He followed behind, reached quickly into his pocket, and came up with a handful of coins. "Here you are," he said. "Why don't you buy yourselves some sweets."

The woman behind the counter, probably the same one he'd talked to on the phone yesterday, raised her voice angrily. "Out, out, both of you!" she scolded. "There'll be no begging here!"

The little girl, bold as brass, answered back. "We've a message for someone. We'll tell it to you, if you give us a copper."

"A likely story!" the woman scoffed. "You've got your coppers already. Be off with you now!"

The lanky priest who'd been sitting at the counter rose and came over. Smiling beatifically at the ragamuffins, he said, "Is it from Miss Henley for Father O'Hare, you've a message? If 'tis, I'm your man."

5

Somewhere close by, a woman was screaming. She couldn't seem to stop. The disembodied sounds bounced off the walls and flew back at her, beating a devil's tattoo in her head. She wondered how long the woman could go on. Surely her voice must be shattered by now. Her own throat ached. She wanted to tell the pour soul it was no use. She herself was helpless and there was no one there likely to come to her aid.

Someone slapped her across the face and said, "Be still now, or you'll get worse!" The screaming stopped abruptly. A relief! But the sudden stillness frightened her. She wept silently, tried to pray. She felt destroyed in her deepest being. The hardest part was trying to understand the horror that was growing inside her like a cancer. The thought that they were human — they were, weren't they? — and she was human too, flesh and blood, just like them. They were one and the same, bound together in the complicity of their innermost nature — an indissoluble bond of violence and hatred. Which made her culpable too. For she longed to torture them, destroy them as they were destroying her.

"Elaine!" he called to her. "Elaine, the lily maid of Astolat turned whore!" he said jeering. Was she worried about getting a baby? She needn't be. They had other plans for her; there wouldn't be time.

That was Owens, he was the worst. He and Peel kept on at her before, during, and after.

How often had she given pussy to that papist bastard O'Hare?

Why had she informed on her brother?

What had she told the cops in Dublin?

Whose names had she given them?

Didn't she know that death was the penalty for squealers?

She took heart at that. If only they'd leave her in peace, kill her, and be done with it.

Peel on top of her whispered, "Come on! You know I'm better at fucking than that rotten Teague cop. Admit it!" he begged her.

She tried to forget her body, kept trying to dredge up a wisp of memory of a time when as a little girl she'd been happy. She remembered her mother bathing her, dressing her in a fresh starched pinafore, brushing her hair, kissing her, calling her "dear sweet child." Oh, that lovely feeling of cleanness, of being loved, cared for!

Even the one who'd seemed kinder at first took his turn. And he was the one who took the clippers and shaved her head down to the scalp. When he was through, they put on her blouse and skirt, but not her underwear or her stockings or shoes, and dragged her out to the car. She caught a glimpse of the sky, gray with dark clouds. She couldn't stop shivering, the air was so cold. They drove for a while, then stopped in front of a church — Catholic. She recognized it, St. Jude's on Jarmyn Street. They pulled her out of the car and, one on either side of her, propelled her across the pavement. She felt she was falling but they held her upright while they tied her to the staked iron fence in front of the church and left her there.

She had no idea what time of the day it was, it was so dark. The church gates were open. A few people came out, perhaps from morning mass, and went hurrying by, not looking, pretending not to see her. They probably thought her a Catholic girl who'd got caught going out with a British soldier. It was not uncommon for the Provos to tar and feather girls who'd committed that crime and put them on display as a warning to the other young Catholic women in the parish so they wouldn't be similarly tempted. She'd heard that most priests didn't approve of the practice. Maybe someone would go in and tell the priest at St. Jude's. If only they would, he might come out and release her. But no one did. No one stopped. No one saw her. She felt she'd become invisible. Perhaps the terrible sight of her blinded them. Still, she hadn't been tarred and feathered, only her head shorn. She wondered would they have stopped to gape if she'd been stripped naked? Why did she blame them? She'd seen a girl once, tied up the same way, and hadn't stopped either, had offered no protest, no comforting word, but heart beating wildly had run off instead. Though once she'd stopped running, she'd had the sense to call the police.

The north wind blew hard and the rain came savagely. In a minute her blouse and skirt were soaked through. A man in a trench coat, hat pulled low, passed her by and muttered something, she couldn't quite make out what but thought he'd called her an ugly name. It didn't matter. She was grateful. It was the only attention anyone had paid her.

The clock in the church steeple clanged, startling her. She counted to ten and thought of O'Hare and wondered if he'd kept the appointment and hoped he was safe. She prayed that he wouldn't find her, and laughed at the thought of how she would look to him now, and cried at this last sad vestige of her pitiful vanity.

6

He was feeling rotten. His stomach was still upset. The porridge he'd taken had done little to soothe it, and to add to his misery he'd got caught in the downpour. His mac was soaked through and his pants legs were dripping.

He could see the rickety sign that said "Rafferty's Café" from where he sat in the car. There was no sign of O'Hare. If it wasn't for the rain he'd be tempted to get out and go looking for him. Waiting wasn't his style; he wasn't built for it. What he wanted was some action.

Patience, he told himself, you've got to learn patience. Play it cool. Like O'Hare. The bastard never turned so much as a hair last night when he learned Black was dead. Even went in to feel for the pulse in the corpse's bloodied neck.

He noticed the two gypsy kids standing jiggling in the shelter of the telephone kiosk on the corner. A man came by and pushed in with them. There wasn't enough room for the three of them. The man was talking to them, giving them some coins, probably trying to get rid of them, maybe wanting to make a phone call. In a minute, the ragamuffins ran off. The man stood there awhile watching, made his call, then disappeared in the rain.

The wind rattled the car, and the rain was falling in sheets. "Ah, it's only the angels pissing," his father used to tell him. The image had tickled him. But today the angels were pissing a flood, and how was he supposed to be keeping a lookout with this deluge surrounding the car like a shroud? He set the wipers going, hoping they wouldn't run down the battery, opened the window a drop, and tried to peer out. Corn Market Street was quiet, virtually empty. A few stragglers taking refuge in shop doorways. Sensible people would be warm and cozy indoors. He stirred irritably and looked at his watch. Ten-fifteen. O'Hare must be with her by now, though he hadn't caught sight of either one of them. The windscreen was misted over inside and he had to keep wiping it. The enclosed air of the car was making him drowsy. Bullets of rain drummed on the roof. He was finding it hard to keep his eyes open.

"Paddy Morphy, is it?" a voice boomed in his ear. "And how's the family?"

Startled, he looked up and, seeing the priest, rolled the window all the way down. Did he know him? He was about to answer that his dad had died last year, and his mother and sister were doing as well as could be expected, but before he could get out a word, the reverend Father poked his head in and without changing his genial expression was saying softly, "O'Meara, R.U.C. The meeting place's been changed. St. Jude's on Jarmyn Street. O'Hare's walking. I'll follow. Drive slowly." And raising his free hand in benediction, moved speedily off down the street under his umbrella.

Excited, he turned the key and pressed the accelerator. The motor refused to turn over. Cursing, he switched off the wipers, waited a few seconds, and tried again. Luckily it caught. In the rear-view mirror he caught a glimpse of O'Meara, hobbled by his skirts, skipping along Corn Market Street, then disappearing around the far corner. He made a wild U-turn, almost hitting a truck, and followed. His heart was beating hard, he could feel the adrenaline pumping. This was more like it.

He caught sight of O'Hare up ahead, coat whipped by the wind, pushing steadily along, O'Meara not far behind on the opposite side. Remembering O'Meara's instructions, he slowed to a crawl, hoping the Rover wouldn't stall. He crept along at what seemed a snail's pace for two blocks, saw the sign "Jarmyn Street," and watched O'Hare turn in.

The three of them must have caught sight of her at almost the same moment — a woman, head shorn, tied to the railing in front of the church. O'Hare quickened his pace. O'Meara, skirts flying, started to cross the street. A fierce gust caught his umbrella, turning it inside out, and he tossed it away. Lifted by the wind, it bowled fitfully along the pavement.

O'Hare had just reached her when the delivery van appeared, coming fast from the other end of Jarmyn. Startled, Paddy watched it, saw the long nose of the Sten poking out of the side window. Without thinking twice, he gunned the motor, turned the wheel hard, swung the Rover around blocking the path of the oncoming van, and jammed on the brakes. There was a crash and a spatter of bullets. He could feel his ribs crack as he hit the steering wheel.

Dazed, he saw the few passers-by freeze, then scatter in every direction. A British lorry, Klaxon sounding, wheels screeching, came racing around the corner. A voice on a bullhorn called, "Clear the street! Clear the street!" There was a burst of machine-gun fire. He felt the heat before he could see the flames.

Pinned by time, like the hands of the broken clock on the panel, he had this terrible longing to know if O'Hare had made it. Pain seared his chest like a hot iron. He was finding it hard to breathe. Someone was reaching for him, trying to pull him free of the wheel, out of the car. He recognized O'Hare and was astonished at the sudden fierce wave of love and gratitude that swept over him as, voice croaking, he said, "What took you so long, y'old bastard?"

7

She came out of the long dark tunnel into a burst of light. Someone was holding her hand, leaning toward her. Her heart gave a leap of joy and pain. He was here, unhurt. She reached up to touch his dear face and, suddenly remembering, turned away and burst into tears, struggling to cover her face and shorn head with the sheet.

"Eileen," he said pleading, "Eileen, don't! It's all right. You're safe now." He reached over to draw down the sheet.

She put her hands over her head protectively and startled, gave a little hiccuping laugh. She was wearing some sort of a cap over her naked scalp, a coif like a nun's. Elaine, ex-Lily Maid of Astolat, once Eileen, Protestant Protestor, transformed now into Heloise, Lily Nun of Argenteuil . . . At last, at least now, she would finally be free of him. He couldn't, after all, make love to this nun, even if he wanted to, even if he hadn't been castrated yet.

She opened her eyes and stared at him defiantly. He looked gray and worn, his eyes heavy, with dark rings under them. He took her hand again and pressed it to his face. His beard was rough, bristly. Her eyes stung and her throat ached. Why was he still playing the same old game with her? Kind Thomas, Sweet Thomas, lips dripping sweet poison, acting so tender and loving, till her bones turned to jelly and the heart in her breast melted away. Then in the next moment, off and gone without so much as a fare-thee-well, Two-faced Thomas, racing back to his true ladylove in Dublin.

He was murmuring soft words at her. She couldn't quite make them out. Never mind, she didn't want to hear them. Her mind was made up. She knew she would never again submit to this lustful priest.

A familiar phrase flew from his lips and came to roost, fluttering in her brain . . .

"News for you . . ." he was saying, the very same words he had used that fateful afternoon in Howth, when he'd told her he was thinking of getting married.

". . . good news of your brother. I saw him two days ago. He seems to be holding up pretty well. His counsel's advised him to cooperate with the government, and he's agreed. I think there's a good chance now of getting him off with a fairly light sentence."

It wasn't the news she'd expected but it was good news, better than she could have hoped for, and she thought she ought to thank him. But he went on, saying he knew it wasn't much, but at least there was some hope. And the important thing was for her to recover her strength, not to worry about anything but just to get well.

A gaunt figure in white appeared in the doorway, clapping her hands briskly.

"Time's up! Out! Visiting hours are long over!"

"Ah, Matron," he said, "I was just getting ready to leave."

"You said you'd be only five minutes!"

He stood up and said apologetically, "I won't be more than a moment now," giving her his old crooked grin, the irresistible Tender Thomas smile, ". . . with your kind permission?"

The matron sniffed reproachfully, but tight lips parting in what must have been meant for a smile, apparently relented. "Oh, very well! But mind," she added, tapping his arm sharply, "I'm holding you to your word this time!"

"A million thanks," he said and waited till she stalked off before he spoke again.

"If you need anything, anything at all, one of the nurses will call me. I've left my number. And will you promise me you'll try not to worry, but just get well and strong again?"

She wanted to promise him the world, but remembering, shut her eyes and turned away. He bent down and kissed her on top of the coif. "I'll be back again in a few days to see you."

She watched him walk out the door and called out, "Don't come back, Thomas!"

She wasn't certain that he'd heard her. He turned back, waved to her, and was gone.

Furious, she shouted after him, "I said, don't come back!"

But she didn't mean it.

6

Doubts are worse than the worst of truths.
MOLIÈRE
Le Misanthrope

1

She knows she has got to stop putting it off, and in a bustle of resolution dresses herself up fit to kill—the first time in a week she's been out of her nightdress—and flies out of the house and up the High Street to attend to the two chores she's been dreading, stopping off first at Delehanty's to inform him the engagement party will have to be postponed. Only for a little while, she assures him, and she hopes it's not a terrible imposition. No, she shrugs apologetically, indicating her helplessness, she can't say exactly when yet, but as P.A. undoubtedly knows, the trial seems to be dragging on forever, and O'Hare, poor man, is drowning in work. All the while thinking to herself, wouldn't O'Hare the bastard be pleased if he could just hear her now, for she's not only a liar, but a sanctimonious hypocrite as well.

P.A.'s manner, discreetly sympathetic, unnerves her. Does she detect a maleficent gleam in the little man's eye as he smilingly professes, " 'Tis no problem, no problem a'tall, dear lady!" And if

she could just manage to notify him, say a week in advance, so
he'd be sure to have everything in perfect readiness?

Barely stopping to thank him, fearful her cheerful facade may
crumble at any moment, she hurries out of the shop with him
calling out after her, "Do give my warmest regard to the
esteemed captain! And of course, to the darlin' sweet child!"

So on her second errand, the cold October wind speeding her
along to St. Anne's where she arrives feeling braced by the brisk
walk and in somewhat better control, only to discover dealing
with Father Malachy is another kettle of fish altogether.

"But why!" Father Malachy asks in astonishment, his wire-
frame glasses sliding down to perch precariously at the tip of his
bony pink nose. She is determined not to go into details and has
told him only that she and O'Hare have decided it might be a
good idea to put off the second posting of the banns for a bit.

"Why?" she parries. "Och, it's nothing at all, Father, nothing
serious! Only a minor matter that needs to be straightened out."

"Ah?" he says and waits patiently.

"It's only we both feel we need a little more time."

"Oh?" he says. A long silence.

"Just a chance to think things over," she smiles brightly, ". . . a
slight misunderstanding . . . nothing that can't be mended!"

"Ah!" he says and continues to wait, his mouth pursed, his
eyes peering quizzically at her over his spectacles as she goes
nattering on, aware she has already said too much, about how she
and O'Hare have decided they both need a little while longer to
sort things out and have agreed on . . . a sort of trial separation
you might call it. Better sooner than later, she's sure the good
Father would agree . . .

"I don't suppose," he says smoothly, "you'd care to give me
some small idea, say, of what this slight misunderstanding might
be about?"

Exasperated at her failure to detour the priest's escalating
curiosity, she answers more sharply than she intends that she'd
prefer not to go into it at the moment. The truth is, the whole
affair, naturally, has been somewhat upsetting.

"A-hah!" he says, looking pleased. "Let me see have I got it straight now. This trial separation, as you call it, appears to be not such a minor matter after all? And the truth it seems is, you're quite upset about it?"

"Yes," she says faintly, and lets out a wail. And before she can stop herself, is telling him that the separation was all O'Hare's idea; that she hasn't had a word from the man since the day before he took off for Belfast, and not so much as a whisper since he's returned; it's as though he's banished her from the face of the earth; and if it wasn't for the news of him in the damned newspapers—excuse it please, Father—she'd be thinking he'd vanished himself into thin air!

"There, there, Mrs. O'Connell dear," he says, taking her hand comfortingly, "sure'n 'tis only a lover's tiff!" At which point she dissolves entirely and is carried off in a river of tears.

All sympathy now, Father Malachy is patting her hand and in a moment goes spouting off, explaining O'Hare to her—how the poor man must be totally weighted down these days, what with the trial and the testimony and all the tribulations of bringing the terrible assassins to justice. And wasn't it a wonder how he'd caught up with those miserable scoundrels! And how once the whole business was over, he'd be sure to be coming round again—wait and see—and the two of them back together again, happy as a pair of lovebirds once more!

She can't find her handkerchief. He offers her his, freshly laundered, she's relieved to discover. She is grateful, too, that he now seems somewhat diverted from ferreting out any further information and that so far, thank heaven, she's managed to let fall no word of her fearful secret . . . Ten days late, and no wiser than her two lovers who the true father may be . . . Dear Mary, Mother of God, let it be an early Change! she prays fervently.

"Now then, are we feelin' a bit better?" he asks. She smiles wanly and, in gratitude, offers him a fair list of her trespasses, including sloth and depression.

The crux of the matter, she tells him, what she really needs his advice on, is the state of her mind. She seems to have lost all sense of herself since O'Hare's been gone. All she does these days is dither about the house, mooning over the past, is a harridan with her poor small son . . .

"Now, now, we can't have that!" he admonishes gently. And pacing the room, proceeds to lecture her.

"Good works!" he propounds, "good works, my dear Mrs. O'Connell, are a powerful antidote to gloom and despair. To quote the immortal Dante, 'There is no virtue in gloom, which is the easiest hiding place for languid idleness!'" He pauses dramatically, and approaching her, places his hand on her shoulder. "Go out into the world, my dear," he exhorts her. "Tend the sick, the aged, the infirm! Care for the poor orphan, perform good works, and you'll soon rout all the devils of doubt and despair. And in no time a'tall, take my word for it, you will find your sweet optimism and your lovely natural zest for life completely restored!" And blessing her with the one hand, he presses her shoulder soulfully with the other.

"Thanks ever so much, Father," she says, returning his handkerchief.

So much for the comforts of religion, she thinks, walking home in a daze. The wind has turned sharp, and she hugs her coat tight around her.

2

A gray Sunday. Bleak Belfast dark and sooty, but quiet. Will she or won't she, he wonders. Whatever the outcome, he's determined to get on with it, do the right thing. He's thought it through carefully, thought of little else all the week. *There is no obstacle that cannot be overcome, given the will,* he reminds himself. Or at least circumvented. His heart trumpets a call to arms. Resolution, the order of the day.

The entrance hall is awash with sad-eyed visitors, whispering. He doesn't wait for the elevator but mounts the stairs two at a time in a quick burst of energy and, admonished by a Sister, finger to lips, reminding him of the need for quiet, tiptoes into her room decorously, bearing the fruit and flowers he's brought with him from Dublin.

The minute he sees her his heart clinches again with pity, though there's no doubt she looks a lot better—frail and wan still, but her eyes clear now under the cap she still wears—and she smiles at him as he proffers the bouquet. A sharp memory of another Sunday nips at him—a bright sunlit day when, carrying posies and wheeling the bike for her son, he'd proposed to the other one. Luckily he's come to his senses since, and knows now he is doing the right thing. This gentle, decent, loyal young woman needs his strong arm and loving support. This sad young girl needs him, and he longs to protect her, care for her.

"I didn't expect you," she says. "Thanks for the flowers."

"You're looking lovely," he tells her, feeling heavy and awkward. "And how are you feeling?"

"Much stronger," she answers. "I thought for a while there they'd taken my brains away when they shaved off my hair, but I seem to be able to use them again. Anyway, I'm sorry I was so rude the last time. Sit down, won't you?"

He draws up a chair and puts the fruit and the flowers on the night table next to her bed.

They are both silent awhile.

"Eileen," he says tenderly and stops.

She waits. "Yes?" she says, encouraging him.

He draws a deep breath. "How are they treating you here?"

"Everyone's very kind."

"Well, that's good. Would you like a glass of water?"

"No thanks, but help yourself."

He pours a glass from the carafe on the bedside table and drinks it slowly.

"What's happening with the trial?" she asks. "I've been following the news, but I'm anxious to hear how you think it's going."

"Not too bad. Kelsey Owens has admitted the bomb your brother left at the airport was intended to catch Prime Minister Haughey as he deplaned. Only it never went off. Owens claims it was his buddy Peel, killed in the fracas on Jarmyn Street, who planted the bombs at the bank and the bridge. It seems the O.F.F.

figured if they didn't get the P.M. at the airport, they'd catch him on his way to the Dail. Luckily for him, Haughey caught a later plane and managed to escape both explosions."

"Owens's testimony should help!"

Better not raise her hopes too high. "It could, if we can believe Owens."

"You're not optimistic?" she says, looking worried.

"It's early on yet, but there's still a fair chance your brother could get off with a minimum sentence." He stirs restlessly.

"These days must be putting a great strain on you. You're looking tired, Thomas. Are you feeling all right?"

He laughs nervously. "I'm okay!" Why can't he just come straight out with it? "Would you believe it," he says with a burst of energy, "it looks like I'm to remain a solitary bachelor after all! The wedding's off!"

"Oh! You must be upset. What happened? . . . Or would you rather not talk about it?"

"I don't mind. There's not much to tell. We just agreed to disagree."

"Perhaps you'll patch it up."

"Not likely. In a way, I guess I'm relieved. Being free again could have certain advantages . . ." He looks at her hopefully.

She looks startled. "Could it?" she says.

"Well, for one, I might be coming up to Belfast more often."

She hesitates, says finally, "Are you propositioning me, Thomas?"

He flushes. "Not exactly," he says sheepishly, "but would you mind if I was?"

"No," she laughs. "I'd turn you down, but I'd be pleased!" Then adds in a teasing voice, "For a minute there, I thought you might be wanting to make a good woman of me."

It's turning out all wrong. He's thought all week about asking her to marry him. Why can't he do it!

He takes her hand. "You *are* a good woman, Eileen, the best that I know," he says sincerely. Then with a tremor of conscience, blurts out, "I love you, Eileen!" There, he's done it! "I'd ask you to marry me, if I thought you'd say yes." And now, shamelessly, is weasling his way out of it.

He has a sudden sharp sense of loss. "I don't want to give you up, Eileen."

"Maybe you won't have to," she says. She puts his hand to her face. "Maybe, if we're lucky, we can become good friends." Eyes shining, she lies back on her pillow, letting him go.

He stands up, misty-eyed. "I'll stay in touch," he says.

"I'll be counting on it," she tells him.

He trips over the chair and blunders out of the room. He feels drained. What he wants is to go out and get drunk. But in Belfast on Sundays all the pubs are shut tight. Besides, Morphy, upstairs in the men's wing, is expecting him.

3

He was one sick son of Eire, a high-burning Hibernian. He felt rotten. He had two broken ribs, some second-degree burns, and a puncture in his left lung, but he was going to get well and would be feeling a lot better, given time, the doctor has told him. The puncture was small and the operation a success. He'd been reminded of a joke about the stalk of celery who'd just undergone an operation and, waking from the anesthetic, asked the surgeon, "How am I, Doc?" The surgeon replied, "Well, I've some good news for you, and some bad. First the good news. The operation was a success. The bad news, I'm afraid you'll remain a vegetable for the rest of your life."

He'd told the joke to Dr. McInerney, a dour Scot who'd barely cracked a smile, but assured him earnestly he wasn't going to be a vegetable for the rest of his life. The prognosis was good, he just had to be patient. He'd asked how long it would be before he was up and around. A month, McInerney told him, maybe three weeks if he kept on improving at this rate.

Three whole weeks or more of lying flat on his back in this bleak hole of a hospital, he thought miserably. Patience wasn't one of his strong points. He'd be demented by that time, with nothing to do but lie still and stare at the cracks in the dirty ceiling. There was no relief from the monotony and the drabness, the dank cold and the gloom, and it still hurt him to take a deep breath. Even the nurses were drab, dried-up, unsmiling old witches, though there was one young student nurse who brought him his meals and fed him, and sometimes laughed at his sallies, saying "Ah, it's a devil you are, Mr. Morphy, you truly are!"

The nights were the worst. He had nightmares still, remembering the searing pain, the scorching heat of the flames, reliving the panic in those last minutes before O'Hare had pulled him free of the wheel and out of the burning Rover.

O'Hare had ridden with him in the ambulance to the hospital. He had a vague memory of swearing to O'Hare then that there'd never been anything serious between him and Agnes. It was a noble lie, a sort of last Act of Contrition, because he thought he was dying and wanted to ease the man's mind. O'Hare stayed with him until they wheeled him into the operating theater. Later, when he came to, he had a kind of a dream of O'Hare bending over his bed, saying, "You're going to be fine. I'll be back before you know it. Hang in there, Paddy." He hopes it wasn't a dream. He'll be glad to see the old buzzard again.

Funny how his feelings for O'Hare have changed. Sad to say, they haven't for the future Mrs. O'Hare. Sick as he is, his prick still perks up at the thought of her. It's all this lying around in the bed that does it, the sheet and the blankets pressing down on his cock making him hornier than a rutting goat. Impossible to vent his ravening lust. It is Sunday; there are a lot of visitors about. He finds himself envisioning various graphic possibilities as he gropes for her, fondles her, enters her. And starts guiltily on seeing her fiancé standing quietly at the foot of his bed.

He shuts his eyes quickly, hoping O'Hare hasn't glimpsed the images mirrored there.

"Hi," he says weakly

"Sorry I woke you. Shall I come back later?"

"No, stay, I was just dreamin'."

"I've brought you some clips from the Dublin papers to cheer you. Full of your heroic exploits. They'll be givin' you a parade with a brass band when you get back."

O'Hare hands him the packet and a book as well. "And here's something for improving your mind, some love stories of Edna O'Brien's."

"Love stories?" he says startled. Just what he needs . . . "Thanks, O'Hare." He'd like to look at the clips but puts them aside thinking he'll save them for later to fill the time when O'Hare's gone and he's alone.

"Don't think I'm ungrateful," he tells him, "but I'd rather have a manual instructing me on how to get out of here."

"What's wrong?"

"I can't stand the place. Couldn't you pull some strings to spring me?"

"You're better off in the hospital till the lung's healed."

"I'd settle gladly for Mercy Hospital, if I have to. I can't stand these frigid foreigners. They never smile."

"You're looking good, complexion pink as a newborn babe's."

"I'm feverish with longing for dear old Dublin."

"I'll try to see what can be done. But you don't want to rush things. Incidentally, your mother and sister send love. They talked with the doctor and he told them to wait a bit before coming to visit. It worried them."

"I asked him to put them off for a while. I don't think I could stand the moanin' and snifflin'."

"I promised I'd drive them up when you're feeling stronger, next week maybe."

"Don't. I'd only have a relapse."

O'Hare gives him a grin, but looks to him sad and beat up, like a worn-out old pugilist. "Are you okay?" he asks. "You look like you could use a bit of hospital care yourself. I'd be glad to let you have my bed, though I don't recommend the place."

"I'm all right, overworked is all. The station's a lunatic asylum these days. Riley's wild with the glory of the capture of Henley's compatriots. Can't stop giving interviews to the newspapers.

You'd think he caught them himself, single-handed. If we weren't a Republic, I'm sure he'd expect to be knighted."

Paddy raises himself on his elbows. "Ah sure'n the man's already benighted!" he quips, and gasps as a sharp pain shoots through his chest.

Looking anxious, O'Hare takes hold of him. "Easy there! Don't be jumpin' around!" And adjusting the pillow, eases him back gently till he's prone again.

"It only hurts when I laugh," he says.

The pain, a reminder of his precarious mortality, turns him serious.

"I never got to say thanks for saving my life."

"I owe you the same. I wouldn't be here if you hadn't been so quick. You did a fine job, you know. First time out and handled yourself like a pro. You're a good partner."

Strong praise from O'Hare! He is unnerved by a sense of his unworthiness, yearns desperately to be decent, virtuous. Like O'Hare, who'd even given blood for him. They were the same blood type. Who would have thought it?

O'Hare muses, "They say when you save a man's life, you're responsible for him for the rest of your time."

Embattled enemies hardly a week ago, now Damon and Pythias! Closer—blood brothers! He feels he's about to start blubbering. It must be the pain and the damned feeling of weakness. "Do they now?" he manages.

"I'm afraid you're stuck with me for life," O'Hare grins.

"I guess that holds true for the two of us," he answers and tenders his hand. They shake solemnly.

O'Hare is getting up, ready to leave. "Soon as you're fit to travel, I'll see can I get you transferred to Mercy."

He hates to see him go. "I hope I'll be out in time for the wedding." He wonders now that they've become sworn buddies if O'Hare will ask him to be best man.

O'Hare, putting on his coat, seems not to have heard.

"Has the date for the nuptials been set yet?" he persists.

"No," O'Hare answers, "not yet."

He is tempted to say "Give my regards to sweet Aggie O'Connell!" but restrains himself discreetly.

4

Well, she'd finally acted on Father Malachy's advice, grudgingly at first she has to admit, and has been amazed to discover that the priest is entirely right, and that her new role as an angel of mercy at Mercy Hospital is remarkably gratifying. Luckily, she doesn't often have to deal with the bedpans.

Assigned as a volunteer aide on the men's ward, she reads to the patients, chats them up, listens to their complaints, soothes their worries, and dispenses good cheer and comfort with an open, not to say profligate, hand. And the men, sick as they are, strive manfully to rise to her tender ministrations. The doctors on staff, too, are all lovely to her.

Making rounds this morning, Dr. Darcy O'Neill takes her aside and, staring deep into her eyes, says with great sincerity, "You have, without a doubt, my dear, what we've come to know as 'the therapeutic personality.' Morale on the ward has improved wonderfully since your arrival! By the way, would you care to have a bite of supper with me tonight?"

She knows he is married and fobs him off, expressing regret. So sorry, she has a small son and is reluctant to leave him at night.

Well, why not lunch one day soon at Caesar's? Lovely place, does she know it? Or perhaps an early dinner, which might give them a little more time together?

She looks doubtful.

"I'm sure we could lay on a sitter for the evening," he urges.

She has no intention of becoming involved with the good doctor, whose reputation as a demon lover has flown far and wide beyond the hospital walls, but is nonetheless titillated by his attentions. Perhaps if she gets to know him better, she might ask him to give her the rabbit test. Could she trust him to be discreet?

She promises to let him know. He presses her shoulder with a soulful expression, brushing her breast delicately as he drops his hand.

Smiling adieu, she walks purposefully back toward the ward and, feeling his eyes tickling her back, cannot resist taking a look. Sure enough, there he stands, dreamy-eyed. (He has, as a matter of fact, been hypnotized by the play of her buttocks as they move silkily under her blue poplin uniform.) He wiggles his fingers at her as he catches her catching him watching her.

Turning, she almost runs into a patient on a gurney being wheeled into one of the private rooms. Of all people — Paddy Morphy! — his color good, his red hair aflame on the white pillow, stirring bittersweet memories. He is alert, looking cheerful, recognizes her.

"Aggie-Maggie," he murmurs, "is it yourself?"

"It is," she says. "And you're looking heroic!"

"Have you come to welcome me back to dear dirty Dublin?"

"I would've, had I known you were coming. I'm working here now."

"What a stroke of luck for me! Can you stop and visit awhile?"

"I'll come back when I get off duty. Around three."

"I'll try to wait patiently," he says, giving her his number one grin.

She knows he can't resist flirting; it's second nature to him. When he's on his deathbed, with the priest administering the last rites, he'll still be trying to make a move on some woman. She's learned recently that he's the sole support of his widowed mother and unmarried sister, and thinks, Poor luv, he'll stay a bachelor the rest of his life.

Strangely enough, she bears him no grudge, even though he's ruined the great opportunity she had for restoring her life. Any bitterness she feels now is strictly reserved for O'Hare. If that big galumph ever truly loved her, he'd never have walked out of her house, out of her life the cold way he did. Even the saints sinned and were forgiven!

The memory of their last meeting still has the power to rise up and torture her.

Back on the ward, she is abstracted with her charges, her mind busy sorting out possibilities for resolving her problems, rehearsing a scene in which O'Hare, pining with love for her, returns in despair to beg *her* forgiveness. *"My love for you is dead," she tells him. "I could never put my trust in you again. Besides, I've found someone else. We're to be married very soon." He gets down on his knees to her, but she is sweetly adamant. "It's too late," she tells him* . . . as pandemonium breaks loose in the ward.

Perky Frankie Finnerty, usually the soul of sweetness and good nature, has suddenly turned cantankerous. Feeling neglected, he is shouting demands and reproaches. Caught up in a contagion of dissatisfaction, half the men have started acting up. Even poor timid old Mr. Malloy, disturbed by her lack of attention, cries out anxiously and in desperation wets his bed. "Too late, too late!" he weeps softly. The words toll like a bell in her head as she changes his sheets. She manages to soothe the men down and restore some semblance of order, but is glad when it's finally three o'clock.

As she pushes open the door to Paddy's room, she sees he has two women visitors. "I didn't know you'd company," she says, stopping in the doorway. "I don't want to make a crowd."

"Not a'tall, not a'tall," the one sitting by the bed says, and gets up from her chair. "We were just leaving. Come in, come in."

Paddy introduces his mother and sister. The two women look drab and drawn, as like as two peas in a pod, except the mother turns out to be garrulous, and the daughter fidgety quiet.

"I'm afraid we've worn him out with our worrying," Mrs. Morphy goes on. "I'm sure he'll be glad of a fresh face. And such a pretty one!" She addresses these remarks at Paddy, speaking loud and slow as if he were deaf or a moron, meanwhile darting anxious glances at Agnes.

"Well, we'd better be off. Say good-bye to your brother, Fiona. We'll come by again in the morning, Son. You won't let him get lonely now, will you, Mrs. O'Connell?" She pats the bed nervously where Paddy's feet stick up under the covers. He winces slightly, shifting his feet to safety.

"Well, come along now, Fiona."

The sister, looking glum, says, "Pleased to make your acquaintance," and flounces out. At the door, Mrs. Morphy whispers to Agnes, "If you could spare a moment, I'd be glad of a word with you," and draws her out into the corridor where the daughter is waiting, frowning and twisting her gloves.

"Is he going to be all right, do you think?" the mother asks anxiously. "The doctor says he's a punctured lung but it's healing nicely." She sighs heavily. "Can you believe what they tell you?"

"Ah, Mrs. Morphy, I'm sure the doctor wouldn't deceive you. And he looks so well, doesn't he? A good sign! They'd never have let him make the trip down from Belfast if he wasn't mending."

"Bless you, bless you!" the mother says. "Go into him now. He'll be sore at me for taking you away. He loves company— always did. And I know you won't tire him." She smiles sadly and says, "Are you ready then, Fiona? Come along then."

"How's O'Hare these days?" is the first thing he says to her.

"I couldn't say," she answers fliply. "I haven't seen him in nearly a month. It looks like the engagement is off."

"Dear Jesus!" he says. "Is that the truth?"

"So far," she says, "it looks like it is."

"Oh Lord, Aggie, I'm sorrier than I can say."

"I thought you'd be glad," she responds dryly.

He flushes. "I guess I deserve that." He takes her hand and holds it. Not flirtatious now, he seems as earnest as a young acolyte taking his vows. "You know, O'Hare saved my life. I owe him something for that."

"I heard you saved his."

"They tell me I did. Which makes the tie between us even stronger."

She remembers a tie of another sort between the three of them, but holds her tongue.

"O'Hare says, when you save a man's life, you're responsible for him for the rest of your days."

Has he taken to quoting O'Hare now?

"And when I needed a transfusion, he was the one gave his blood for me."

He looks at her pleadingly. "I'm crazy about you, Aggie, I guess I always will be, but you know I'm not free to marry. And O'Hare's by far the better man."

And is he now pressing O'Hare's suit?

"My one wish is for the three of us to be friends."

Rejected by O'Hare and deserted now by Paddy with this bland offer! Pulling her hand free, she says, "Well, you're two-thirds there. I'm your friend and it seems you and O'Hare are friends, but I doubt O'Hare and I will ever complete that circle!"

A devil of mischief lights up his face. "I'm counting on it. When the ambulance was taking me along to the hospital in Belfast, O'Hare came along with me. I swore to him then with my dying breath that nothing ever happened twixt the two of us."

"You didn't! He never believed you?"

"He assured me he did."

"You'll wind up in hell, Paddy Morphy!"

"Then we're likely to meet there. You never told him the truth either, it seems, did you?"

"No, not exactly. But I've every intention of!"

"Don't do it, Aggie! 'A truth that's told with mean intent, beats all the lies you might invent.' The man's still in love with you, Aggie. He's sure to come back."

Confusion and disorder! O'Hare, back a month, believes her innocent and never called her? Surely O'Hare must have known Paddy was lying!

Her heart battering away, she manages a laugh. "Hah! I'm not sure I'd have him now if he came crawling to me on his knees!"

Does she mean it?

Mulling it over on the bus going home, she tries to still her bewildered heart, to sort out her feelings — is there a grain of truth in what she'd just said to Paddy, that she wouldn't have O'Hare back if he came to her on his knees? — and is suddenly convinced there is! But what if he were to return, not begging, but — surely the more likely possibility, if he ever came back at all — offering nobly instead to forgive her? . . .

She sees him, Thomas St. Francis O'Hare, not on his knees this time, but standing over her as she lies prostrate at his feet.

"Rise up, Agnes Magdalen," he says, lifting her up compassionately. "I've come to forgive you . . ." His figure shimmers in a nimbus of light, his halo blinds her. "I've erased from my memory all trace of your past transgressions. We'll start afresh, shall we? After all, who among us has not fallen from grace? And loving means forgiving, doesn't it?"

Agnes Magdalen, eyes brimming, stands mutely, humbly before him. Why doesn't she answer? What can she be thinking? Hasn't she been waiting all along for this golden moment of reconciliation?

A wild turbulence stirs in her breast as she gets off the bus. The idea of spending the rest of her life as a peccant sinner, apologizing for every move she makes, O'Hare watchful of every step she takes, makes her gorge rise! Yes, she longs for him to come back, yearns for that sweet moment when, in response to his puling offer to forgive her, she answers vengefully, "No thanks, O'Hare! You can take your kind of love and stick it!"

Timmy is home and champing at the bit when she arrives after five. He is contentious these days, often angry with her, misses O'Hare. But she feels she's become better with him. The men on the ward have schooled her in patience.

"You promised you'd help with my costume!" he greets her, scolding. "You're always late!"

It's All Hallow's Eve. She's completely forgotten! "Sorry, luv!" she says, "I got held up paying a sick call on a friend."

"Is it O'Hare?" he asks anxiously. "He's not sick, is he?"

"Not O'Hare, his buddy, Detective Lieutenant Patrick Morphy. Remember? We read about him in the papers."

"There's good news," he says, suddenly brightening. "Have you heard? The trial's over!"

"Is it?" she asks, her heart quickening. "Where'd you hear that?"

"I bet O'Hare'll start coming round again, now that he's not so busy."

"I wouldn't count on it."

"Why not?"

"I told you. We had a disagreement."

"But P.A. says you'll be having the engagement party any day now. He mentioned he has a grand surprise for me, and I'll be getting it then."

"What were you doing in Delehanty's?"

"Nothing. I wasn't in Delehanty's. I was just passing by. He was outside and caught me on my way back from school." He looks at her coaxingly. "Why don't you call O'Hare and ask him over?"

"I'm not about to do that."

"Why not? You're always saying when I have a disagreement to talk it out, not to fight. How about if I call him for you?"

"Thanks, luv, but no."

"You never follow the advice you give me!"

She's worn out with his pestering. "Have you eaten?"

"I had a snack." He looks at her sullenly.

"Is Michael Finnegan going along with you? I don't want you roamin' the streets alone."

"Yes! And I'm late!. What am I goin' to dress up in? I'm supposed to meet him in five minutes!"

"Calm down. We'll have you set in no time."

He continues to fume as she dresses him in an old black silk skirt of hers that comes down to his ankles, and ties it at the midriff with a crimson scarf. She adds a long-sleeved red jersey and a plaid wool stole, wrapped around his shoulders and waist to keep the chill off. He refuses to wear his anorak. His Adidas peek out below the skirt.

"Hurry up, will you?" he keeps saying. She dabs a spot of rouge on each cheek, pencils a beauty mark at the corner of his sweet mouth. A harlequin mask completes the disguise.

He looks absurd and gorgeous.

He stares at himself in the hall mirror. "I look awful!" he wails.

"You look grand!" She hands him one of her tote bags lined with plastic for his booty. "Remember, no candy! Or cookies! Just coins for the Children's Fund. Here's the box."

He disappears into his room for a moment, riffles through a drawer, while she trails after, spouting advice. "You can take fruit for yourself, if it's offered. But don't eat anything till you get home and I see it's all right. And I want you back not later than eight. That's an order!"

"You're always giving me orders!"

"Sorry, luv," she says, "I should have said please," and tries to hug him. He brushes her off and escapes, slamming the door.

From the window she watches him running off down the street, wrapped in scarves and anger.

5

He's sure Mike'll be waiting outside for him, hopping mad because he's late, but there's no sign of him, though there are lots of kids out on the street, and when he rings the bell, he hears Mr. Finnegan booming out from inside, "Will the damn doorbell never stop ringing this night? If it keeps up, I'll disconnect it, I swear!"

"Ah, be quiet, will you?" Mrs. Finnegan shouts back as she comes to the door, looking red in the face and cross. She stares at him for a minute and says doubtfully, "Is it you, Timothy O'Connell?"

He's pleased she has trouble recognizing him; his disguise must be better than he thought. "Is Mike ready?" he asks.

"Mike's going nowhere tonight, I'm sorry to tell you!" She doesn't seem sorry at all, just angry. "He's being punished, and I'm keeping him in."

Baffled, he says lamely, "Ah, too bad. I was sort of counting on him." He thinks he can hear Mike from somewhere inside snuffling away, and wonders should he ask to come in, but decides better not. He stands on the stoop, uncertain whether to ask for a treat, then says, "Well, I'll be off then."

"Hold on a minute," she tells him and, fishing in her apron pocket, comes up with a couple of coins which she drops in the UNICEF box. "I'm clean out of cookies," she says. "Will you have a banana?" and she pulls one off the bunch in a bowl on a table in the foyer and holds it out to him. He pops it into the tote bag and says, "Thanks, Mrs. Finnegan. Tell Mike I'll see him tomorrow," and skips off.

It's still fairly light when he gets to the High Street, though clouds are scudding up, covering the weak glow of the sun. A gang of kids is roaming about, shouting and laughing, going in and out of the shops, and he feels a bit lonely out on his own, but he goes along swinging his tote bag and rattling his box at the grown-ups passing by, some of them stopping to drop a few coppers in, which cheers him a bit.

He feels sort of funny dressed up as a girl, but it's an important part of the scam he's thought up to fool O'Hare. He'd gotten the idea from a story O'Hare once told him about a thief who'd disguised himself as a woman and hocked his loot under a false name. The name he planned to use was Scarlett O'Hare. It seemed such a clever ruse, and people were always telling his mother how smart he was for a kid only eight. He wasn't sure he'd be able to fool O'Hare, wasn't sure he really wanted to. It was like playing the game of hide-and-seek with him — he loved the excitement and didn't mind it when O'Hare caught him, maybe even enjoyed it more.

Passing Delehanty's crowded with kids, he decides not to go in till later. The place he's headed for might be closing soon. Turning down Sheriff Street, he runs along for two or three blocks till he spots the three gold balls, shining through the dusk. The streets are quieter here. Lifting his skirt, he digs out the small packet he has in his pants pocket, then moves in to peer through the grilled glass door.

The pawnshop looks empty. The bell over the door sets off a rackety clamor, startling him as he pushes the door open. The quiet that follows makes him even more jumpy. He tries to remember the name of the pawnbroker. He saw it outside a number of times while he was casing the joint. Why can't he recall it now?

He calls out "Mister?" — his voice echoing back at him in the musty dark. "Anyone here?" Some musical instruments, suspended from the ceiling, sway overhead.

A wraith rises from behind the counter. He wants to run, but its piercing black eyes are sending off sparks at him through the gloom, pinning him to the spot.

"We-ell," the specter says to him, "is it Halloween we're celebr-r-ratin'? 'Tis not a holiday I favor-r. I buy things and sell things—never-r give 'em away. I'm not in business for char-r-rity!"

The scratchy burr pricks his memory, bringing the pawnbroker's name to mind. "Mr. McGregor?" He stops, uncertain how to go on. He hadn't expected the man to be so scary.

Mr. McGregor leans over the counter. "We-ell, what d'ye have to say, little missy? Ar-re ye goin' to stand ther-re all night, wastin' your-r time and me own?"

Little missy! The words stir him to life. "I've something to pawn, sir," he says, pushing the packet onto the counter.

"Now, what have we he-r-re?" the pawnbroker says, unwrapping it. "Some jewel-r-ry, is it?" And poking a small black casing into his eye, proceeds to examine the earring.

"It's a beauty," he says, dropping the black glass from his eye. "Whe-r-re's the other-r?"

"I've only the one," Tim says.

"I couldn't give ye aught for it, without its mate."

"But it's a real diamond. It must be worth something."

"Tr-rue. But if anyone was inclined to be buyin' it, they'd be wantin' the pair-r."

"I don't mean to sell it. I'm only pawning it."

"Sor-r-ry, dear-rie," he says. "I've no use for a single ear-r-ring." He puts it back in the paper but continues to hold on to it.

What a fiasco! There's another hockshop not too far off. Maybe he'll try there, if it isn't too late.

He reaches out for the packet.

"On the other-r hand, I might be inter-rested in the br-racelet ye'r-re wearin'. That could be wor-rth quite a few shillin's. R-real silver-r, is it?" He points to the medic-alert bracelet Tim is wearing. His mother'd given it to him after the first time he'd been in the hospital and he'd be glad to be rid of it, but he isn't about to let the man see it. It has a stick with wings at the top and two snakes curling round it engraved on one side, and his name on the other with some code that says what's wrong with him.

He isn't expecting the grab the pawnbroker makes for his wrist, but he reacts like lightning, pulling his arm free, and before the man has a chance to take a good look at it, he goes bolting out of the shop, not stopping till he's back on the High Street, when he suddenly realizes — worst luck — he's gone and left the earring behind!

What to do!

O'Hare would know. He could give him a call. Maybe P.A. will let him use his telephone. He won't be able to say much with Delehanty listening in; he'll just say he needs to see him. O'Hare would certainly be able to get the earring back.

If his Mum ever finds out, she'll never let him hear the end of it! Maybe O'Hare wouldn't have to tell her. It could be their secret.

A flash of glitter lights up the sky — a red, blue, and silver rocket. A sudden burst of firecrackers goes off, sounding like the rat-a-tat-tat of a machine gun.

Two white-sheeted ghosts and a skeleton straggle by, calling "Trick or treat! Trick or treat!" A big kid, not in costume, is spraying dirty words on shop walls and the sidewalk. He stops to watch. The guy calls out "Hi, Sweetie!" and aims the can at him. "Bug off!" he shouts boldly and runs off, heading for Delehanty's.

A Hair perhaps, Divides the False and
True . . .

OMAR KHAYYÁM

1

O'Hare is in at the bar at O'Donaghues's at five o'clock on All
Hallow's Eve, ostensibly celebrating the triumphant termina-
tion of the state's case against the O.F.F. terrorists. He is having
a few farewell pints with his good friend O'Meara, who's due
to catch the six-forty-five back to Belfast. The place is mobbed,
the crowd rowdy with excitement, strangers slapping him on
the back, buying him drinks. Presently into his sixth, or is it
his seventh pint, he should by rights be flying through the air
with the greatest of ease by now, but is instead still weightily
earthbound; is, in fact, suffering from an acute case of the
megrims.

O'Meara, on the other hand, is drunk as a lord and loftily
holding court at the bar. "The cockatrice," O'Meara is pontificat-
ing over the din, "though resembling the cockroach in some
ways, belongs to another *spe-cious* altogether!" He takes a long
draught from his glass and goes on. "It is, in fact, a serpent with a
deadly glance, hatched by a reptile from a cock's egg on a

dunghill." O'Meara has been trying to cheer him, but so far has made little headway.

It has been, admittedly, a rough several weeks, but all in all, things have turned out better than anyone, himself included, could have expected—the Belfast mission a success; Kelsey Owens captured, convicted, and sent up for life; Peel dead, shot by one of the Queen's soldiers, sparing the Republic the trouble and expense of trying him; Henley, testifying as a state's witness, given ten years with possible time off for good behavior; Paddy Morphy recovering, moved down just this morning from Belfast to Mercy Hospital; and Eileen, though still convalescent, now out of danger. One possible flaw—the man known as the Wizard, responsible according to Owens for masterminding the Dublin plot, may have slipped through the net, though rumor has it he was actually the third personna of the man known as John White/ Jonny Black. Case closed. The culprits dead or behind bars. And he and Morphy to be cited as heroes by the P.M. at a ceremony scheduled for the next week, when Paddy's due to be let out of hospital. Everything neatly wrapped up and tied with a ribbon. Why, in God's name, should he be feeling so melancholy?

"Now, ain't that a marvelous piece of information!" one of the men standing next to O'Meara remarks. "Tell me, have you ever seen ary one of 'em."

"One of which?" O'Meara asks.

"Them cock-a-trices?"

"Not in recent memory," O'Meara answers. "And would you like me to be tellin' you why?"

"Would you do that?"

"For the simple reason there's not a one left in the whole of Ireland! Neither cockatrices, nor serpents neither. St. Patrick got rid of the lot of 'em for us, together with the snakes, sent them all slitherin' into the sea. And that's the true of it—scuttling into the sea from Lough Derg, County Donegal. And wasn't it on that very day his miraculous vision of purgatory came to him? Now, if you've ever been to Lough Derg, you'd know why that perilous sight appeared to him in that place. For 'tis an exact replica of the entrance to Hades." Draining his glass, O'Meara says, "Here, let's have another round."

"Don't be sayin' a word against Donegal, Mr. O'Meara, if you please," the barkeep interjects. "Me sainted mother was born there."

"My sincere apologies, Mike. Would you make it two double Jamesons for me and the brave captain here? And could we have them at the table over there?" He bows to the crowd with grave dignity, "If you'll excuse us?" and, taking O'Hare in tow, pushes through to a table in the far corner. A waiter follows with the drinks.

"*Slainté!*" O'Meara says, raising his glass.

"*Slainté!*" O'Hare answers. He picks up his glass, then puts it down again without drinking.

"Drink up!"

"I'll nurse it a bit."

"I've got to be off in a few minutes. I hate to leave you, the state that you're in."

"I'm all right, just tired is all."

"You look about as cheerful as a pallbearer at your best friend's funeral. Is it my imminent departure that's troubling you?"

"Not a bit. I'll be only too glad to be rid of the sight of you."

"Well, parting's not always sweet sorrow. Why don't you give her a call?"

"Who?"

"The lady from Clontarf."

"Lay off, O'Meara," he says irritably.

"D'ya want to hear old Doc O'Meara's diagnosis?"

"You'll be late for your train."

"Postpartum depression, on two counts," O'Meara goes on. "The case of the state versus Henley and Owens is over and you're feeling let down after all the excitement. It's natural, but only temporary. But the case of O'Hare versus O'Connell is still pending, and that seems harder to settle."

"It's over, I tell you! Finished! Ended!"

"Maybe. But it appears she's still much in your mind."

"Only at moments like this!" he lies and goes on angrily, "What do you expect? I was going to marry her! I thought she was in love with me." He gulps half his whiskey and, cocking his head comically, sputters out his venom. "It seems she was only in lust with me!"

"Don't knock it, O'Hare."

Once O'Meara has got him going, he finds it hard to leave off. He empties his glass. He can feel himself melting, turning maudlin.

"You know, for a while there, she lit a candle in my heart."

"That's a lovely thought."

"She was a blaze of a woman!" Why is he talking about her as if she's dead? "And completely immoral!"

"A hard combination to beat . . ."

"Laugh, if you want to! You know what I miss the most?"

"I can guess."

He grins ruefully, "That, too. No, it's the boy. I miss Tim. I feel I've let him down. And I miss the damn arguments! Did I tell you she'd a terrible temper?"

"Once or twice. It may be that you're well rid of her. There's nothing worse than a peevish shrew, though I gather she had other virtues."

"Tell you the truth, I can't think of a one." He tries, but all he can recall is her devilish beguiling smile and all the other terrible faults that had seduced him. "T'hell with it all, O'Meara! Let's have another drink."

O'Meara looks at his watch. "I've about ten minutes to catch my train."

"Och, they're always late!"

They stop at the bar for a quick one. "Two for the road. On the house," Mike says as he pours.

O'Meara proposes, "Here's to old friends and new loves!"

"To old friends!" O'Hare says.

They clink glasses.

"I'll be taking a cab to the station. Can I drop you?"

"No, I'll walk. I could use the air."

They exit together.

After the snug heat of the bar, the cold air of the street hits him a blow. He sees O'Meara into a cab and leans toward him, his head swimming. "Give my love to Peg."

"Come up to Belfast soon. And take care of yourself!"

"Thanks, O'Meara."

They shake hands.

Feeling suddenly lorn, he watches the cab disappear. He wonders if he ought to have another pint to fend off the chill, but decides against it. Three miles to home — a long way to those cheerless two rooms. Never mind, the walk will do him good.

He pulls back his shoulders, buttons his jacket, turns up his collar, and tossing the scarf round his neck, lurches boldly forward — cutting, he feels, a jaunty figure. Missing the curb, he stumbles and, feet flying, finds himself sprawled in the gutter.

A cascade of multicolored sparks lights up the sky — Roman candles exploding over gray Dublin. A gang of witches and pirates, brandishing sparklers, shooting off cap pistols, surrounds him, shrieking for tribute. They help him up. He distributes coins lavishly. A blond pirate reminds him a little of Tim.

Is the boy out trick-or-treating tonight, he wonders. Why not call and find out?

Is he daft, or what! It's the drink playing tricks on him. But after all, why not? She'd said, "Call if you feel like it, when you get back." Well, he's back almost a month, and hasn't felt like it! Not true! He's had the impulse a dozen times, but managed each time to stop himself, determined not to give in to his weakness. Even dialed the number once, but hung up at the last minute, afraid if he heard her voice again, he'd be gone again, lost to all reason.

Luckily he's over that now. Now that he's no longer in love with her, what's the risk?

He might give her a ring — not tonight, in a week or so maybe — to ask after Tim, inquire if he could take the boy off for an afternoon's outing. Courteous, polite. None of that desperate "I-miss-you-m'cushlah" stuff.

You were *in love with* her once, you never *loved* her, he admonishes himself sternly. Remember that! And remembering, goes tittupping through the tulips of his memories, gathering up all the garish red, yellow, and purple blossoms of their wondrous days and nights together . . .

The sight of her rump and her horse's, romping in rhythm through the mist of the early morning, when they'd gone riding through the woods in Galway . . . The lost look on her face as she leaned out of the cab, the day of the explosion when Timmy was missing, begging him "Call soon, O'Hare!" . . . The happiness he'd felt — it seems only yesterday, it seems eons gone — when, heart beating high, he'd stood on her doorstep and said, "Will you have me, Aggie? Say yes! Say you will!" . . .

Well, that was all over and done with! He'd closed the iron door on her! But she was still clamoring away, locked in the dungeon of his heart.

In Belfast, on his way to the hospital, Paddy had sworn nothing had happened between the two of them. The poor bugger thought he was dying. He wouldn't be lying if he thought he was dying, would he?

Och! They were all liars, himself included! Hadn't he lied to Paddy when he said he believed him? And to Eileen in her hospital bed, with her heartbreaking smile and her poor shorn head, telling her he loved her, yet unable to bring himself to ask her to marry him. He'd even, like the idiot he was, half-suggested they might still be lovers. She'd had the good sense to fob him off, but the offer had seemed to cheer her. And after all, what was so wrong with that?

And hadn't he lied to Agnes the last miserable time he saw her, when he said he could understand her taking Paddy into her bed, that what he minded was her not trusting him enough to tell him the truth and, worse than that, her corrupting the child? She'd sworn then that she'd never asked Timmy to lie for her. Somehow he believed that part, though it wasn't much solace.

But the biggest lie of all was hers—when she'd said, "It's you I love, Thom! God knows that's the truth!"

Of all the great liars, Aggie's the Queen
The only one not a liar is gentle Eileen . . .

Wrong! Even Eileen had lied, lied to him about her name. But she'd only done it to protect her brother. And how could you fault her for that?

There were all sorts of lies it seems. Some were pure evil, some seemed right, or at least justified. Maybe some lies were better than the truth?

He looks up at the sky, seeking a judgment. The harvest moon, low on the horizon, glows like a lamp, but does not light his way. The stars twinkle indifferently. His legs weary with walking, his mind a muddle of doubt and confusion, he sits down on the curb and stares up at her house.

No lights on.

Early in their courtship he'd advised her to leave a night light burning, a simple precaution against burglars. She'd looked at him, her eyes laughing, mocking him. "I'm sometimes lonely," she said. "I don't think I'd mind, so long as he was a friendly robber."

Even her bedroom upstairs is dark. He stares at the window and before he can blot out the image, sees her again, standing there before the mirror, brushing her hair . . . How he longs to be shut of her, to be rid of her face, her grace, and with them, all of her haunting witchery! But he still feels this terrible need to lace it into her for betraying him, lying to him.

He may be peloothered, but he knows now what he needs to do. He'll knock down her door, drag her out, and give her the bashing she deserves!

In three quick strides he's across the street and ringing her doorbell.

Silence.

He rings again, two long peals.

Still no answer.

Past supper time and no one at home! Where has she got to? And where's the child? Shipped off to some neighbor while she's off gallivanting somewhere?

He hammers the door with his fist. It swings open.

Unlocked? What kind of a reckless fool is she, leaving the door off the latch, an invitation to any mad thug skulking about, waiting his chance to come in and ravish her!

He hears footsteps overhead, hears her voice calling down "Timmy?" and sees her at last, swiftly descending the stair, her face flushed and earnest. She is wearing her green silken robe and, with a towel, drying her hair, a tousle of burnished gold.

She stops at the foot of the stair, her eyes wide and startled.

"Dea te saich," he says, his voice sounding strange and boorish in his ears. "May I come in?" But he is already inside, not waiting for her reply.

"You left your door open!" he says angrily.

"I didn't!" she answers. "You battered it in with your banging!"

"I've come here to settle a few things between us!"

"Settle away!" she says hotly, folding her arms over her bosom, standing there waiting, the brazen chippie, defying him.

He leans over her, his eyes dark with threat, feels her quick angry breath warm on his cheek—and as if in a dream, puts his hands on her hips and moves her close to him.

She drops the towel and lets out a cry.

Why is she weeping? He hasn't hit her!

He crushes her close, kissing her breasts through her robe. She throws her arms round his neck, kissing him wildly all over his face.

Still holding her, he tries to disentangle his scarf, remove his jacket.

"No, no," she pleads, "Tim will be back any minute." But she continues to kiss him.

"She loves me!" he tells his astonished heart.

Her robe falls away.

She's in a rage to be loved.

He's in a rush to comply.

2

When he gets to Delehanty's, he finds the shop closed and shuttered. His heart sinks. Now what? If he could get one of the coppers out of his box, he might call O'Hare from one of the coin phones up the street. He shakes it, turning it upside down, but nothing comes out. He needs wire or a pin, something to fish it out with. He'd once watched some kids stick some chewing gum on the end of a bent wire hanger and lift some coins up with it from under a grating, but he doesn't have gum or a wire, and anyway it wouldn't work for this. A magnet on a string maybe, but it would have to be small enough to slip through the box's slim opening. Anyway, he can forget that idea. He hasn't the money to buy a magnet and Madigan's is closed by now, so he couldn't even try to filch one.

He rattles the door, hoping P.A. will hear him, then beats a tattoo on the glass with the rim of the box.

"Hah! Got you!" a voice says loud in his ear. Someone's grabbed him from behind and is holding him tight.

He's scared to death, but only for a second till he recognizes the voice. "Hi!" he says quickly, twisting around. "It's only me, Timmy O'Connell!" He remembers Delehanty being robbed awhile back, and wonders if the little baker thought he was trying to break in.

"Let's have a look at you!" says P.A., holding on to him. "Now why would a pretty little girl like you be pretending she's Timothy O'Connell?"

"No, really!" he says, stripping off his mask. "It's really me!"

P.A. makes a face of comical astonishment. "Timmy? You rascal! Who could have guessed? You had me deceived entirely!"

"Did I now?" he says, enjoying the game though he guesses P.A. is only pretending.

"I was hoping you'd stop by," Delehanty tells him. "I was just out to pick up the late papers and was afraid I might miss you."

"I can't stay long," he says as P.A. lets go and starts to unlock the door. "I promised my Mum I'd be home by eight." He'd like to ask if he can use the phone right away, but doesn't want to seem rude.

"Ah, it's not nearly that yet, you've plenty of time. Come along in, I've something to show you."

Holding his hand, Delehanty leads him through the shop and into the back room full of shelves stacked with cakes and candies and goodies. The delicious smells in the closed shop make his head swim.

"Let's fill up your bag first, shall we? Here, let me have it."

"I'm not supposed to have sweets."

"Don't I know that!" P.A. takes a box down from a shelf. "These were made *pour toi, surtout* — just for you, Tim — no sugar, no chocolate, and *delicieux.*" He starts to open the box, then quickly closes it and sets it down on the table. "If you give us a kiss, I'll let you see what's inside."

Tim gives him a quick peck on the cheek. P.A. sits down on a bench and draws him close. "Here, let's take off some of these wraps first. Much too warm in here for all this. Wouldn't want you to be catching cold now, would we?" Unwinding the scarf and opening Tim's shirt a button or two, P.A. runs his fingers inside, along Tim's neck and chest, rubbing gently. "What a sweet child you are," he murmurs, his jolly face turning pink with pleasure. "Shall we take a look now?" he says as he continues to pet him. "Go on, open it!"

The sight inside takes Tim's breath away, a tiny menagerie with a lion and a tiger and a funny baboon and all sorts of marvelous miniature creatures smelling of peppermint and vanilla and some other heavenly scents. His eyes wide, his mouth watering, Tim says, "Oh, P.A.! They're wonderful! Are they all for me?"

"They are, every one. Now how about a hug?" He pulls Tim over, gathering him onto his lap, and gives him a long wet kiss on the mouth, at the same time rocking him in his arms.

Tim squirms, wanting to get away, but is held fast.

"I'm not a baby, you know!" he gasps, trying to wriggle free.

"I know," the baker says breathlessly, "but don't you like to be cuddled? Even grown-ups like to be petted and cuddled some-times. Here, wouldn't you like a taste of one of them?"

"I promised my Mum I wouldn't till I got home." He hasn't had a chance to ask for the phone, but all he wants now is to get out of the place. He picks up his scarf and starts to wind it around himself, but Delehanty is hanging on to the ends. "I'd better be off."

"Ah, you don't want to be going already," P.A. says. "You've only just come. Did I ever tell you about the robbery and how those hoodlums tried to rob me and how I scared them half out of their wits till they ran shaking out of the shop?"

P.A. hurriedly opens a cabinet, burrows about, and draws out a long object covered with cloths. Unwrapping it, he holds it up for Tim to see. It's an old musket, oiled and polished, and almost as long as P.A. is high. He lays the rifle down carefully.

"Now that word's got around that I've got this, ready and loaded, no scallywag's likely to come round and try again! And take a look here." He darts up and pulls out a tray. "Here's something I know you've been wanting for the longest while." Nestling in his hand is a chocolate mouse — perfectly molded, its spun-sugar tail and whiskers quivering as though it's alive. "Now what do you say to that?"

"It's a marvel," he says. "But I've really got to get home."

Delehanty, looking disappointed, sets the mouse down on the table. "Don't you like it?"

"I do!"

"It's yours."

Tim is buttoning his jersey.

"Let's have a last kiss then, before you take off," P.A. says and, pulling Tim by the ends of his scarf, starts kissing him on the mouth and the eyes and the neck, hugging and rubbing him, sighing and groaning as if he's having a fit.

"Hey!" Tim says when he's finally able to catch his breath. "Could I just ask you something?"

Should he ask to use the phone? Not now! Pushing hard, he backs his way out of P.A.'s arms and, in an effort to distract the baker and avoid any further clutching, picks up the gun.

"Does it really shoot?"

★ ★ ★

He barely touched the trigger. The recoil knocked him clean off his feet, the blast so loud it kept echoing in his head — waves of sound lapping all about him. There was a haze of blue smoke, and when the air cleared, he saw P.A. lying sprawled out, looking for all the world like a raggedy doll, but it wasn't sawdust seeping out of him. And there were gobs of red spattered all over the shelves, decorating the cakes and the heaped-up cookies and the whipped cream tarts. The box with his menagerie had fallen and the animals lay scattered all over the floor. In a daze, he got up and his eye caught sight of the chocolate mouse, still on the table. He took it up carefully. Luckily, it hadn't been spoiled. He sat down on the floor again, away from P.A., feeling suddenly very tired.

He wished he'd been able to reach O'Hare earlier, but he wasn't at all sure he wanted O'Hare to track him down now.

3

The phone rang.

"I'll get it," he said.

"No, I will," she said and stirred indolently. "What time is it?"

"Just after eight."

She kissed him. "Don't make a move." She picked up her green robe from where it lay on the floor and said smiling, "I'll be back before you know it," and went out of the room.

He put on his pants and went down after her and heard her cry out, "Is it Timmy? Is it my Tim?"

She let out a moan, dropped the phone with a clatter, and sat down on the floor.

"Mrs. O'Connell? Mrs. O'Connell? Are you there?" the voice clicked away on the other end.

He raised her up and, holding her, picked up the phone.

"Who is this?" he said. "What's wrong with Tim? What's happened?"

"Officer Mulroony here. There's been an accident down at Delehanty's. The boy's not hurt—had a bit of a shock. Who's this?"

"Detective Thom O'Hare," he said. "I'll be right down. Tell the boy I said I'll be right there, will you?"

"Yes sir, Captain. I'll do that, sir. Not to worry. Shall I send the squad car for you?"

"Please."

"Tim's all right, Aggie," he told her. "Do you feel up to coming with me?"

"Yes!" she said. "Yes, I'll come! I'll be quick. Let me just find a dress." She stirred herself and, holding on to the rail, climbed the stairs.

An ambulance, lights flashing, stood in front of the place when they got there. Someone slammed a door, and the ambulance took off, siren clanging.

"Have they taken the child without me?" she said fearfully, jumping out of the car.

A crowd of people and some children in Halloween get-up were standing around watching.

A garda in uniform came over. "Captain O'Hare?" he said, saluting.

"Where's the boy?" O'Hare said.

"Inside. The doctor's with him."

"What happened?"

"Delehanty's been shot with that old blunderbuss of his. They just took him off in the ambulance. The child's all right, the doc says. A bit dazed, but you can see for yourself." He took O'Hare aside. "I don't think Mrs. O'Connell ought to go in. The place is a mess."

O'Hare turned to Aggie and said, "Will you wait in the car a minute? I'll bring him out to you."

She let herself be led to the car.

He pushed past the crowd and into the shop. All the lights were on. Tim, wrapped in a blanket, was sitting on one of the counters, not moving, his eyes blank. A man was standing next to him. O'Hare recognized Nolan, the police surgeon.

"Hi, O'Hare," Nolan said, snapping his bag shut. "I've just given him a shot. I spoke to Dr. Vogel, his physician. He thinks the child ought to be hospitalized for observation for a day or so."

"Thanks, Nolan," he said. "I'll take him in the squad car, if that's okay with you."

"Fine."

O'Hare touched the boy. "Tim, lad," he said, "the doctor says you're all right. You're going to be fine."

Tim stared at him dully, then looked away.

He picked the child up, cradling him in his arms.

"I'm not a damn baby, you know!" Tim said. "Have you come back to stay?" he asked angrily.

"Damn right on both counts!" O'Hare said.

The boy laid his head on O'Hare's shoulder and gave him a faint flickering smile.

8

Daily and hourly alarms
Lest the truth should out . . .

THOMAS HARDY

1

After all the excitement with P.A. almost murdered by little Timothy O'Connell, it seems to Jenny O'Flaherty (and she is sure to every other decent soul in Clontarf) *unseemly,* to say the least, for the child's mother to be in such a wild rush to be married. But no doubt the woman has her reasons.

It is to be a small quiet wedding, pushed down to just before Christmas, with only the family and a few close friends in attendance, according to Father Malachy. She herself and her mother, who've always considered themselves close friends and good neighbors, have not received an invitation. Not that they would have dreamed of accepting, knowing what they know of the constant shameless carryings-on in the widow's house next door. O'Hare's son will be best man and his wife (a Prod!) matron of honor, and a colleague of O'Hare's by the name of O'Meara (a Jew!) has been chosen to give the bride away. But the final outrageous note — the concubine's fancy man, the very one she'd seen creeping out of the widow's back door not two months ago, has been invited to attend the ceremony! The bride will be wearing a beige satin gown, made-to-order, in which she looks totally ravishing. (This last maddening detail supplied courtesy of Miss Lizzie Branigan, saleswoman at the MacGuire's Bridal Shop.) If it were up to Jenny, the bride would be dressed in black tar trimmed with feathers, and have a scarlet *A* branded on her bosom.

A hot flush of guilt sweeps over her. And who is it that must bear the responsibility for this miserable mis-marriage? Who else but innocent, tenderhearted, foolish Jenny O'Flaherty! For wasn't it she herself, God forgive her, who'd first introduced O'Hare to the woman?

If only the poor betrayed bridegroom-to-be had answered the letter she'd sent him, things would surely have turned out differently. Sad to say, it appears she has waited until too late to profitably pursue the matter, and Delehanty, whom she'd counted on to spread the word, has turned out to be no help at all. Shot not long after she'd let him in on the scandal, he's been *hors de combat* ever since, his shop still shuttered and rumors flying that the little man is planning to sell out and take up permanent residence abroad.

So much for good deeds and noble intentions!

Until recently, she still believed, still felt in her bones, that something would happen to stop the wedding. And when P.A. was shot by the woman's son, her hopes rose. She was sure that would do it. But she was mistaken, for the ceremony has been scheduled for the twentieth at noon, less than a week off now. So little time . . . And yet, is it really too late?

There is something that certainly smells to high heaven about the whole business of the shooting. She didn't believe for a moment P.A. was a "paedasterist"—or whatever name it was people were calling him—a degenerate traducer of small children. It couldn't be true, could it? Why, he looked hardly more than a plump child himself! Yet, how could one be sure? Anything was possible with a Frenchman (and a half-caste at that). And evil abounded everywhere, cropping up in the most unexpected places, even in Clontarf, as she knew only too well. In

America, she'd heard, child molestation was a common practice, daily reported in the newspapers. But what could you expect in a country where tales of nuns marrying priests were advertised in the headlines!

If one discarded, temporarily, Timmy's resistance to P.A.'s lewd advances as a possible motive, then what? If the authorities thought P.A. was guilty, they would certainly have arrested him by now, wouldn't they? *What could have happened to make the child shoot the baker?*

She has been racking her brain for alternative possibilities.

Assuming P.A. is innocent of "paedastery" — or whatever — doesn't necessarily make him innocent of all sin, does it?

What if she'd been mistaken in thinking P.A. had wanted to help her? What if he'd gone straight to the widow and traitorously confided the scandalous news Jenny'd given him? Perhaps even cited its source! Or (she feels she is hot on the scent now), suppose he'd threatened to blackmail the woman!

Could the child, urged on by his mother in a desperate effort to save her forthcoming marriage, have been suborned into shooting the blackmailer? What if the whole story of Delehanty's dreadful diddling was an out-and-out lie, made up by Agnes O'Connell to justify the attempted murder? Her mind reels under a new terrible possibility. If P.A. had named her as his source, her life too may even now be in danger!

She has to find out what actually happened! She has to get at the bottom of it!

She goes to visit P.A., phoning first, a few days before the ceremony.

2

He'd had no regular visitors since he got home, outside of Father Malachy, the old priest who'd come by twice in this week offering to take his confession (he'd declined politely), and so is surprised to hear from, of all people, the old maid O'Flaherty, sounding so genial over the telephone, saying she'd love to stop by for a visit, just to chat, and to bring him some nourishing broth her mother has made specially for him. Beware *une commère* bearing gifts, he thinks, but says yes, please to come, he'd be delighted — impelled more by curiosity than by any desire for her company, though *le bon Dieu* knows how lonely he is these days with the shop closed, missing the bustle and excitement of the old days, no customers coming and going, no shouts and laughter of children running in and out of the shop.

His two employees paid him a visit yesterday, ostensibly to inquire after his health, but actually to collect back wages and to find out if there might be a chance of employment in Paris, once he's opened his shop there. He said perhaps, indicating chances were slim, knowing chances were nil. He is determined to start a new life, make a clean break, sever all connections to Clontarf . . . if he doesn't die of a broken heart first. The gaping wound in his side is almost healed, but there are other wounds from which he fears he may never recover.

Still and all, he feels he has handled things well, considering the circumstances. In hospital, sick as he was, questioned by Captain O'Hare, he'd taken a firm stand. *Under no circumstances was the child to be blamed; the fault for the accident was entirely his own.* He'd known the carbine was loaded, but was certain the catch was locked when Timmy asked to look at the gun. Had no idea how it could have been released. A freak, an unfortunate accident! And he was tormented by the thought that the dear child had been put through such a terrible ordeal, might still be suffering from guilt or concern about what had happened. Still, all's well that ends well, and he himself was already on the mend. And he only hoped the boy would be able to put the whole incident out of his mind and not dwell on it.

Did O'Hare seem satisfied? He wasn't certain. But a few days later, when Mrs. O'Connell came in to see him, whispering that Timmy sent his regards and regrets, and was there anything he might be needing, anything at all she could do for him, he'd felt somewhat easier.

She'd even paid him a second visit, arriving this time with her usual high spirits and friendly air, to tell him the good news — the wedding date had been set to just before Christmas, less than a month off now! O'Hare's family, including the grandchildren, were all coming down from Galway, and they would be having the wedding dinner in the private dining room at Caesar's, and her only regret was that P.A. wouldn't be catering the affair. She'd laughed, protesting, when he said he'd be out of hospital in a few days and he'd love to make her and O'Hare their wedding cake, as a gift, of course. "Oh, P.A.," she'd said, "it would be wonderful! What a dear sweet generous soul you are! But I couldn't dream of letting you go to the bother!" With a bit of persuasion, he'd been able to convince her it would be pure pleasure for him, and no bother at all. And he'd spent the time since he'd gotten home working out the design for the cake. But his plans for a surprise for Tim, and of course the other children, were even more exciting.

He has been testing the special ingredients and has just started working on the molds when he hears a rattle at the front door. Absorbed in his task, he is annoyed at the interruption but, wiping his hands, moves swiftly through the darkened shop to the front door and peers through the shuttered glass. The old maid is standing there, clutching a bulky brown parcel to her chest.

"*Entrez, entrez,* my dear Miss O'Flaherty," he says, unlocking the door, drawing her in and locking the door behind her. "How *gentille* of you to visit this lonely invalid!"

She stands there like a scrawny bird, looking startled.

"Oh," she says, "not at all! Mother and I were so sorry not to have managed to visit you in hospital. Well! You look grand, just grand, Mr. Delehanty."

He knows his complexion is gray. He feels grim these days and looks it, though he's lost some five kilo in weight, which makes his figure appear somewhat sleeker. But how can she tell how he looks in the dark of the shop?

"It's the R and R," he says, leading her carefully through the gloom and up the back stairs to the small front parlor of his flat where the table is already set.

"A new tonic, is it?" she asks, her eyes darting about with curiosity.

"No, just rest and relaxation." He pulls out her chair. "I've made us a tisane — herbal tea. Or would you prefer the Irish? And we've some of your favorite scones."

"The herbal, I think," she says doubtfully.

He passes her the sweet butter and strawberry jam.

"You shouldn't have gone to such bother! Ah here, I almost forgot! Mother's broth." She holds out the parcel, then aware his hands are occupied, sets it down on the table.

"How thoughtful! Please extend my thanks to her, won't you?" he says, pouring.

She drinks, eyeing him anxiously over the rim of her cup, and eats with little bird pecks, picking up the crumbs and licking them carefully from her fingers. He sips his tisane slowly in silence, waiting to learn why she has come. On her third buttered strawberried scone, she leans toward him and says effusively, "I hope you'll be opening the shop again soon. We desperately miss your wonderful pastries." He smiles. She and her mother had hardly ever bought anything — on a few rare occasions, a few scones or a quarter kilo of the inexpensive boiled sweets he'd kept in stock to give away to the neighborhood children.

"I'm thinking of traveling abroad."

"For a holiday?"

"*Qui sait?* Who knows? We shall see. Perhaps I shall open a shop in Paris."

"So I've heard," she says. "Oh dear, what a pity! Not that I blame you, of course. You must long to be off and away, far from Clontarf and all the terrible gossip."

"The gossip?" he says, his heart freezing.

"About the shooting," she says. "So dreadful! It's only natural you'd want to leave with all the rumors flying about, people putting the worst possible interpretations on things."

"My dear Miss O'Flaherty, what are you saying?"

"Of course, I've my own theory. But I wonder. First, could you answer a question frankly?"

His mind reeling, he says, "What question?"

"I'm certain you must recall my mentioning a certain incident concerning our next-door neighbor that took place at her house on a Sunday in broad daylight, not too long ago?"

A vague memory stirs. "I'm not sure . . ." Is she talking about Mrs. O'Connell?

"Oh, Mr. Delehanty, you must remember! You were so shocked to learn that that person was — how shall I put it — openly, flagrantly, carrying on with another man at the same time that she was intimately involved with her fiancé?"

Quelle idiote! What is she rattling on about? "What is the question, Miss O'Flaherty?"

She pauses, leans toward him conspiratorially and asks softly, "Why do you think the child shot you?"

He rises abruptly and shoves back his chair, knocking it over. "Are you here on behalf of the police, Mademoiselle? I've already answered their questions. But I'll tell you what I told them. It was simply an unfortunate accident."

She stares at him anxiously, but persists. "Is that what you think?" Eyes blinking rapidly, she says, "I believe it was a planned — a deliberate — attempt at murder."

The woman must be mad — *vraiment folle!* "You think the child planned to murder me? Timothy O'Connell? Why would he do that? The child loves me! I'm his dearest friend!"

"Because his mother must have known that you knew all about her scandalous behavior, and if word got around, any possibility for her upcoming marriage would certainly have been destroyed. It was she who planned it."

He picks up the chair, sits down on it, and suddenly starts to laugh. She looks at him in silent astonishment a moment, then says earnestly, "I know how this must upset you, Mr. Delehanty. But I believe it's true. Did you ever tell her it was I who passed on to you that dangerous information?"

"No, Miss O'Flaherty, never." He wipes his eyes with his napkin. "As a matter of fact, dear Miss O'Flaherty, Mrs. O'Connell visited me twice in the hospital. And when you arrived, I was at work designing her wedding cake, my gift to the happy couple!"

He is startled by the look of rage and despair on her face as she rises. Her mission a patent fiasco, she says through tight lips, "Thank you for the tea," picks up the parcel from the table and makes for the stairs.

He follows her down, grateful that she has decided to deprive him of her mother's nourishing broth. As he opens the door to let her out, she hesitates a moment, then says defiantly, "Perhaps I was mistaken about you and your 'unfortunate accident,' but one thing is perfectly clear. That marriage is certainly doomed!"

He watches as she scurries off, shoulders hunched, and is suddenly sad for her. *La pauvre vieille fille* — she has never known what it is to love, the glory of it, however star-crossed! And remembering, his heart love-sick, tremulous with grief and aborted passion, whispers longingly, "Oh my sweet love! My darling! . . ."

3

"Your turn, Uncle Timmy," Sheila says shyly.

"No, it's not!" says Shaemus, looking at his sister murderously. "It's still mine!"

"You missed!" Sheila says.

"I did not!" shouts her brother, punching her on the arm.

Sheila lets out a squall of pain.

"Leave her alone," Timmy tells him. He is tired of entertaining the twins. He has been playing pick-up-sticks with them, but they're not much good at it and Shaemus keeps trying to cheat.

"And he's not our uncle!" Shaemus says.

Sheila, sniffling but defiant, persists. "He is so! Or he will be after the wedding, won't you, Timmy?"

The twins' mother, who is upstairs helping his mother get dressed, comes out on the landing and calls down a warning.

"Can't you children behave yourselves? Or do I have to come down to you?"

"Isn't she ready yet, Aunt Della?" he calls back.

"Almost," Della answers and disappears back into the bedroom.

"Aunt Della!" Shaemus mimics. "Hah! If you're our uncle, how come our mother's your aunt?"

He ponders an answer but can't come up with a good one. All these new relatives are driving him crazy. If Jamie, who's married to Della, is going to be his step-brother, once O'Hare adopts him, what does that make Della? His step-sister? No, his cousin maybe. Och, she must be his aunt! Else why wouldn't she have corrected him? Anyway, most older women relatives were called "Aunt," weren't they?

In a temper, Shaemus has swept the sticks off the kitchen table onto the floor.

"Shaemus, you're mean!" Sheila says and, getting down on her knees, starts to pick them up. Tim helps silently. Sulking, Shaemus declines to join in the clean-up. The task completed, Sheila pleads, "Can't we go out in the garden and play?"

"No. Your mother said you're just to sit here and stay clean."

He gets up and goes into his room to see if he can find some crayons and coloring books to keep the twins quiet. He digs out a couple of battered ones with some pages still uncolored from the bottom shelf of his bookcase and locates a few broken crayons in his pencil jar. "Here," he says firmly, setting the lot down on the table. "Get to work on these." He is expecting some opposition and is surprised at how obediently they both respond. They're not bad kids, he thinks, just babyish.

The twins occupied, at least for the moment, he wanders restlessly through the hall to peer out the front door. All quiet. No sign yet of the limo that's supposed to be picking them up. Turning, he catches a glimpse of himself in the hall mirror. He looks good, kind of grown-up. O'Hare had taken him to pick out the outfit: gray flannel trousers, navy blazer, white linen shirt, and polka-dot tie — a four-in-hand, O'Hare called it. He notices the tie looks sort of funny. O'Hare'd spent some time showing him how to knot it and he thought he'd got the hang of it, but it doesn't look right somehow. The underneath end is trailing way below the upper one. Maybe his mother can fix it, if she ever gets finished dressing.

He's suddenly reminded of his mother helping him get dressed up for Halloween, the day he'd tried to pawn her diamond earring and run off and left it behind. He'd finally told O'Hare about it and O'Hare had gone and gotten it back from the pawnbroker. He'd been pretty worried about what his mother would say if she found out, but O'Hare said they'd have to tell her the truth.

"Why did you do it, Tim?" O'Hare asked, and embarrassed, he'd admitted he'd wanted to see could O'Hare track him down. It was just for a lark.

Well, O'Hare told him, if he promised never to try anything like it again, maybe they could put off telling his mother for a while, at least till after the wedding when things weren't so hectic.

"What if she needs it for the wedding?" he'd asked.

"I've got a plan," O'Hare told him.

His mother let out a great cry of joy when O'Hare "discovered" the earring under one of the cushions in the parlor sofa, and then burst out crying. (If getting married's so great, he wonders, why was she so nervous these days?) Afterward she kept saying the earring must have been hiding there for over two months, and O'Hare must think her some dreadful kind of a housekeeper!

He wonders if O'Hare is taking as long as his mother to dress for the wedding, or if he's as nervous. Probably not. Men were different. Though he'd been pretty jittery himself there for a while after the business with Delehanty. He could hardly remember what had happened, didn't like to think about it, only knew he'd been scared to death at the time, certain the baker was dead, that the gun going off had killed him. Luckily, it turned out he'd only been wounded, though he'd had to be in the hospital a long time. His mother had made him send P.A. a card saying how sorry he was and that he hoped P.A. would soon be better, and the little man had sent him a message through O'Hare that he mustn't worry or blame himself, it had just been an accident, pure and simple. Still, he didn't feel easy about it. He liked Delehanty well enough, he was a good egg, and "generous to a fault" as his mother kept saying, yet somehow he always felt jumpy with him.

Someone is coming down the stairs. It's only Della. "Hi, Tim," she says, "your Mum'll be down in a minute. Thanks for watching out for the twins. Are they behaving themselves?"

"They're out in the kitchen coloring picture books," he says, feeling guilty. She gives him a hug. "Are you going to be my aunt?" he asks her.

"Your sister-in-law, I think, but you can call me Aunt Della, if you like."

"Okay." he says, feeling relieved. He follows her out to the kitchen.

Della lets out a shriek, "Oh Sheila!" Sheila, stretched out on the floor busily crayoning, gets up quickly.

"Look at you, look at your dress!"

It doesn't look so bad to him, maybe a bit crumpled.

"Where's Shaemus?" their mother asks, taking Sheila in tow.

"I think he went to the bathroom," Sheila says.

He trails after them as Della heads for the bathroom, where they find Shaemus mashing his crayons into a paste in the basin.

"Oh Lord!" says Della. "Let's get this mess and the both of you cleaned up."

Embarrassed — he knows he should have been keeping an eye on them — he is saved by the doorbell. "I'll get it," he says quickly.

It's O'Meara, a nice guy, O'Hare's friend. No relation, thank goodness.

"Well, you're looking pretty spiffy," O'Meara greets him.

"Hello, Mr. O'Meara. Say, I think something's wrong with my tie. Could you fix it?"

"We'll have it right in a moment," O'Meara says, loosening the knot and adjusting the ends so they're even. "There you are! Now, where's everyone?"

"Mum's upstairs. Aunt Della's in the back bathroom giving the kids a wash-up." O'Meara heads for the rear.

Feeling the need for a bit of fresh air, he opens the door and steps outside. Parked right in front of their house is the shiny black limo, a uniformed chauffeur standing stiffly beside it. Pretty classy!

The man sees him, raises his hand smartly to the tip of his hat in greeting. "A lovely day for the wedding," he says. "Air very balmy for December."

"Yes," he agrees, "very balmy!"

4

Dressing for the ceremony, he can't find his cuff links. Where in hell are they? The pants of the new tuxedo are too tight, pinch at the crotch. Jamie insists again on straightening his tie, is making him nervous. He's too old for this sort of thing. Cuff links in, tie adjusted, dressed and ready, he finds he has to go to the bathroom. Picks up yesterday's paper to help take his mind off dangerous thoughts. The headline reads:

SDLP WINS 14 SEATS
SINN FEIN 5

"Over 60 percent of the people have cast their vote for non-violence." The Lord Mayor of Derry, John Tierney, is quoted: "Peace through accommodation of differences is well on the way." Calls it "a great victory for hope!"

If the extremists in the North can be reconciled, surely he and Agnes can work out their differences. What are they? Piddling after all, compared to the larger picture. Her tendency on occasion to evade the truth? Her volatile temper? All nonsense. Love is the answer. Love can work miracles.

Never thought he'd be a father again. She's pregnant, told him last night. He hadn't the nerve to ask her how long, only if she was sorry. No, glad, she told him. Pushing fifty, he'll be raising a second brood. Well, it'll give him new life. He'll be good to the child. Doesn't he love Tim as if the boy were his own?

Jamie bangs on the door. "Be out in a minute," he says.

Thinking of Timmy, he wonders if he's made a mistake in not pursuing the Delehanty business. A freak accident, the little man swore. And according to Tim, nothing untoward actually took place. Admits there were a few kisses. He'd always felt there was something fishy there — P.A. too mushy, too bushy-tailed with the kids. He'd mentioned his suspicions to Agnes, but she pooh-poohed the idea. Since when was kissing a child a crime? she'd said. Hasn't he done the same? True, but likely not in quite the same way, he believes. Anyway, the baker was selling out and moving to Paris. Let the French authorities keep an eye on him. He'll drop a note to Maigret . . .

He comes out of the john. Jamie is hovering at the door with his coat, helping him into it. A knock at the hall door. Jamie goes to answer it. Paddy there comes in and claps him on the back. A trifle too heartily, perhaps? Does he still suspect Paddy and Aggie of . . . ? Forget it! No way to make sure.

He has a sudden terrible urge to see Agnes before the wedding, catch just a glimpse of her. One quick searching look deep into those luminous eyes could help settle his mind. Or — unsettle it?

"I need to stop off to see Agnes," he says.

Jamie, sounding exasperated, says, "We don't have the time, Dad. Besides, you know it's bad luck for the groom to see the bride just before the ceremony."

He and Paddy each take him by an arm. "Let go!" he says irritably.

In at the back of the church to the vestry, where Father Malachy shakes his hand enthusiastically, makes the sign of the cross over him, and informs him that the bride has not yet arrived, but will surely be there any minute. It is chilly, the room draughty, but he is sweating. Jamie helps him off with his overcoat and leads him, as though he is blind, down the long hall to the entranceway. Paddy holds the door for them, then slips into a seat in the rear.

The deafening strains of the organ — "Love's Dream" — pealing forth, washing over him. Father Malachy at the altar. Two dozen people in the front rows, all turning to peer at him. In a little while, if he doesn't speak up, call it off before it's too late, they'll be man and wife, tied for life.

Jamie walking him down the aisle, keeping a tight grip on his arm, holding him to a measured pace, as rehearsed, in time with the music. Arrived at last in front of the priest, he turns round to watch for the bride's entrance. Late, as always. Why is she taking so long? Has she changed her mind? He sees himself, old fool that he is, deserted at the last minute, left stranded at the altar . . .

5

Helping her dress for the ceremony, Della picks up the diamond earring she's just dropped for the second time and smiling says, "Here, let me."

Both earrings in, they wink brilliantly at her from the mirror.

"You look lovely," Della says. "All set?"

"Almost," she answers breathlessly, "but I can manage the rest on my own. I have to go to the bathroom." This past week, she's been having to pee every five minutes.

"I'll just go check up on the children," says Della and leaves her. Mindful of keeping her dress from creasing or letting it trail on the bathroom floor, she sits carefully, heart palpitating, and decides she can't go through with it.

Why in God's name hasn't she told him the truth!

Whatever for? Simply to stir up trouble?

O'Hare knows she's pregnant. She told him last night. He'd taken it quietly, but flushed to the ears. She couldn't make out was it shock or what, though after a moment he'd asked was she sorry or glad. Glad, she told him, and he'd kissed her tenderly. She felt like a Judas, was sorely tempted to spill the whole truth then and there. But what purpose on earth could it possibly serve to tell him the child might not be his? When she's not even sure herself!

Of course, a simple blood test could determine paternity. She could always ask Paddy—quietly, once the baby was born—if he'd take the blood test. Then if they found out he wasn't the one, there'd be no need to carry on about it, no need to tell O'Hare anything! But suppose the child turned out to be Paddy's?

She hears Della calling from downstairs, "It's almost twelve, Agnes!"

Why is she worrying about it at this moment? She'll be late for her own wedding! There'll be plenty of time to straighten it out after they're married. A woman ought to be able to tell her own husband she once made a slip—before he'd even proposed!

But what if she's previously denied it? And what if the slip has had consequences?

Would O'Hare want the marriage annulled once he knew? Let him! Her mind is made up. She'll tell him the truth. Let the chips fall where they may! She'll tell him tonight, or whenever an opportune moment presents itself.

She flushes the toilet.

In the bedroom, she takes a long searching look at herself in the mirror and is startled by the wild-eyed woman staring back at her.

A knock at the door. O'Meara's voice, "Are you decent?"

"I'm ready," she says, pulls herself together, and opens the door, smiling. O'Meara stares at her, eyes bright with admiration. "The sight of you could take a man's breath away," he says softly. "Isn't O'Hare the lucky devil?" A stab to the heart . . . He takes her hand and leads her carefully down the stairs. A ring at the front door. Della goes to answer. Jimmy Scanlon, O'Rourke's delivery boy standing there, his face almost concealed by two huge boxes.

"The wedding cake from Delehanty's," he announces. "And he says to tell you there's a special treat in this one for the children. There's a note for you, Mrs. O'Connell." O'Meara takes the boxes and tips the boy, who seems reluctant to leave. O'Meara ushers him out.

"How will we ever get them to Caesar's?" she cries out in a voice that might trumpet the end of the world.

Della pats her arm, "Not to worry. All will be taken care of."

"What does it say?"

Della takes the note and reads, "For Mr. and Mrs. O'Hare — Congratulations and very best wishes. Sincerely, P. A. Delehanty. P.S. The contents of the smaller carton are for the children — made *sans* chocolate, *sans* sugar."

Shaemus shouts, "Can we see?" The twins crowd round as Della places the carton on the hall table and opens it. "Ohhh . . . !" a long drawn-out breath from Della. "Aren't they marvelous!"

Squeals of excitement from Sheila. Shaemus bug-eyed. Tim standing off a little way, appearing indifferent, but can't resist watching as Della removes the surrounding tissue to reveal, under a protective clear plastic dome, a whole orchestra of shiny chocolate mice. They are performing on violins, violas, a cello, oboes, bassoons, a French horn, on cymbals, timpani, even a piano, their eyes directed toward the conductor who, whiskers quivering, holds his baton aloft.

"The man's a genius!" says Della.

"He is that!" Agnes answers, recalling as if she were tasting it now the marvelous scent and flavor of that first chocolate mouse she'd bought for Timmy, but never got to give him because she'd just learned he had diabetes. Remembering how she'd wept as she ate it, and the way O'Hare had comforted her that night, their first time together . . .

Timmy comes over and takes her hand. "Will I be allowed to have one?"

She hugs him. "Of course. More than one, if you like." Her first-born, she'll always love him the best.

"I want the one playing the piano!" Sheila says.

"We'll see," her mother tells her.

The chauffeur from the limousine O'Meara has hired, spiffy in his pressed uniform and polished boots, appears in the doorway, brilliantined hair plastered close to his scalp, hat in hand, to inform them it's already past twelve.

O'Meara tells him they're all set to go and hands him both boxes.

"Oh, do be careful with them," Della pleads.

The man clicks his heels smartly and heads for the car. Herded by Della, the children troop out after him. O'Meara is handing her into the gleaming limo, Timmy next to her, Della beside Tim. The twins, delighted, assigned to the jump seats. O'Meara rides in front with the chauffeur.

And they're off at last! Cinderella cum entourage in the golden coach, bearing her to the palace to marry her prince. All her dreams of happiness about to come true. Why does she feel like screaming?

The clock on the glistening front panel reads twelve-fifteen. They're terribly late! But the chauffeur, proud of his equipage, drives at a funereal pace, nodding grandly to Sunday strollers. O'Hare will be furious; she's always late.

Arriving finally in front of the church at twelve-eighteen, to race up the steps and through the front entrance. She can hear the organ pumping out "Love's Dream," and stops at the font to catch her breath. Her conscience is killing her. Her shoes are too tight. O'Meara's beside her, moving her swiftly along.

Paddy Morphy of the flaming red hair there, O'Hare's good friend, opening the doors for them. The music stops, then peals out anew, heralding the bride's entrance. And she knows at last she has to tell O'Hare the truth, the whole truth, renounce once and for all the sweet dream of being his wife. She will confess all at the altar, announce her guilt, abjure all her sins, bare her breast before him and all the assembled guests.

Paddy, a hand on her arm, whispers, "Good luck, Aggie!"

Frozen, she stares at him blankly.

And in a thunderclap of divine insight, recalls something he'd told her that day in the hospital: "O'Hare gave his blood for me . . ."

A sign from heaven! He and O'Hare have the same blood type! God's babe, whoever the father . . .

Della helping to lower her veil, then stepping back. Ready for the procession. She turns to thank her. In her hyacinth-blue gown, Della looks wonderful! The three bright-eyed angels cluster behind.

She takes O'Meara's arm and starts down the aisle. She sees O'Hare, face turned toward her, watching, waiting for her . . .

6

Jamie, in a whisper, is admonishing him, "Eyes front, Dad!" but he ignores him. Some bustle now in the back. A murmurous buzz, a stirring of excitement and renewed interest from the restless guests. Has she finally arrived?

"The Wedding March" replaces "Love's Dream." And here comes the bride, a vision in shimmering satin and frosty veiling. Breasts high, waistline trim as ever—no sign yet. He watches, pulse quickening, as she floats down the aisle. Midway she pauses, raises her veil, and brazenly winks at him!

Light-headed, high-hearted, he gives her a grin, then turns to face front. Shaking off his son's arm, he says, "I'm all right, Jamie. Have you got the ring?"

Epilogue

Remembering how it was in the old days, Aggie looks at her three men smugly and says, "It's hard to believe how everything's changed."

"Och! Nothing has changed, except for the better," her husband says, misunderstanding her. "Look at you. You're more beautiful than ever."

And while O'Hare may be exaggerating a bit, Paddy agrees. Aggie in her sixties is still a fine-looking woman! His own life has changed considerably, for though he has never married, he has settled down and become quite domesticated. He and Aggie and O'Hare have been close friends now for all of twenty-five years, and for a number of reasons, he has come to be considered a member of the family.

Timothy O'Connell, M.D., research pathologist, smiles at his three elders. At thirty-three, he is on the brink of discovering a cure for diabetes and has just been awarded a sizable national grant to continue his work, an event they are presently celebrating with champagne in Aggie's garden behind the same little house in Crompton Road where he grew up. "Mum's right," he says. "Who would have believed when I was a kid we'd have a United States of Ireland? And a Protestant candidate for P.M.!"

"Eileen will be proud as a peacock if Ian gets in," O'Hare says.

"She ought to be," says Aggie generously. "She did a fine job of bringing him up." With your help, she thinks.

"He hasn't got in yet," Paddy, the diehard, says hopefully.

"He will," says Tim. "All the polls say so."

"It won't be so bad," Aggie reassures Paddy. "At least these days we're not killing each other every minute."

"There's less need," says O'Hare. "We're united by a common enemy — the government, made up in equal parts of Prods and Teagues — against whom we can all now complain bitterly!"

They laugh.

"Guess what?" Tim says. "I got a card from Delehanty the other day congratulating me on the grant and suggesting I stop off and see him if ever I get to Paris."

"That little man was a pawky baker!" Aggie says nostalgically.

"Among other things," Tim says.

"I wish Dee-Dee could be here. Nothing's the same without her," Paddy complains. "Why did she have to run off to America?"

"You're not the only one who misses her," Aggie sighs. "But she's due back for a visit at Christmas."

"To our Deirdre!" O'Hare toasts.

"To Sis!" seconds Timmy, raising his glass, which is almost empty.

O'Hare pours champagne all around.

Jenny O'Flaherty, living alone since her mother died, peers out of her window, sees her neighbors carrying on merrily in their garden and wonders why God in His infinite wisdom has seen fit to reward the evildoers and punish the virtuous, but strives quickly to wipe out the envious thought. May the saints forgive her, they know she's not one to complain . . .